THE SUN RISES

THE SUN RISES

MARIO A KASAPI

Sun Rise Books
Vancouver, BC

Cover design and book layout by Mario A Kasapi

ISBN-10: 148188008X
ISBN-13: 978-1481880084

This book is a work of fiction. The characters and events are fictitious. Any similarity to actual persons, living or dead, is coincidental.

First Edition

www.thesunrisesnovel.com

for Vicki, Anthony, Alexandra and Jessica

❧ CHAPTER ONE ❦

Kaleb

*What man of you, having a hundred sheep, if he
has lost one of them, does not leave the ninety-nine in
the wilderness, and go after the one which is lost, until
he finds it?
And when he has found it, he lays it on his
shoulders, rejoicing.
And when he comes home, he calls together his
friends and his neighbors, saying to them, 'Rejoice
with me, for I have found my sheep which was lost.'*

Holy Bible, Luke 15:3-7

Mary placed the tattered Bible on her lap—its crisp age-yellowed pages parted at a thin, leather bookmark.

'Mumma, will you read to me from my book?' the young boy lying in the bed next to her said in a soft voice.

'Soon, angel,' she replied, touching his arm. 'Let's read just a little bit more from this book, and then we'll start reading again from yours. Okay?'

'Okay,' he sighed, 'but I don't like those stories. They give me nightmares.'

Mary smiled lightly. 'What are your nightmares about?'

'I don't remember,' he whispered.

'Well,' Mary said, brushing the hair away from his forehead, 'if you remember, you tell me. All right?'

He nodded.

Mary gazed at her son and the network of narrow tubes that violated his body: clear, synthetic veins through which were delivered vital fluids and chemical relief from pain. Many months ago, during their first stay in hospital, they delivered terrible liquids into him, strong poisons tailored by science to destroy the advanced malevolence that now ravaged his small body. Poisons so dangerous they were dyed bright red to prevent accidental administration. He bit his lower lip as he toyed with his woolen blanket.

'Do you hurt?' Mary said.

'No.'

She placed her hand on his cheek. 'What is it, Kabe?'

'Nothing,' he whispered.

'You know I can always tell when something's bothering you. What is it?'

He gazed uncertainly at his mother. 'I—saw him again.'

'Who?' she said, but knew the answer before he spoke.

'Puppa.'

Her stomach tightened. This new issue had strayed into their path like a suffering animal to which she could offer little assistance. No matter how she tried to address it, still it haunted them. 'You're sure it was Puppa?'

He nodded.

'Did he say anything this time?'

'No, he was just sitting over there and staring at the ground,' Kaleb said, pointing near the door.

Her eyes followed his finger to the closed door. Through the glass window in its upper section she could see one of the ward nurses talking casually in the hallway.

'You had a high fever last night, Kabe,' she said, caressing his cheek. 'High fevers can sometimes make you see things that aren't really there.' She moved to the door and sighed at her tired reflection.

'Do you see yourself in the glass?' she asked, pointing at the window.

He lifted his head from the pillow and stretched his neck, but only the reflection of the white plastered wall opposite his bed was visible.

He nodded.

'Well, that's what you saw,' she reassured him with a smile. 'You look so much like Puppa, when you saw your reflection in the glass, you thought it was him.'

Mary waited for his reaction, wondering if the white lie would take effect, but he remained silent. Her son shared few of his father's well-defined facial features. It was Mary with whom he bore a striking resemblance; his wavy, dark brown hair and large, chestnut eyes were unmistakably hers. She moved to his side.

The afternoon sun was perched high above the small town, but the weight of the day was already leaning heavily upon her. Covering her mouth with her hand, she yawned silently. She smiled as his eyes closed and then snapped defiantly open, relieved that sleep was descending upon him. But she knew his surrender would not be easily achieved. She placed the Bible on the small table beside her.

'Mumma?' he said.

'Close your eyes and go to sleep now,' she said, resting on the edge of his bed.

'Would He still make an earthquake?'

'Who?'

'God.'

'What do you mean?'

'Would He make an earthquake and smash the hospital while we're in it?'

'Of course not. Why would you ask such a thing?'

'In the story you told me yesterday, He made an earthquake to kill His son.'

'No, Kabe. He made the earthquake *after* his son died. Remember? And He did it only to scare the people, because

He was angry with them. He would never hurt you.'

'Oh,' he sighed. 'He must have been really mad at them.'

'I'm sure He was.'

'And strong, too.'

Kaleb lightly squeezed his lips together between his thumb and index finger; a habit that Mary knew accompanied intense concentration.

'If He could make an earthquake,' he said, 'why did He let them hurt Him?'

Mary smiled and slowly shook her head. 'Why is it always at bedtime that you come up with these questions?'

To her endless frustration, they were also usually particularly difficult queries, for which she often didn't have the answers.

'It must have been part of His plan, angel.'

'What was His plan?'

'Why don't we read more from the Bible later and you can find out then? But right now, I want you to take a little nap. Okay?'

'I don't want to go to sleep, Mumma. I'm bored.'

Mary sighed into the still, stale air and moved to a tall, wood-framed window deep within the outer wall. But she knew it would offer little relief. The old granite building had originally functioned as a sanatorium, whose founder had all the windows sealed, believing that by starving disease of air it could be confined within the stone walls. Most of the windows had been returned to their original state, but the one in Kaleb's room could be only partly opened. She lifted the pane and rested her hands upon the sill, which was rough from the many layers of chipped and cracked paint that covered the ageing wood beneath.

Winter's coming, she thought as she peered through the thin, leaded glass. *Soon the summer's warmth will abandon us again and the rains will come in its place, bringing with them extended periods of darkness.* And she would welcome it.

Snapping her eyes shut, she tried to rid her mind of those recurring thoughts that threatened to erode her spirits. But keeping them at bay was becoming increasingly difficult.

'Don't go, Mumma,' Kaleb whispered from behind her. 'I can't sleep.'

She moved to him and took his face into her hands, kissing his forehead. 'I'm here, sweetheart. You don't need to worry— - I won't leave you. I'm always close by, even when you can't see me.'

'Will you stay here until I fall asleep?'

Mary nodded and sank into a large, brown leather chair near his bed. She took the Bible from the table and placed it open on her lap.

'Are you going to read some more?'

'I'll do some silent reading while you take a nap. Okay?'

'Okay,' he breathed and closed his eyes. Over his eyelids lay dark shadows that contrasted starkly against the pale features of his small face.

The leather seat crunched beneath Mary as she shifted her weight over him and kissed his eyes. Sitting back into the chair, she allowed herself the rare pleasure of becoming absorbed into the soft comfort of her seat. She gazed upon her son and watched him fall asleep.

Unconsciously, she reached for a silver pendant that hung from her neck at the end of a long, delicate chain and slowly turned it over in her fingers. The heart-shaped pendant was one of a matching pair—her son wore the other. They were the last vestiges of her late husband, and mother and son wore them always. Her thoughts drifted as exhaustion took hold, and the sounds and colors around her faded away.

The burnt orange sun hovered high above Mary in a bright summer sky. Thick waves of heat rising from the field that surrounded her blurred the horizon into an ever-changing gradient of dull yellow. A gentle breeze arrived from ahead, rustling the tall, yellow grass that swayed like waves in a golden sea. The only sound was the weak hiss of the dry grass as the breeze passed through it. She moved through the field, skimming the palms of her hands along the soft, feathery tops of the grass, taking long, deep breaths and filling her lungs with the sweet, warm air.

The strange serenity reminded her of a place from her childhood: a vast field near her house where she would often play. But there was something different here. The grass, which whispered all around her, seemed to conceal an imperceptible foreboding.

The dry earth of the narrow path that led through the field was worn barren by the feet of many who had passed through before her. From where she stood it was not possible to see where the path led. But there was only one way, for with each step forward the path closed in behind her.

Suddenly, she was gripped with panic. *Kaleb!* she thought. *Where's Kaleb?!*

Her heart pounded as she quickly scanned the field, but it slowed when she saw him running through the grass far off in the distance. She called to him, but he didn't respond. Over and over she called out his name, until her voice was lost, but he did not acknowledge her. As she called silently to him in the distance, ominous red and black clouds collected above, and his tiny silhouette was swallowed by a growing darkness.

The air suddenly thickened with a foul, sulfurous odor. She tried to call out again, but as she sucked in the dense air, it burned the back of her throat. As she gagged into the redness, a large, grey cloud of tiny midges slowly approached. She looked through it to where her son had been, but he was gone. Desperately, she listened for his sounds, but there was nothing except the hiss of the field.

It appeared as a flash from the tall grass beside her: a tiger-like animal that moved with unnatural speed. In its wake loomed blurred streaks of burnt yellow and scarlet. The beast struck her on one side and she fell hard into the grass. Immediately it was upon her, sinking its great talons deep into her chest, pinning her to the flattened grass under its infinite weight. A long, scaled tail swayed from side to side as it reared its head and opened massive jaws. Inside its mouth were rows upon rows of long, black teeth. Hot, putrid breath spilled over her as it released a terrible scream: a pulsing sound mixed with the shrill squeals of animal and machine. Bright, red light danced maniacally in its reptilian eyes as they rolled back in their sockets, and the beast lowered its gaping mouth toward her neck.

For a brief moment there was complete silence, and during that moment, Mary surrendered to her fate and exposed her jugular to the beast. She closed her eyes and waited, but at the instant she expected to feel its teeth puncture her skin, there came a muffled thud from one side of the animal. Her body twisted violently as its long talons tore from her. It tumbled into the field, screaming horribly, with thick crimson streaming from its side. Then the beast scrambled to its feet and fixed its gaze upon her briefly before disappearing into the grass.

It was then that Mary heard the crack of gunpowder from the distance. Large, jet-black birds lit from all around her, as though erupting from the soil. As the birds took to the air, the sky blackened with their numbers and echoed with their cries. In the far distance she saw a human form silhouetted against the dark red sky. It lowered something it held in its hands and then dissolved into the dark waves of rising heat. The air buzzed electrically.

Warm blood soaked the top of her dress, but she felt no pain. Slowly, she moved the shreds of torn fabric away from her body. A gaping void now lay on one side of her chest. She stared into its vastness and felt herself being drawn into it. Just as she was about to surrender to its immense power, her son appeared beside her. He touched her arm and spoke, but the voice was not his.

'Mary?'

Mrs. McLeary, the head ward nurse, stood red-faced over her.

'I'm sorry to disturb you, Mary, but there's someone here to see you.'

Mary's heart seemed to stumble in her chest. Quickly, she turned toward her son's bed. He was sound asleep. She exhaled fully as thoughts of her real world filled her mind again and displaced the unwanted images of her dream. Through the open door flowed in cool, welcome air that passed soothingly over her. With her left hand she reached over and touched the right side of her chest. Nothing had changed.

Her breast was gone.

❧ CHAPTER TWO ❧

Kadesh

In the early days of her son's first hospital stay, all visitors were required to report to the nurse station at the end of a long hallway east of his room. As time passed, the nurses of the children's ward became familiar with his few regular visitors. But as the duration of her son's second stay extended from days to weeks to months, so too grew the length of time between visits. Days would often pass without the companionship of a single friend, and so the arrival of an unexpected visitor awoke in Mary a long-forgotten curiosity.

'Who is it?' Mary whispered, wishing for a mirror and a few private moments.

'I don't know, I've never seen him before,' McLeary said.

Pressing down on the broad, soft arms of the leather chair, Mary rose to her feet and wiped the sleep from her eyes. After a quick check of her dress, she stepped lightly toward the door. McLeary hurried ahead of her into the hallway, stepped to one side and gestured for the visitor to enter.

Mary waited anxiously just inside the doorway, but moments passed and no one entered. She saw McLeary again beckon for the visitor to enter, but the only response was an indiscernible murmur. After a few more moments, Mary swept her hair back and stepped hesitantly into the hallway.

Leaning awkwardly against the wall adjacent to her son's room was a middle-aged man. A well-worn and wrinkled, dark grey wool suit covered a stout but broad frame. Over the suit jacket hung a long, brown overcoat, the collar of which stood up comically on one side. A slightly askew grey fedora adorned with a black grosgrain band partly covered his medium-length, greying hair. When Mary made eye contact with him, he quickly turned his gaze downwards, doffed his hat and smiled at the polished linoleum floor.

'Eh, I'm so sorry to intrude on you like this, Maryam,' he said in a colorful voice that was labored with a thick, Middle-Eastern accent.

Mary blushed at the sound of her birth name. Although it had been many years since she had been referenced with it, she liked the sound of it warmly embraced by his accent.

Holding his hat by its soft felt brim, he pressed it against his chest and bowed his head. His hair thinned considerably at the top rear-most section of his head. He took a quick peek at Mary and then returned his gaze to his scuffed brown leather shoes, which seemed to afflict upon him infinitely less discomfort.

She knew she had met him before. His profound shyness and strong accent seemed very familiar. But the faded memory of their previous encounter remained well hidden within the recesses of her mind, along with the many happier moments of her past.

'Eh, we have met before—some years ago,' he said, stealing another glance at her.

Again she searched for the context of his face, but she couldn't place him. He shifted uneasily and licked his lips as her eyes swept over him and the silence grew. Her patience lost in the awkwardness of the moment, McLeary placed her large hands on the man's shoulders and reoriented him toward the exit. He turned suddenly and extended his arm to Mary.

'Kadesh,' he announced, smiling, '—Gabe Kadesh.'

Like a long-forgotten song within which had been

encapsulated a strong emotion, his name released the distant memory that Mary sought. 'Yes,' she said shaking his hand. 'I remember you. We met at one of my husband's functions—a long time ago. I'm sorry I didn't recognize you right away.'

'No problem, no problem,' he said, waving the apology away. 'Your memory is much better than mine—to remember an old man among so many people that night.'

Again he returned his gaze to the floor. 'I'm sorry about Aaron. He was a very good man—an altruistic man—the type who is very difficult to find these days.'

With heavy sadness Mary recalled her last moments with her husband and the rare fight that had erupted when, in an uncharacteristic dissent, she objected to him joining a volunteer team of medical doctors about to depart on a ten-week assignment to a chronically troubled land. 'Thank you,' she murmured.

He shuffled toward her. 'Eh, I wonder if I could have a moment with you—alone?'

McLeary's jaw dropped and an expression of grave disapproval took shape. But after a reassuring nod from Mary and a few more awkward moments of silence, she trudged back to her station and sat glaring at Kadesh from the end of the hallway.

'Eh, I wonder if you also remember that I am a detective?' he inquired of Mary's feet.

'No, I'm sorry—I didn't recall.'

'Of course not, of course not,' he said, shaking his head and waving his hands. 'Well, I *am* a detective and I have been for a very long time.' He paced as he spoke and ran his fingers along the rim of his hat, which remained pressed against his chest.

'Eh, you see, I am working on something which is very important—and it is interesting that I should think of you now.'

He glanced up at Mary who, although she was not tall by any standard, stood nearly four inches taller. 'You see, I find myself in desperate need of your assistance.'

She stared at him incredulously. 'My assistance?'

He raised his head slightly and for the first time made deliberate eye contact with her. 'Well, as you know, you are a psychiatrist.'

Mary reflected for a moment, struggling with the meaning of his words that seemed somehow distant and faded.

'Yes,' she said softly.

'Well, I very much require your assistance. You see, I have a man in my custody whom I have been interrogating for some time, but now I am afraid that I have reached the limit of my skills.'

Dazed and mildly disoriented, Mary blinked in disbelief. His request seemed surreal. It could not be that this near-stranger would be making such a request of her in this place, at this time.

'The problem is,' he continued, 'he seems to remember very little about his past. More importantly, I do not think he wishes to recall the details that I most desperately need of him.'

'He has amnesia?'

'I do not know—maybe. I am not a doctor. This is precisely why I need you. You have the skills to determine such things and to help me find a way into his mind.'

'I don't understand,' she said, slowly shaking her head. 'Don't you have access to your own psychiatrists?'

'Eh, normally yes, but this situation is very different. It is a long and complicated story, really, and I would like very much to have the opportunity to explain my circumstances to you. Do you think you could spare just a little time to help me with this endeavor?'

The detective looked down the narrow hallway toward the marble stairs that led to the foyer two floors below, as if at any moment the walls might close in and permanently isolate him from his task.

'*Now?*' Mary said.

'Yes, please.'

'I'm sorry, Mr. Kadesh, but I can't possibly go with you.

You couldn't have come at a worse time.' She looked over her shoulder into her son's room, where he slept heavily.

Kadesh lowered his head. 'I appreciate what is happening here—'

'With all due respect, Mr. Kadesh, I don't think you do—or you wouldn't have come here.'

He consulted with the floor for a few moments, his face blushing with a light shade of crimson. 'Please understand that I would not be here if my situation were not dire. I know your family has suffered greatly—and your suffering continues still—but I do not ask this of you for me alone. There is very much at stake here and my window of opportunity to effect change has almost closed.'

In his voice she could perceive the purest tone of sincere desperation: a compelling, almost hypnotic sound amplified by the intense discomfort he was clearly experiencing. He looked up at her, struggling again to meet her eyes, and did so.

'I know about your son,' he said softly, 'and that your dedication to him is unyielding. But I hope you can appreciate that I would not come here at this time with this exceptional request if it were not of the utmost importance and urgency. I do not require much of your time. If you will trust in me with this matter and grant me this magnanimous favor, it is very possible you will return to your son before he awakens.'

She stood absolutely still, listening closely to the pacifying rhythm of his voice. Deep within the turbulence of her confused emotions dwelled a strange but powerful desire to go with him: a selfish need to escape from the suffocating atmosphere that permeated every room and hallway of the hospital, and to distance herself from her endless nightmare. And something else was mixed within those feelings— something completely unexpected: a strong desire for adult companionship. *Male* companionship. To hear the deep, reassuring sound of a man's voice and to speak about things far removed from the context of that place. Things she could affect. Things she might have control of. The police station was not far away and she knew her son's midday sleep could last for an hour or more. And then, as if it came from someone else, from another woman who experienced feelings other than pain and despair—a woman who struggled to be free from all of this—she heard herself whisper, 'Okay.'

Kadesh smiled.

The events that soon followed later reassembled in Mary's mind like pieces of a fragmented dream. Kadesh gesticulated as he spoke and they walked together down the hallway. Her heart raced while they descended the marble stairs, but Kadesh's voice played in her ear like soft, calming music, and all distress remained isolated and distant. It wasn't until she met the chill of the outside air that she hesitated and gazed into the outer world, which seemed to have forsaken her long ago. Suddenly, she was gripped with intense guilt and stepped back into the foyer.

'It's not far,' Kadesh said, placing a reassuring hand on her arm. 'The air is unusually cold today. I will go upstairs and retrieve your cloak.'

'No,' she spoke into the damp, heavy air, which transformed her breath into a fine white mist. 'I'm all right.'

As the chilled air engulfed them, her thoughts softened and the police station became almost tangible within them. She didn't protest as Kadesh removed his coat and draped it over her, gently brushing the shoulders with the back of his hand. He took her arm and led her through the arched doorway, down the wide stone steps and headed westward along the narrow cobblestone street. Mary glanced over her shoulder and saw the limestone gargoyles perched on the roof of the hospital looking down upon her, wearing grotesque expressions of delight.

The quiet street was lined with small shops: narrow red brick and stone structures that shared at least one common wall with an adjacent business. Yet each one presented itself with a singular, distinctive architectural personality. Every merchant's sign was meticulously hand-painted or carved from wooden or stone slabs and tastefully mounted above the doorway. The cold but functional materials that formed their façades contrasted starkly with the warm orange-yellow glow and inviting scents that emanated from within.

'Who is he?' Mary said as they moved quickly along the walkway.

'He is someone who had disappeared but has now reappeared—a man whom I have been seeking for quite some time.'

'Can you be a little more specific?'

'Eh, he is a person of international interest.'

From the corner of her eye she could see that he was looking at her. Gradually, he slowed his pace until they stopped in the middle of the walkway, where he gazed, transfixed, at Mary's face. She turned away and blushed. Immediately, he snapped back into his animated chatter and gestured with his hand toward the short length of road.

'Eh, where was I?' he said, resuming their walk.

'You were telling me about your prisoner.'

'Oh yes, well, I am afraid there is not much more that I can tell you.'

'Do you mean you don't know anything more, or that you won't tell me?' She eased her arms into Kadesh's coat, and slid her hands into the flannel warmth of its pockets.

'Eh, perhaps a little of both,' he smiled. 'I know who he is, of course, but for reasons that must remain confidential, I cannot tell you. I hope you understand, Maryam.'

'It's just Mary. I haven't been called Maryam since I was a young girl.'

'Oh,' he sighed. 'I am sorry. It is a beautiful name.'

Across the street, a mangy-looking grey dog lay in the doorway of a small butcher shop, chewing on a long piece of leather. Upon noticing them it slowly rose to its feet, head lowered and back arched. Even from a distance Mary could hear the low rumble of its growl. She tensed as it stiffened and appeared readying to charge. Kadesh also noticed its reaction but seemed unconcerned and continued their conversation, without Mary's full attention. As they turned the corner and headed northward, she kept a keen eye on the aggravated animal that followed them with its stare until it fell far behind in the distance.

Moving quickly into a light headwind, they soon arrived outside the police station: a pale grey structure guarded on each side by large marble statues of men poised with long swords held high in triumph. As Mary and Kadesh stood in front of the stone building, the seemingly indelible look of enthusiasm faded from his face.

'So, he was arrested and brought here,' he said in a somber voice.

Now in the presence of the megalithic building, Mary became anxious. 'Is he dangerous?' she said.

'I don't believe so—not in his current state.'

His tone was not convincing. She stared at the stone statues, wondering how she had come to be there, as Kadesh walked toward the building.

'I have been with him for many hours,' Kadesh called to her. 'I ask now that you trust in me and accept that what I have told you is the truth. Will you do this?'

'All right,' she said, slightly embarrassed by her doubt. Kadesh's even tone and humble demeanor commanded complete confidence.

He moved quickly toward her, his face awash with a look of grave concern. 'I wish to restate that this opportunity is almost finished. That is why I have come to you now. And I am very grateful for your assistance.'

'Aren't there others who can help you? People who normally help you with these things?'

'They are of no use to me in this matter,' he said, waving his hand. 'This man can be very convincing. It is easy to believe that he does not deserve much attention. This is how he has remained hidden for so long.'

'What do you believe?'

'I do not just believe—I *know*. There is knowledge locked within his mind that is of paramount importance. This knowledge must be released before there is irreparable loss. What I *do* believe is that you can help me to do this.'

Mary didn't fail to notice that even with all his talk, Kadesh had revealed almost nothing about his prisoner. What little he did say only prompted more questions. There was also something unusual about him. Not something that invoked nervousness or suspicion, but a strange demeanor that suggested he was hiding something important—something she *should* know. But the more he spoke, the more familiar his voice seemed and the more at ease she felt in his presence. The unusually crisp air that seeped through Kadesh's coat had an equally powerful effect on her, and she was becoming increasingly anxious to get inside. Noticing her discomfort, Kadesh gestured toward the building, but instead of leading her up the wide, concrete steps that led to the grand main entrance, he escorted her to the side of the building. They walked a short distance along a gradually sloped pebble alley and stopped in front of an inconspicuous door, weakly illuminated by a single, precariously suspended lamp. As Kadesh tried in vain to unlock the door, producing key after key from his pockets, Mary shifted uneasily, hoping that with each attempt the lock would finally surrender.

Light rain began to fall.

After several minutes, Kadesh abandoned his handful of keys, and after a thorough search of every pocket of his suit, he smiled at Mary.

'Eh, I wonder …' Kadesh said, gesturing at his coat.

Mary placed her hand into the right pocket and produced a long, brass key.

'Thank you,' he said, taking it from her. The key fit into the lock and rattled loosely as it passed through the tumbler. As Kadesh fiddled, Mary began to doubt that he had the right key. She was relieved when a muffled click finally sounded.

'Please,' Kadesh gestured to the open door.

Before her eyes had time to adjust to the new lighting, she was greeted by a musty smell of mildew and heavy dampness. The grey concrete floor of the narrow hallway was heavily marred and extensively cracked. If the rough plaster walls had ever borne color, it was impossible to tell in the modest light.

As Kadesh closed the door behind her, she felt a sudden tightening in her throat, but his friendly expression put her quickly at ease.

'Thank you for coming, Mary,' he said quietly. 'Again, please know that if this was not of the utmost urgency, I would not have called upon you—especially now.'

He led her down the hallway to a narrow, unmarked door and stood for a moment in front of it, as if waiting for it to open on its own accord. He turned his gaze downward and lightly scratched his head. 'I have only until morning,' he said softly, '—after that, it will be too late.'

He held out the key and flipped it over the back of his fingers, making it appear to walk over his hand. Holding it up between his thumb and index finger, he smiled. 'Ah,' he said and reached behind Mary's ear. He withdrew his hand closed tightly into a fist and when he opened it, a different key lay in his palm.

Mary smiled.

In one fluid movement, he inserted the new key into the lock and opened the door.

'Eh, there is one more thing. I may have to end the visit prematurely if he becomes—*agitated*. Please do not be offended if this happens.'

A cold wave passed over her shoulders, and the fine hairs on the back of her neck stood on end. Disturbing images of what might await them behind the door permeated her thoughts. But before she could react, she was ushered through the doorway and into the interrogation room. As her eyes adjusted to the new lighting, she heard the bolt slide in the door behind her.

The interrogation room was even cooler and darker than the outer hallway, but the air was considerably drier and lighter. The sweet scent of jasmine incense lingered pleasantly. Stark, grey concrete walls rose up from an unfinished, yellowed floor. A single lamp burned dimly at one corner. At a long wooden table just to her left, a lone man sat with his head bent down. Thick, dark hair hung lankly over his forehead. He was unrestrained and unguarded. Her instincts called immediately to her—something about him was wrong. His stare was too intense, his attention strangely unchanged by their sudden presence. He seemed drugged.

Gently taking her arm, Kadesh led her toward the table. He spoke softly to her as they moved toward the man, and although his voice was soothing, she didn't listen to him. She was focused on the man, who remained unresponsive and detached even as they drew near. It wasn't until they were standing directly in front of the table that he slowly raised his head and looked at her.

She relaxed slightly when they made eye contact. His drawn and haggard appearance only partly masked a pleasantly handsome face that, like Kadesh's, bore an enigmatic familiarity. In many ways Mary and the prisoner looked alike, sharing the same large, dark eyes and angled facial features. But a strange emptiness lay behind his eyes that now gazed gravely upon her.

There was a brief moment of stillness and complete silence as they looked at each other. An odd expression passed across his face and then, without the slightest warning, he lunged at Mary.

At that moment, her thoughts melted and she was standing in the tall grass of her dream. The beast was upon her again, its flared talons clawing at her chest.

'*This is not for man!*' she heard it cry.

Reflexively, she pulled back, stumbled and fell hard to the concrete floor. The man was reaching for her across the table.

'No!' Kadesh cried and rushed to her. 'Mary, are you all right?'

With her gaze locked on the prisoner, she crawled backwards on her hands and feet away from him. Her bottom lip quivered; her eyes were wide and wild.

'I am so sorry, Mary,' Kadesh said, reaching for her.

Taking hold of his arm, Mary pivoted on it and pulled herself up in one quick movement. She ran to the door and heaved on the handle, but it wouldn't open. She fumbled with each of the many locks as the sound of her heart pounded in her ears. Her mouth opened to release a scream, but before it could escape, Kadesh's hand reached past her and turned one of the locks. The door popped open and Mary fled down the hallway. Behind her, the prisoner called out in a low, powerful voice.

'Tlitha!'

And she was gone.

✢ CHAPTER THREE ✣

Home

M ary ran.
  She ran like the time in grade school when a classmate had produced a live grass snake from a lunch sack. Like the time a grey cloud of enraged wasps had poured from a broken nest to deliver retribution. Faster and faster her legs moved, feeding the growing expanse between her and Kadesh's prisoner. But even as the old building shrank into the distance, she could still hear his hiss in her ear:

This is not for man!

She was inanimate: a lifeless thing without meaning, without feeling, without purpose. She thought of the disfiguring scar beneath her dress and she knew what he said was true. She was undesirable—a broken doll at the bottom of an old wooden chest—only the remnant of a woman, no longer appealing to any man. In her mind she heard him cry over and over again, each time his words stinging like incensed wasps tangled in her hair.

And he had touched her.

His hand had been where no other man but her husband had been. She ran not just from the man, but also from her shame. With her poor judgment and unforgivable recklessness, she had compromised her safety and so had failed not only herself, but also her son.

The spectacle of a young woman running down the midday street of the small town attracted considerable attention. Several of the merchants left their shops and called out to her. The stray dog outside the butcher shop rose as she approached, but quickly lost interest and returned to its leather as she passed.

Soon, the hospital loomed ahead of her like an unsavory old acquaintance waiting for her return. Demoralized and drained of all energy, she stopped across the street, placed her hands on her thighs and tried to catch her breath. As she stood bent over, listening to the sound of her own breath, a diffuse ache radiated throughout the bones of her upper legs. Her chest expanded and contracted like a bellows, feeding the burning in her lungs. The heat of her slim body collected around her and prickled her skin. Realizing that she was still wearing Kadesh's coat, she removed it and invited the cool, midday air against her body.

When her heart slowed, Mary looked up at the old grey building that was their surrogate home. The stone gargoyles that earlier had appeared to laugh now smiled smugly at her. Tears pressed their way to the corners of her eyes and she trembled with anger, knowing that if she passed through the arched entranceway in her current state, she would face a barrage of unwanted questions from the hospital staff and endless looks of disapproval from McLeary.

Mary looked westward down the narrow road toward the commercial district of town and then eastward toward a large forest about a quarter mile away. From where she stood, she could just make out the tips of the tall trees that stood at the end of the road like guardians of the forest, their broad-lobed leaves green and full. As she walked toward the forest, strange thoughts and images ebbed through her mind: the prisoner's blank stare, Kadesh's strange and almost comical demeanor. Each of the men seemed to be a part of the same dream, long-since forgotten and buried deep within her memories.

With each step the familiarities haunted her like an unwanted companion, distracting her thoughts. With almost no recollection of the journey to the road's end, she arrived at the humble brick structure that was their home.

Like most of the houses of the neighborhood, theirs was bordered by a low stone fence, on both sides of which stood tall, majestic oaks. A narrow flagstone walkway wound through an array of small flower gardens once meticulously tended but now overgrown with noxious weeds and thick, hardy grasses. Under a cloudy sky, brittle, orange-brown leaves swirled and tumbled across her path, caught in a light breeze that passed over the farmers' fields to the south. She followed the walkway to the foot of a weathered wooden stairway and gazed up at the place that had once been their sanctuary, filled with warm memories and comforting scents, but which now appeared stark and unwelcoming amidst the neglect. As though it had developed a will of its own in their long absence, their home had reverted to a house.

Mary climbed the short stairway and stood nervously before an unpretentious wooden door. Gazing at the wrought iron lock, she placed her hands in her pockets and sharply realized she didn't have the key. She sighed and was about to leave, but then placed her hand on the black door handle and squeezed the latch. The door opened.

The sweet scents of dry wood and dusty fabric embraced her like an old friend as she stepped into the foyer of her home. Natural light that passed through the many large windows of the main and upper floors provided ample illumination as she moved across the main floor to the kitchen. There she opened a window framed just above a deep soapstone sink. Standing on the dark-stained hardwood floor in a pleasing current of fresh air, she sighed at the familiar surroundings: the small softwood table circled by four simple chairs, the large rack of dried herbs in small tins and functional assortment of hanging pots and pans. She closed her eyes and breathed in slowly and deeply, savoring the tranquility of the long-lost moments.

Adjacent to the kitchen was a small family room that looked over an abandoned vegetable garden and toward a well-tended neighboring home. In the middle of the room sat a wooden rocking chair and an audience of assorted toys. In the southwest corner of the house was a small room that had once served as a study. A large maple desk stood abandoned in front of a northward-facing window that looked along a narrow street. The room's two windows admitted a considerable amount of light, so even on that grey day the study was well illuminated. A stained-glass desk lamp—now covered in dust—was normally employed only at night and on dark winter days.

Adorned on the cream-colored plaster walls of the study was an array of brightly colored paintings and illustrations: vague renditions of family, friends and home that represented her son's foray into the forgiving world of art. Amidst the artwork hung Aaron's and Mary's degrees, each pressed behind a clear glass plate and bordered by a dark, hardwood frame.

Except for the study, Mary's artwork covered most of the vertical surfaces of the main floor, so that the modest house resembled a small art gallery of oil and watercolor paintings on canvas and charcoal drawings on linen paper. To Mary, each piece held a special significance and was a milestone achievement in her life. As she moved through the foyer, examining her work—the themes almost exclusively wildlife—she drew in slow, deep breaths, inhaling the experiences and emotions that fed her creations. She stopped in front of a large oil painting and admired the soft colors and confident brush strokes that defined her earlier work.

To those unfamiliar with the piece, the painting appeared to be a representation of a simple landscape: a large field of long, golden grass reflecting the light of a midday sun set high in a clear, yellow-blue sky. She could almost hear the hiss of the light wind as it passed over the feathery tops of the dry grass. But to the attentive eye, the still face of a Bengal tiger stared into the eyes of the observer from within the tall grass of the foreground.

So it's you who's been haunting me in my sleep, she thought … My old friend.

The cryptic animal held its stare. I am your creation, of your design, it seemed to reply.

Lowering her eyes, she conceded to the great cat and backed away from the painting.

To the right of the front entrance hung a set of elegant French doors that divided the main foyer and the living room. As she passed through them, she recalled the painstaking care that Aaron had put into soldering the brass frame that held the fifteen glass panels in each door. In the center of the living room stretched a beige lambskin rug, its soft texture contrasting with the dark hardwood floor beneath it. On the wall opposite, Mary had hung a large mirror bordered by an intricately carved ebony frame. She stepped toward it, but stopped short and stared from the distance at her reflection. It peered back at her through a thick layer of dust. Slowly, she backed out of the room and gently closed the doors behind her, as if endeavoring not to wake a sleeping child.

Not far down the foyer lay a narrow wooden staircase that led to the upper floor. As she placed her foot on the bottom step, it wiggled loosely under her weight, sounding a painful reminder of the many unfinished chores that would remain unattended to indefinitely. The staircase creaked and moaned as she ascended, as though speaking to her in a language only she could understand. When she reached the landing, she paused to examine the top railing post that bore screw-hole scars where a child gate had once been mounted.

To the left of the landing was her son's room, the larger of the two bedrooms. The extra space had been deemed useful as a play area, needed one day with the arrival of a sibling. In the far corner of the room was a small bed. A wool blanket lay stretched taut over it and tucked tightly under the mattress. Upon the bed was arranged a group of stuffed toy animals. A variety of colorful, painted wooden toys lay neatly in groups around the edges of the room. They too seemed to be waiting for the return of the small hands that would once again bring them to life.

From the ceiling above the bed hung a small papier mâché mobile: Mary's hand-made gift to her newborn son. Suspended by nearly invisible fine black thread were dozens of intricately painted butterflies that once had glided above the bed in perfect balance but now hung motionless in the still air. She closed her eyes, and in the darkness behind them, she could see her young child lying on his back, gently blowing at the figures, freeing them from their tethers and giving them flight, so they might join the multitude of other animals that were painted onto the walls of his room. As she looked at the elaborate murals, she recalled the story that she had once told her son about how the animals came to appear there. It began:

> The house was once home to a wizard and his family. The wizard had a son who, like her son, was terrorized by the dark and so couldn't be left in his room alone. The wizard made various potions and cast many spells but try as he may, he couldn't alleviate his son's anxiety. He even bought his son a dog to protect him from the night things, but when the dog was asleep the boy would again become frightened. One day the clever wizard summoned his animal friends from land, sea and sky to the boy's room and asked them if they would help his son overcome his fears. They loved the boy and so they all agreed. With a simple spell and a wave of the wizard's wand, the animals were transformed into images on the walls and there they would remain to watch over the boy to protect him from any harm, until they were no longer needed by the boy—or by any other child who slept there.

Perched on top of a tall wooden dresser was a small picture frame, within which beamed the smiling image of her son. His hair was short and tidy, his young face full and bright. Taking the frame in her hands, she kissed the dusty glass plate, removed the picture and placed it carefully in her pocket. She lay the empty frame down on the dresser, removed her wedding ring and placed it next to the frame. Gently, she closed the door to the bedroom and moved to the master bedroom at the southeast corner of the house. She gripped the cool brass doorknob and after a brief moment of hesitation, opened the door.

The bedchamber appeared eerie and still, frozen in time like an old museum display. She almost expected to see a thick, red velvet rope hanging across the doorway and to hear the voice of an acquainted tour guide narrate a captivating story of the young family who had lived here in happier times. But the room was off-limits to her now. For in that placid space were objects that harbored unendurable memories, waiting to strike like coiled, venomous snakes: an antique wristwatch that used to keep track of the passage of minutes and hours when they mattered; an antique hand-carved wooden box full of old letters—tokens from a lost husband. There the memories would remain undisturbed, bound to the inanimate objects with which they were associated, until she could one day again permit them into her thoughts.

But one memory was inescapable.

As she turned away, a brightly colored object caught her attention: a seashell necklace that lay incidentally in the shape of a figure eight upon a round bedside table. She gazed across the room at the mixed colors of the small shells. Entangled within them was a profound memory: a series of images that flickered in her thoughts like an old movie film.

The beach was stifling that day. The tide was low. A large area of white sand that stretched for miles lay exposed to the sun by the retreated sea. Waves of hot, salty air carried a gentle breeze over the sparkling sand. Aaron lay to Mary's left, propped up on his elbows, soaking up the late-morning sun like a pink cactus. He wore nothing but a baggy pair of khaki shorts and a slight grin. He squinted toward the distant clouds in the horizon. A pair of dusty leather sandals lay cast to one side, half-buried in the hot sand. It was the young family's first vacation together and although it had been a great ordeal for them to reach their destination, they were now deeply immersed in the relaxation commanded by the ubiquitous sand and gentle sounds of the sea.

Mary sat cross-legged on a grass beach mat spread under the shade cast by a large parasol, wearing a white sun dress and a large, beige, floppy hat. She stared toward the glistening ocean where Kaleb played in the still, shallow salt water that snaked between sandbars. Then she pinched some of the fine, white sand between her fingers and, smiling deviously, released the grains into the pit of Aaron's bellybutton.

'Hey,' Aaron moaned.

She laughed and kissed him on the lips just as a small voice called out beside her.

'Seashell necklace?'

Shading her eyes with her hand, Mary looked toward the sun. A girl about nine years old stood next to Mary, her thin arms adorned from shoulder to wrist with necklaces of small, colorful seashells threaded together like beads. With fine brown hair highlighted by the sun that shone above her, emerald-green eyes and golden-brown skin, she looked as though she had been born of the sand itself.

'They're beautiful,' Aaron said, leaning toward the young girl. He gently took her by her wrists and she stepped over Mary toward him. As she presented the necklaces to Aaron, Mary endeavored to wipe the sand from her oil-covered legs and threw Aaron a mildly dirty look.

'There goes any chance of negotiating a fair price,' Mary smiled at Aaron. 'How much?'

'I make them myself with shells from the sea,' the girl said in a thick Spanish accent. 'They bring good luck.'

Kaleb stood facing the beach on a small sandbar about twenty-five yards away, his small belly protruding from under his narrow chest. His back had turned a dark shade of brown in response to the incessant sun and the blinding rays that reflected off the water. Wet sand covered his bare buttocks. Aaron waved to his son and called to him. The toddler squatted without responding and flicked up the wet sand with his tiny fingers.

'What's your name?' Mary said.

'Sofia.'

'That's a pretty name. Do you live near here?' Mary said, scanning the sparsely populated seashore.

'Si,' the girl replied. The shells dangling from her arms shook and mixed together, making a soft, musical sound as she pointed down an empty stretch of beach.

Mary reached up and touched the smooth shells. 'They *are* beautiful,' she said.

Aaron threw Mary a dirty look and she laughed.

Kaleb nearly lost his balance as he stood up. The sand on the edge of the sandbar was soft and offered little support even for his small body. He turned toward the shore and squatted again, peering into the clear water of a narrow channel that coursed slowly between two large sandbars. Suddenly, a tiny fish darted past. As he stepped into the water, the fish disappeared in the beige cloud of sand that surrounded his foot. A second later it bolted from the cloud, like a firefighter emerging from the smoke of a burning building. Yelping with delight, the young boy pursued the fish, following it along the snaking waterway that weaved between sandbars. Periodically, he stepped out of the channel and squatted on the sand to avoid the sun's reflection off the water. He had just steadied his hand above his quarry when it vanished into dark water. Surprised by the unexpected disappearance, he stood up, snuffed into the salty air and stepped after it, plunging deep into the cool darkness.

The young girl stood smiling as Aaron ran his hands over

the assortment of smooth, threaded shells, twisting and turning them between his fingers.

'I will pick one to match your skin,' the girl said finally.

'I think it would look more appropriate on our son, don't you, Aaron?'

'What son?' the girl said, looking toward the water.

Mary pointed at the sand where Kaleb had been playing, but he was gone. 'Aaron!' she cried and jumped to her feet.

Aaron bolted toward the sea, white sand flying from his feet. Peering at the spot where her son had been playing, Mary squeezed the sun from her eyes, but the space was now vacant. It was as though the sand had swallowed him whole. Her instincts screamed at her to run. Every muscle was contracted, every tendon taut. But there was nowhere to run. The shore that only moments earlier had washed tranquility over the beach now appeared vast and unfamiliar, unwilling to surrender its terrible secret. Desperately, she scanned the waters for a sign of her son, but there was nothing.

Without the slightest hesitation, Aaron flew past the spot where Mary had last seen Kaleb and he rushed into the sea. It was now apparent that the vast water had been advancing toward them, like a predator moving silently toward its prey. When Aaron was well past the point where she had seen Kaleb only seconds earlier she called out to him, but he didn't respond.

Blood pounded in her ears as her husband stormed into the sea, water splashing and churning all around him. Time accelerated and all sounds became muffled except for a solitary, high-pitched tone that rang in her ears. In the far distance she could hear herself calling, 'Kaleb! Kaleb!' but the voice was no longer hers. Heat waves rising from the sand obscured her vision. The beach was closing in on them, engulfing its inhabitants in a dream-like world. Her legs folded beneath her and she collapsed to her knees. Her face turned pale, her mouth drained of all moisture. And then, almost one hundred and fifty feet away, Aaron plunged his arm deep into the blue water and reclaimed their son from the sea.

Tucking Kaleb under his arm in a nearly upside-down position, Aaron ran toward the beach. Salt water slowly drained from Kaleb's mouth. With Aaron's left hand he supported Kaleb's shoulders and neck, preventing the young boy's head from swinging as he ran. With his middle finger he checked for a pulse. From the beach, Mary could see Aaron endeavoring to resuscitate their son as he ran by rhythmically compressing his chest with his right forearm. Suddenly, Kaleb coughed and salt water and vomit spewed from his mouth. By the time Aaron laid their son in Mary's arms, Kaleb was crying.

Mary pressed Kaleb to her chest. Rocking him back and forth, she began to weep. Aaron knelt next to them, panting, his hands placed firmly on their shoulders.

'I love you,' Mary whispered, her face buried in Kaleb's cheek.

When the tears stopped, Mary looked for the young girl, but she was nowhere to be seen. She had disappeared as silently as she had appeared. Mary needed to find her—to reassure her that Kaleb was okay. She would buy a necklace from her. But the girl's business with them had already been concluded, for upon Mary's beach mat was a brightly colored seashell necklace.

Mary stepped lightly into the master bedroom, retrieved the seashell necklace and backed into the hallway. As she tilted it in the palm of her hand, the shells rolled over one another, making the familiar musical sound. She kissed the shells, placed them into the pocket of her dress and descended the stairs. With only a brief pause to glance through the quiet house, she stepped outside and closed the door behind her. The great oaks swayed in the wind before her. Taking a deep breath, she stepped onto the stone path and left all but one memory behind.

❧ CHAPTER FOUR ❧

Innocence

'Arianne, have you seen Mary?'

Startled by the sudden appearance of the Head Pediatrics Nurse, the receptionist placed a paper bookmark into her novel and slid it into the hutch in front of her. 'Mary who?' she said, smiling.

McLeary scowled. She was clearly in no mood for humor.

'No, not today,' Arianne said. 'Why?'

'I'm starting to worry about her,' McLeary replied, looking toward the main entrance. 'A strange man called on her about an hour ago and I haven't seen her since. It's not like her to leave suddenly, and she's never been gone for this long. You didn't see her leave?'

'No. I just came on shift about twenty minutes ago. Is something wrong?'

'No,' McLeary said slowly, shaking her head. 'I've got too much to do today to worry about this now!' McLeary placed her hands firmly on the countertop and looked sternly over her spectacles. 'Listen, Arianne, if you see her I want you to come and tell me. And if you see the man she was with, I want you to find me right away. I don't want to hear about the rules. Understood?'

'I will. But how will I recognize him? What does he look like?'

'He's an odd one … a funny-looking sort.'

'I see lots of funny-looking people,' she giggled.

'You'll know him when you see him,' McLeary snapped. After a final glower at the front doors, she turned on her heels and lumbered back up the stairs.

As soon as McLeary disappeared from sight, Arianne opened the top right drawer of her desk, placed the novel inside and retrieved a long, triangular block. She looked culpably toward the east and west wings of the building and, after a brief assessment, placed the wooden block on the counter, its etched side facing outwards:

BACK IN 10 MINUTES

She left the reception area, quickly passing over the smooth marble tile floor of the central foyer. After a final glance over her shoulder, she pushed opened one of two large doors of the hospital chapel.

The chapel stood at the rear of the building, where the two wings of the hospital met. A long row of intricately patterned stained-glass skylights mounted high above the altar created a stunning mosaic of color, but the northern sky provided little ambient light for the tall room on even the brightest of days. Instead, large windows above the hospital's south-facing entrance permitted the sun's light to pass through the central foyer. Two large stained glass windows over the chapel entrance transformed the light into bright hues of orange, red and blue that scattered under a high-vaulted nave and shallow transepts. At one side of the chapel altar stood a wooden table over which was draped an intricately embroidered white linen cloth. In the centre of the table was placed a small marble statue of the virgin mother, around which were laid wax effigies: pale white representations of various body parts, macabre offerings to a power far greater than the skills of those who toiled just beyond its walls.

Arianne stepped lightly over the marble floor, patterned with alternating dark and light tiles like a giant checkerboard. She gazed around the impressive architecture as though noticing it for the first time. Only one other person was present, an elderly woman in a powder blue housecoat who sat to the right of the wide aisle. Her crumpled hands rested shoulder-width apart on the back of the wooden pew in front of her. The old woman gazed directly ahead at a large, golden cross suspended behind the altar. Sensing Arianne's presence, the woman turned to her and smiled brightly.

'Hello, Arianne,' she said in a fragile voice.

'Hello, Mrs. Timble. I'm—looking for someone.'

'Well, you're not going to find him in here, dear,' she said, grinning, '—at least, not at this time of day.'

'I'm looking for Mary,' Arianne blushed. 'Have you seen her?'

'I haven't. I don't think I've ever seen her in here, dear. If she's not with her boy, she's probably in the guest room. Have you looked there?'

She shook her head. 'No.'

The old woman placed a hand to her lips. 'For heaven's sake,' she whispered, 'I can't remember his name. What is his name, dear?'

'Kaleb.'

'Oh yes, of course. *Kaleb*. Such an uncommon name— you'd think I'd be able to remember it. He's such a beautiful boy.'

The old woman lowered her eyes and sat silent for a moment, her hand resting lightly against her cheek.

'How are you, Mrs. Timble?' Arianne said.

Most of the hospital staff knew that the old woman suffered from a multitude of painful ailments, including severe rheumatoid arthritis. She had survived two strokes relatively unscathed, but at ninety-six, her heart was tired and failing. It was widely believed that, having outlived her husband and both her children, it was not for the return of good health that she now prayed.

Suddenly, the old woman sprang back to life and her demeanor switched, like a well-rehearsed actress entering a stage.

'I'm feeling fine, Arianne—right as rain. Thank you so much for asking, dear.'

'You look good, Mrs. Timble.'

'This is the Lord's house, Arianne. Mind the truth now,' she said with a coy smile.

'My conscience is clear.'

'Why are you looking for Mary?' Her expression turned suddenly grave. 'Nothing's happened to the boy, I hope.'

'No, nothing's happened.'

'Oh, good. Now see, I can't remember his name again.'

'Kaleb,' Arianne said, fighting back a smile.

'Oh yes. Of course.'

'Mary's been gone for a while and we don't know where she is. Nurse McLeary's worried about her.'

'That woman makes it her business to worry about people—her patients *and* their relatives. You know, most people are afraid of her, but I'm certain that beneath her gruff façade and imposing frame beats a proportionately large heart. She has a lot of empathy, that woman does—she just doesn't know how to show it.'

'I think you're right. She's certainly worried about Mary.'

'I'm sure Mary's fine. She's very sharp. I don't know her well, but I can tell she can take care of herself. She probably just needed some air. The Lord knows what she's gone through and how much she's sacrificed for her son.' The old woman squinted. 'Does she have a husband? I've never seen her in the company of a man, come to think of it.'

'I think he died. I believe he was a doctor and he died in a war somewhere.'

'Oh, I hope you're wrong, dear. No, that just wouldn't be fair at all.'

The flames from a row of beige beeswax candles that burned at the altar reflected off the wireframe spectacles that dangled from the old woman's neck on a heavy string.

'She's so beautiful, isn't she?'

'Yes, she is,' Arianne blushed.

'I'm just lucky that you two weren't around when I was young … or I'd never have found a husband!' she laughed.

Arianne smiled as the seventy-eight year difference between them dissolved into that thought.

'She reminds me of my mother,' Mrs. Timble said. 'Isn't that funny—a beautiful young woman reminding an old woman of her mother? Bless my soul!'

'No, not at all. I think I know what you mean. I'd like to hear more about your mother some time, but I'd better get back to my post before they find out that I left. It was nice talking with you, Mrs. Timble. I'm so glad to see you up and about again.'

'Thank you, Arianne. You're so kind. Come up to chat anytime.'

Arianne walked up the narrow strip of red and gold carpet that defined the aisle and stood at the foot of the altar. She bowed her head and made the sign of the cross over her chest with her thumb, index and middle fingers pressed together at their tips. Using the flame of a candle, she lit another and placed it in a small, fine-grain sandbox that sat on a raised table next to the aisle. Groping in her pockets, she searched for a coin but then noticed the donation box was missing. She turned and hurried down the aisle, smiling at Mrs. Timble as she passed.

Mary felt like an unwelcome stranger as she stood before the tall, cathedral-like entrance of the hospital. Just as her home had appeared different, so too the hospital seemed less familiar. But her spirits were much higher than the last time she had gazed upon it, and she now had the confidence to plunge back into her responsibilities. She took a deep breath and passed under the stone archway.

'Where have you been?' Arianne said as Mary walked through the foyer.

'I went out for some fresh air.'

'Well, it looks like you got plenty of *fresh*,' she said, smiling at the coat in Mary's arms.

Mary looked at Kadesh's coat like it was evidence of a crime. She knew Arianne wouldn't rest until she had a full explanation, but Mary was in no mood for her usual playful conversation. Too much time had passed since she had left the hospital, and she was eager to get to her son before he awoke.

'I'll have to explain another time,' Mary said, moving quickly toward the stairs.

'I can hardly wait,' Arianne smiled. 'Oh, by the way, McLeary's looking for you.'

Mary's chest tightened. 'Why, is something wrong?'

'No, don't worry,' Arianne said, retrieving her book from under the counter. 'She was just worried about you. You know how she gets. I'm supposed to find her as soon as you get back. Be ready for an earful.'

'You're sure nothing's wrong?'

'I'm sure.' Arianne smiled at the pages of her book and glanced at Mary out of the corners of her eyes, her small nostrils flared.

Mary entered a small washroom not far from the reception area, along the lower east wing. Under a flickering yellow light she moved to a mirror that hung over an ivory white porcelain sink, and sighed at the uncharacteristically pale woman staring back at her. Her hair was loose and untamed. Reflexively, she reached for a handbag that wasn't there. She looked for a moment at Kadesh's coat, wondering if a comb might be hidden fortuitously in one of its large pockets, but she couldn't bring herself to search them. She laid the overcoat respectfully onto the lid of the toilet and carefully folded it into a neat cube of brown wool.

The tap squealed in protest as she opened the valve, and it moaned as cold water gurgled through the long neck of the faucet. As the water spilled over her cupped hands, she dipped her face into it, resisting the strong urge to withdraw. The cold was exhilarating, but in that brief moment of icy darkness she also found an overwhelming sense of calm. Slowly, she spread the liquid over her face and neck and repeated the ritual several times. Stray beads of water ran down the smooth skin of her neck and wet the collar of her dress. She wet her hands and combed her fingers slowly through her long, wavy hair. Closing her eyes, she drew in a deep breath and slowly exhaled into her reflection.

Mary reached into the pocket of her dress and withdrew the seashell necklace. She unclasped it and, holding it by its ends, reached behind her neck. As she gazed at the smooth, colorful shells, she noticed that her dress was undone just below the top button. Carefully, she placed the seashell necklace on the narrow edge of the sink. Pinching the buttonhole with her left hand, she moved it over the spot where the button should have been, but there was nothing underneath. She placed her left hand through the opening of her dress and spread out the fabric. Moving her hand in a circular pattern, she inspected the chronically rashed skin beneath. As the dress shifted with her movements, something slid down her front and fell to her feet.

On the faded linoleum floor lay her silver necklace. Relieved to see that the pendant was still there, she picked it up and examined it. The chain was broken at a link near the clasp. She tied the ends of the necklace together and placed it in her pocket, feeling naked without it hanging from her neck. As she retrieved the seashell necklace from the edge of the sink, the shells produced their soft, musical sound. For an instant, within the sound she thought she could perceive voices—the sweet whisper of the young Spanish girl from the beach, and a chilling hiss:

This is not for man.

And then there was silence. Her thoughts became clear and focused, and she was taken unwillingly back to the incident in the interrogation room. The man's hand was upon her, groping at her chest, and again she heard his voice: '*This is not for man!'*

Her hand slipped into the pocket of her dress and her fingers moved unconsciously along the smooth links of the necklace as the event earlier that day reassembled in her thoughts. As though she were observing the slightest movement of a moth that had been camouflaged against the bark of a tree, a new truth seemed to emerge and she was no longer certain about the meaning of the incident. She gazed into the mirror, turning left and right in an endeavor to see if the necklace could have been visible underneath her dress. But the thick material overlapped considerably at the buttons and regardless of how she positioned herself, she could not see beneath the fabric.

But what would it have meant, even if he had seen it? she wondered. *Why would my pendant be of interest to him?*

With those thoughts turning over in her mind, she retrieved the overcoat, opened the door and stepped into the bright hallway.

Kadesh stood at the reception desk, talking quietly with Arianne, his hat held tightly against his chest. His sudden presence seemed somehow out of context and strangely inappropriate. He hadn't yet noticed Mary, and for a brief moment she wondered whether she might be able to escape to the upper floor without detection, but he turned to her and beamed. 'Oh good,' he said. 'I see that you still have my coat!'

'I'm sorry,' Mary said, handing it to him. 'I didn't realize that I still had it on when I—left.'

'That is understandable,' he said, waving his hand, '—quite understandable under the circumstances. It is no longer raining, so I do not need it right now, but I may wish that I had it soon.'

He bowed his head and seemed to collect himself as a long moment of awkward silence passed.

'Eh, I must apologize for what happened,' he said. 'I was caught off guard. I never would have imagined that he would react in such a manner. I am truly sorry. I should not have asked you to come with me. I will not bother you again with my problems.'

He was clearly suffering—not just from remorse, but also from the effort required to speak with her. With each word he squirmed and fidgeted like a guilt-ridden child about to be scolded. It clearly required a monumental effort for him to face her.

'I'm fine, really,' Mary said.

'I do not know what happened. His reaction to you was totally out of character. I have never seen him act aggressively. If I had, I would not have brought you there. I assure you.'

'Do you know why he reacted like that?'

'Eh, no, I do not. He has been, eh, unresponsive since you left.'

Mary produced the broken necklace from her pocket and held it out to Kadesh. As she did, the pendant slid down the chain and swung momentarily at the bottom of its length. The light of the foyer moved across its smooth curves.

'My chain is broken. I think it happened when he grabbed at me. I wonder if he was trying to get it.'

Kadesh stared, transfixed, at the silver pendant. 'I don't know,' he murmured and gently grasped it. 'Where did you get this?'

'It was a gift from my husband,' she said. 'I'm sure it's just a coincidence.'

Kadesh tracked the silver piece as Mary drew it away from him, eyeing it like a hungry dog following a piece of meat.

'Eh, I wonder if I could have that?' he said.

'Why would you want my necklace?' Mary replied, feeling suddenly possessive.

'To—have it examined. It may have some significance.'

'It does. It has great significance to me. What would be the good of you taking it?'

'Please,' Kadesh said, grasping her wrist as she moved the necklace toward her pocket.

Mary froze. She stared, shocked and confused, wondering where his sudden aggression had come from. It then occurred to her that he was by necessity persistent, and that it must often be imperative for him to find a way around or through the many obstacles that would undoubtedly be encountered during the course of his work. When something important was at stake, he could never allow his shyness to interfere and hinder his investigation. Feeling his hand closed firmly around her wrist, she knew that when necessary, he could conquer his handicap. Aaron's gift lay directly in the path of his investigation and it now required his attention.

But curiosity was not his alone. If there was any connection between it and Kadesh's prisoner—no matter how unlikely it may be—she also wanted to know.

'Eh, Mary, you would be doing me another great favor if I could borrow your necklace for just a short while.'

He let go of her wrist and fidgeted nervously with his hands. There was something wholly improper about his discomfort, making it difficult for her to accept that she was its source. She felt like a parent who had inadvertently inflicted pain on her child.

'You won't damage it?' she said.

'Not a scratch—I assure you.'

After a brief hesitation, she held the necklace out to him.

Gently, he took it from her and folded its length across the palm of his hand. He seemed to weigh it for a moment before closing his fingers tightly around it. He smiled awkwardly.

'I will be back within the hour—I promise you,' he said, turning on his heels just as a voice boomed from behind them.

'What's going on here?'

Kadesh reflexively ducked and looked over his shoulder toward the stairs. McLeary was moving quickly toward him.

'I was just leaving!' Kadesh announced, waving his hand in the air, and he disappeared down the outer steps.

Mary stared at the empty doorway, knowing that Kadesh would now endeavor to see if the piece he held in his hand somehow fit within his investigation. Somehow she knew he would be disappointed, and she took pity on him. She reflected on how little she knew about the man—simply because she had never inquired. Mary was disappointed with the person

41

she'd become. Without a word, she slipped past McLeary, who was now preoccupied with Arianne, and quickly ascended the stairs.

'You know, Betty,' Arianne said with a smirk, 'he's nothing like you described him. He's kind of cute.'

'Oh!' McLeary snorted and threw up her hands as she pursued Mary to the third floor.

❧ CHAPTER FIVE ❧

Mukkadesh Atesh

A sinking feeling came over Mary as she neared the door to her son's room. *Please be asleep*, she thought as she slowly pushed the door open.

Propped up in his bed, Kaleb sat concentrating on a small wooden board that lay on a swivel table positioned over his lap. A young woman sat cross-legged on the end of his bed, dropping small pieces onto the board.

'Well, look who's here, Kaleb,' the young woman said, smiling up at Mary.

'Mumma!' Kaleb said, holding out his arms, a wide smile stretched across his face.

'Oh, Kabe,' Mary sighed. 'Why aren't you asleep?' She embraced him, careful to not pull on the array of tubes. 'I'm sorry, Muriel, I didn't realize I'd be away for so long.'

'There's no need to apologize, Mary,' she said, rising from the bed and straightening her dress. 'We've been having lots of fun.'

'We're playing Mancala,' Kaleb announced, spilling some of the small stones onto his lap. He quickly gathered them and placed them back on the game board.

The game consisted of a rectangular piece of wood about

the size of a shoebox lid, and a number of small, polished black stones. The board was fashioned from a single piece of tight-grained hardwood, smoothed and darkened from years of contact with human skin. Two rows of shallow, circular pits were hand-carved into the board, six on each side. At each end was formed a larger, oval pit. As Mary focused on the small stones in the pits, a wave of nausea passed over her. She closed her eyes.

'Watch, Mumma.' Kaleb said. He reached over and grasped the stones from a pit in the row nearer to him.

'I pick up all the seeds from one of my holes and I grow them like this.'

'*Sow* them,' Muriel said as she moved toward the door.

'Sow them,' he said. 'Watch me—'

Still dizzy with nausea, she leaned onto the bed, and with one hand over her mouth she watched as Kaleb placed a stone counterclockwise into each of the round pits. When his hand was empty, he looked to his mother, grinning widely with satisfaction.

'You learn so fast,' Mary said, brushing his hair away from his forehead. 'I'm so proud of you. How long has he been awake, Muriel?'

'I was pretending to be asleep when you left,' Kaleb said. 'I tricked you.'

The inside of Mary's mouth felt parched and sticky. She blushed.

'Please don't get upset, Mary,' Muriel said. 'I've been with him the whole time. We had a wonderful visit, didn't we little monkey?'

He nodded vigorously. 'And I met another boy like me.'

'You did?' Mary said, forcing a smile.

'Yup. His name is Daniel. His mumma says I can visit him whenever I want. He's just down there,' he said, pointing toward the hallway.

'Daniel arrived yesterday,' Muriel said. 'He's in three-sixteen.'

'That's so nice you have a friend now,' Mary replied. 'I'm

very happy. So much has happened in such a short time.'

'And Kaleb was just fine,' Muriel said. 'No need to worry.'

'He's always fine when he's with you, Muriel. What would I do without you?'

'I'm going to teach Daniel how to play Mancala,' Kaleb said. 'He's probably never played before.' He reached into the large oval pit and withdrew about a dozen of the small stones.

'Look how shiny they are, Mumma,' he said, displaying them in the palm of his hand.

'They're like gemstones,' Mary murmured rolling one over on his palm with her fingertip.

'Oh,' he breathed. 'What are those?'

'They're very special rocks.'

'Oh. I think that's what these are.'

'The game is very old,' Muriel said, running her hand along the wooden grain of the board. 'It's been played all over the world for thousands of years. This one was given to the hospital by an old man soon after it was built. The nurses say he'd had it in his family for a long, long time, and that the forty-eight stones in these pits are the same ones that came with the game many years ago. Not one has ever been lost.'

Kaleb listened attentively, mesmerized by Muriel's story. The sound of his heavy breathing could be heard through the brief silence that ensued.

Muriel leaned toward him. 'Do you know how I know?' she asked.

'How?' he whispered.

'These are black onyx stones. They're very difficult to find around here. Forty-eight pieces were made for the game, and forty-eight pieces are still here.'

A small smile touched Mary's lips. It was ludicrous to think that the game had remained intact after passing through the hands of so many children. Yet the board was clearly antique and the patterns of the stones were very similar. It was possible they had all been cut from the same rock. If they all remained after Kaleb was through with it, she would believe Muriel.

'If I leave the game with you for a while, will you promise to take good care of it?'

'I promise. Is the old man still here?'

'I'm sure he's not,' Mary said.

'What happened to him?'

Mary hesitated and shifted her weight uneasily. She smiled lightly at Muriel, inviting a response.

'I don't know,' Muriel said.

Kaleb watched his mother closely. 'Did he die?' he said.

'I—don't know, Kabe,' Mary said, shaking her head. 'I didn't know him.'

'I'm sure he had lots of grandchildren just like you,' Muriel smiled.

'Oh,' he sighed. 'Why didn't he give it to them?'

'He probably had so many grandchildren that he couldn't decide which one to give it to.'

Kaleb stared at the wooden board. 'He must have worked really hard to make it.'

'This game is much older than the man,' Muriel said. 'It was made long before he was born.'

Kaleb carefully placed the stones into one of the larger oval pits.

'I'll leave you two alone,' Muriel smiled and moved to the door. She gave him a sweet wave and left.

'Kabe, I don't ever want you to trick me again.'

His smile faded. 'Okay. Are you angry at me?'

'No, of course not. I just don't like to leave you alone.'

'But I wasn't alone, Mumma. Muriel played with me the whole time. She said I can play Mancala with her whenever I want.'

He pinched a stone between his index finger and thumb and held it up toward the window. 'How do they make the rocks so shiny?' he sighed.

'Hmm. I don't know,' Mary said, picking up a few stones. As she gazed at the rows of shallow pits, rolling the stones over in her fingertips, the game became familiar. From a far corner of her mind approached a memory: a faded image of her squatting in front of rows of small, dusty pits that she had carved into hard clay with her fingertips.

'I think I played this game when I was a little girl,' she said.

'Oh. That was a long time ago.'

'Sometimes it feels like it,' she smiled.

Kaleb picked up a small group of stones from the board and placed them one at a time into the round pits in a counter-clockwise manner. His last stone landed in the oval-shaped pit to his right. He picked up another group of stones from a pit and placed them similarly. When the last stone landed in an empty pit on his side, he removed all of the stones from the opposite pit and placed them into the oval pit to his right. He smiled proudly.

Mary embraced him. 'You are my angel,' she said.

He reciprocated and kissed her hair. 'Mumma,' he whispered in her ear as he curled her hair around his index finger, 'are you sick?'

She pulled back and stared at him, her brow furrowed. 'Of course not,' she said. 'Why would you ask that?'

'I'm sorry, Mumma,' he muttered and bowed his head. He glanced up at her from under his brow, as if expecting to be scolded.

'I'm *not*,' she said stroking his hair. 'And it's not for children to worry about grown-ups. Okay?'

He nodded, gazing at the game and casually moving stones from one pit to another.

'Why don't we start a new game and you can show me how to play?' Mary said.

'Okay,' he smiled.

Mother and child played together until all the pits on Kaleb's side of the board were empty. 'I have eighteen,' he announced after counting the stones in his oval pit. 'How many do you have?'

He eyed Mary's collection, which appeared considerably larger than his.

'I have eighteen, too,' she said. 'We're the same—me and you.'

He beamed as she placed the game on the bedside table.

'You look tired, angel,' she said.

'Just a little bit.'

'Will you try to go to sleep this time?'

He nodded.

'Then lie back and close your eyes. Mumma's here now.'

Mary removed one of the soft down pillows from behind his head and placed it next to him. As he shifted his body underneath the covers, she reclined his bed to a horizontal position. She then moved to the open window and drew the heavy curtains together. The stagnant smell of old fabric wafted over her and she gagged briefly, then parted the curtains slightly to invite in some fresh air. By the time she bent over her son and kissed him on the forehead, he was already asleep. She watched his breathing change to a slow, rhythmic pattern, and then she sank into the soft leather chair beside him.

Her thoughts drifted to Kadesh's prisoner. She couldn't remember whether she had been told his name, but she could see his face clearly. Its image had been etched into her memory forever. As she recalled the curves of his face, she couldn't escape the feeling that there was something familiar about him: an enigmatic familiarity Kadesh also shared, and which made her feel strangely at ease in his presence. At another time she would have been more willing to help the detective, but her son's breathing, slow and labored, was a painful reminder of her priorities. His soft sound muffled all other curiosities.

Mary shifted in the leather seat, searching for a position that offered relief to the aches in her hips. After a few minutes of struggle she stood up, placed her hands behind her hips and arched backward, stretching the muscles of her lower back and abdomen. But as she stared at the ceiling, nausea and dizziness set in again and she sank back into the chair. As the nausea worked its way through her, she placed her hands over her face and her head between her knees. She closed her eyes and waited for the discomforts to pass, but they remained. Sitting doubled-over, she listened to the distant sounds of the hospital ward as her two intimate maladies battled one another for dominance over her misery.

After some time, the discomforts finally faded. She rose from the chair and stretched again. Her son's breathing was deep and even; his eyes moved noticeably behind their thin lids.

Outside, she heard someone speak her name. She followed the voice into the hallway and gazed down its length to where McLeary was gesturing at one of the nurses. As Mary approached, McLeary placed her hands pugnaciously on her hips.

'Well, where have you been?'

'I've been playing Mancala with Kaleb.'

'*Before* that,' McLeary frowned. 'Who was that man with you and what did he want? I can't for the life of me understand how you could up and leave with a complete stranger just like that.'

With no reasonable explanation to offer her, Mary felt ashamed. And the shame was made worse by being lectured like a child in front of a young nurse, who found sudden interest in a stack of papers.

'I guess I just needed a break,' Mary murmured.

McLeary stared at her for a moment, then took the stack of papers away from the nurse and dropped them on the desk.

'Well, I didn't like the look of him, Mary. I don't trust him and I suggest that you don't, either. Who was he, anyways?'

'He's—a detective.'

'Good heavens, Mary. He doesn't look anything like a detective. Why on earth would he come here looking for you? You'd think he'd know better than that. It's completely inappropriate.'

'He thought I could help him.'

'Well, I can't imagine why he needed your help—especially at a time like this. It's ridiculous!' She stepped nearer. 'You have a giving character, Mary. Your type is easily taken advantage of. I know *his* type. He's the taking sort. Don't let him take advantage of you. I have enough to worry about around here—don't make me worry about you, too.'

Mary knew it would be fruitless to try justifying her behavior to McLeary. She couldn't even justify it to herself. And if McLeary learned of the incident at the police station, Mary would never hear the end of it.

'Thank you for your concern, Betty, but you don't need to worry about me.' Mary smiled apologetically at the nurses and headed back toward her son's room, pausing for a moment to gaze along the length of the hallway.

The walls were adorned with colorful illustrations made by children. She had passed by them many times before, but until that moment had never noticed how many there were. Hundreds of drawings on papers of various sizes and colors tiled the walls like a giant mosaic. Each illustration had one of two themes: a group of characters—some small, some large, but all smiling—or a solitary child who was usually in bed. The isolation came clearly through in their artwork, and it weighed heavily upon her. She suffered at the thought of the many children who had inhabited the rooms of that ward, and the hours and days of loneliness they had experienced. She didn't hear Arianne's approach, and was startled when the receptionist suddenly appeared beside her, flustered and out of breath.

'Mr. Kadesh is here for you, Mary. He asked me to come get you.'

Reflexively, Mary touched her pockets, as though expecting to find yet another item of his that had inadvertently come into her possession. But they were empty. She followed Arianne along the hallway and glanced over her shoulder to see whether McLeary was watching.

Her knees felt weak as she descended the stairs. The hardness of the marble was acutely noticeable, and with each step her legs threatened to fold beneath her. The inside of her mouth had become dry as paper. Kadesh's early return could not be a good sign.

When she arrived at the main floor foyer, she rushed to Kadesh, who was seated on a long wooden bench at one side of the entrance. He stood and smiled, but his forced expression was not reassuring.

'Eh, hello Mary. I am sorry to bother you again.'

'That was fast,' she said, trembling slightly.

'Eh, yes. I have completed a preliminary analysis. I thought it important to discuss my findings with you right away.'

'What could you have learned in such a short time?'

He gestured for her to sit next to him. 'Please,' he said, sinking to the bench.

'I'd prefer to stand.'

'Of course,' he said, quickly rising to his feet again. He cleared his throat and shifted his weight from one foot to another.

'Where's my necklace?' Mary asked, noticing his empty hands.

'Well, eh, that is why I am here.'

'Did you lose it?'

'Oh no, of course I still have it.'

'Then what is the matter?' she said, stepping toward him.

He gently grasped her right hand. 'Eh, I am afraid I bear some bad news.'

Mary retracted her hand, but he held firmly. Her stomach tightened.

'How to say this? The pendant you have given to me is *mukkadesh atesh.*'

She breathed a small sigh of relief. 'What does that mean?'

'It is an Arabic phrase. It means, literally, *holy fire.*'

She stared at him for a moment, wondering whether he was confused. His words held no meaning for her. 'I don't understand.'

'Eh, the pendant shows significant radioactivity. It is very dangerous. I believe it to be made of uranium, but I will need to confirm this. If one looks closely, there are two very small inscriptions in Arabic near the tip of the heart that, to the naked eye, appear only as blemishes. But they serve as a warning to those who know their significance. It is told that widows of war shape them into gifts for the enemy. Until today, I had only heard of such a thing.'

Mary stared at Kadesh in silent disbelief. His gibberish still rang empty in her ears and was of no relevance to her. He was talking about something else. And then suddenly, like cold air passing through thin clothing, thoughts of her pendant seeped into her mind: thoughts that slowly congealed into a hideous form, a shape that lay at the nucleus of her suffering.

It was clear now. The pendant's arrival marked the beginning of her illness. It was the keystone of her afflictions: the persistent rash on her chest, her chronic fatigue. It was the fountainhead of misery from which spilled relentless streams of malevolence. Around their necks they had borne the agent of their disease.

'Kaleb!' she cried and fled up the stairs, leaving Kadesh standing alone in the foyer.

It seemed to take an eternity for her to reach her son. Her legs felt filled with lead, swinging through deep salt water. The ground at her feet had become wet sand and passed beneath her in slow motion. Even the air offered new resistance, pushing her away from her child. Finally, she reached the third-floor landing and ran down the hallway toward her son's room.

'What's wrong?' McLeary called out to her from down the wing.

But Mary could hear nothing but the sound of her shoes on the hard floor. She burst open the door to Kaleb's room and flew to the side of her sleeping child. Throwing off his covers, she tore the front of his gown open like a skin that hid the malice beneath. There the serpent thing lay wrapped around her son's thin neck, its mouth open and pressed flat against his chest, slowly and silently releasing its poison into his dwindling body. Its dark, unfeeling eyes stared expressionlessly outward.

Like a popping ember, its spine cracked softly as she tore it from his neck. It coiled and slid around her hand as she slammed the wretched thing upon the floor over and over again. When it remained still and limp in her hand, she ran screaming to the window and cast it down to the street.

Exhausted, Mary crumpled to the floor and began to weep.

McLeary and another nurse rushed into the room. The head nurse attended to Mary, the other went to Kaleb. A third nurse stood just inside the doorway, her hands placed firmly over her mouth.

'Mary dear, what's happened!?' McLeary said.

Tears streamed down Mary's cheeks as she raised her head. 'Aaron,' she breathed, 'he brought this upon us.'

McLeary quickly turned to Kaleb. He sat upright in his bed, crying softly for his mother. The nurse stroked his head while covering his chest with the torn gown.

'You've got to stay strong,' McLeary whispered as she helped Mary to her feet. But Mary stared blankly ahead into nothingness.

'This isn't fair to Kaleb, Mary. You've got to stay strong for him.' The large woman gently shook her. 'Mary, do you understand!?'

For a brief moment there was silence, except for the sound of a child whimpering far in the distance. Mary knew the voice and to whom it belonged. He was the only thing that mattered. 'Kaleb,' she murmured, searching the room with her eyes. When she found him, she ran and embraced him.

'I'm sorry, Kaleb—I'm so sorry…'

Abdul-Majid swept away the larger bits of rubble from the stone tiles on the rooftop of the abandoned building with his hands, and sat in the clearing with his back against the outside wall, his rifle laid across his lap. He flexed his ankles and admired the handsome shape of his boots. Besides these he had only one pair of shoes, and the soles of those were worn through. Although his younger sister often reminded him that it was not truthful to call the boots *new*, as they had been removed from the body of another soldier, they were as good as new to him. He had hesitated to take them at first, believing they would bring bad luck. But after assurance from his leader that it was by God's will that the fallen soldier's feet were larger than his and not smaller, he accepted them. At fifteen, he was the youngest member of *Masha'allah*. As the most recent recruit, he was given first pick of new gear but it had to be found in the battlefield, as the insurgence had few supplies for its recruits.

The sun was directly above him, so he cast little shadow. He twisted his head and, leaning back slightly, peered through an opening about the size of a human head in the stone wall behind him. The lower edge of the hole was worn smooth and blackened by the hands and feet of children who used it as a step to access the top ledge. From that vantage, he had a clear view of the dusty street below.

Shifting his body to a squatting position, he faced the wall and placed his fingers on the edge of the hole. As he peered down at the street, he tensed. About eighty yards away, a tall man approached. Slowly, he pushed his rifle through the opening and rested it on the lower edge. Peering down the rifle's sight, he confirmed that the flag stitched on the man's right shoulder was that of an infidel. He thanked God for leading him to that spot.

He raised his rifle, pressed its butt firmly against his left shoulder and began his breathing exercise, waiting silently as the man approached, tracking him with the rifle. When the man stopped across the road about thirty yards away, he placed his finger over the trigger and began to squeeze slowly and evenly.

Aaron was pleased with his choice of gifts. He was confident that the silver pendants would serve as restitution for the argument he'd had with Mary just before leaving. It had weighed on his conscience over the past few days and seemed to grow more burdensome with the passage of time. It was not like them to fight and he didn't like it. Unconfident in the integrity of the package, he checked it again to ensure that the postage stamps wouldn't separate from the paper wrapping. The stamp glue, which had tasted vaguely like child's paste, was of inferior quality so the stamps wouldn't stick properly to the papyrus. He'd needed to use extra adhesive to get them to stick. An old cobbler had given him some of the glue used for fixing soles to leather shoes. The package still stank of the volatile liquid that also glued the paper together, but he was now confident that the package would hold up to the rough handling it would inevitably be subjected to during the course of its travel. He dropped it into the mailbox.

The rifle fired, kicking hard against Abdul-Majid's shoulder. His body twisted from the force, but he could see that he had hit his mark. The bullet entered the back of the man's neck just to the left of the midline. From the spray of flesh and blood the boy knew it had passed through the front of his neck. He tracked the man's body with his scope as it folded to the ground, and waited for any sign of movement, but the body remained still. He withdrew his rifle from the hole and laid it down at his side.

'Praise God,' he whispered, '—that He would give me the keen eyes of the hawk, the steadiness of the cat and the patience of the spider.'

The boy closed his eyes and sat with his back against the wall as the scene of the killing played over again in his thoughts. He giggled. He had never before seen a man collapse like that. It reminded him of a wooden marionette shaped like a man that his father had found and given to him years ago. He couldn't get the scene out of his thoughts. It came over and over again like an echo through the mountains. The giggle soon turned to laughter. Desperate to muffle his sounds, he buried his face into the sleeve of his left arm and convulsed as tears streamed into the fabric of his jacket.

When the laughter subsided a few minutes later, the boy felt a strange coolness in his groin and realized with horror that he had wet himself. He inspected his darkened pants and cursed softly into the hot air rising off the roof. There he would have to remain until the warmth of his body and the heat of the sun dried his pants. He praised God that none of his fellow soldiers were there to witness the indignity. As he wallowed in shame and anger, the door to the rooftop burst open and half a dozen soldiers streamed out. With his vision still blurred by the tears of laughter he leaned to one side and reached for his gun, but as his fingers clasped the stock of his rifle, the faceless soldiers fired upon him.

The air clapped like thunder. Dozens of bullets entered the boy, seemingly unyielding as they passed through him, erupting out the back of his jacket like a series of small volcanoes spewing flesh and blood like fire. The stone wall behind him was cracked and painted with pieces of flesh and sprays of blood.

The crunching sound of boots on gravel faded into the town as the military escort scattered. Although unable to move, Aaron was acutely aware of his surroundings. He could discern the earthy odor of dusty clay and the weak metallic taste of his own blood. It was strangely quiet. His eyes scanned the heavens as his body starved for air. His chest tightened and he thrashed motionlessly. Soon, the dampened pain subsided and all sensation, all thought, melted together into a consuming state of calm. And then, staring at the pink and orange glow of the desert sky, he yielded his life.

⮞ CHAPTER SIX ⮜

Mary

The nurses worked without speaking as they restored the room to its proper order, toiling silently within a palpable sadness. Before they left, they disconnected the wires and clear, plastic tubing that bound Kaleb to his bed and Mary took him.

With her son pressed lightly against the soft side of her chest and his arms wrapped loosely around her neck, she slowly paced the room, her gaze passing blankly over the floor. Comforted by the gentle movements of her warm body and the soft beating of her heart, the boy soon fell asleep. In her arms she could feel the resolute conviction of the disease that worked on him: his tiny, emaciated body was feather light.

If there was a bottom to the great emptiness that had formed within her, she knew she was near it. Its vast coldness seeped deep into her flesh and extinguished any residual faith in man or religion that had survived her tribulations.

This world was content to leave mother and son—to abandon them in its wake of suffering as it carried on. Old men played backgammon and sipped strong coffee in a crowded room across the street. In the tavern next to it, others drank dark beer. Not far from the edge of town, farmers prepared their fields for the imminent arrival of winter and the cool rains that would follow. Staring out of the window at the grey vastness that stretched before her, she felt insignificant and isolated.

'Mary?' a soft voice called to her.

A thin, middle-aged woman stood at the doorway, smiling at Mary through a sharp but pleasant face. Holding onto the woman's long, floral-patterned dress was a pale boy who, from his modest height and uncertain stance, appeared to be about nine or ten years old. He wore a green hospital gown and a pair of sheepskin slippers, the tops of which were stained with small oil droplets. He had the same sandy-colored hair and narrow face as the woman standing next to him.

'Yes,' Mary said.

'I'm Isabelle and this is my son, Daniel,' she said, placing her hand on the boy's head.

'Hello,' Mary smiled graciously at the boy.

A long moment of silence passed before Isabelle cleared her throat. 'We were wondering if you and your son might like to come with us to the chapel downstairs.'

Chapel. The word stung like a poisoned barb, burning and hissing under her skin. Such places were now nothing more than grand façades that offered false hopes to the naive and simple-minded.

'Why would we want to do that?' Mary said.

Isabelle placed her hand on her son's shoulder and drew him closer to her. The boy placed his arm around her hips and looked up to her for reassurance, but there was none.

'One of the nurses told me that you were interested in the Lord's work,' Isabelle said, looking toward the Bible on the bedside table.

'It's not mine,' Mary said. 'You can have it.'

'Oh—I have one. Thank you,' Isabelle blushed.

'Well, I think we'll pass on the field trip today. Thanks just the same.'

Isabelle looked to Kaleb, who remained motionless with his back to her. 'Perhaps your son would like to come with us?'

she said.

'He's sleeping. And he doesn't have any business down there.'

Isabelle's gaze moved back and forth across the floor for some time. Finally, she advanced a small step toward Mary.

'Don't despair, Mary,' she said in a quivering voice. 'God loves all his children.'

Mary's response was reflexive. It was there before Isabelle appeared. Even before Mary learned of the *mukkadesh atesh*. It had been perched on the tip of her tongue for weeks, waiting for its moment to be released. 'Not this one.' She turned her back to Isabelle as her tears came.

Isabelle placed her hands over her mouth. Kaleb's chin rested on Mary's shoulder, but his stare was on Isabelle. Daniel looked to his mother, his eyes and mouth wide. As tears filled her eyes, Isabelle grasped her son's hand and fled the room.

Within the hour, the nurses had once again tethered Kaleb to the assortment of dangling bottles and electro-mechanical devices that surrounded him like dispassionate spectators. While he sat upright in his bed, forming letters with the Mancala stones on his woolen blanket, Mary sat in the leather chair next to him, staring blankly at the window. Random thoughts and disjointed images passed through her mind: the fight with her husband; her mother sitting at the kitchen table, holding her head in her hands; Mary walking through the field of tall grass, her beast hiding within it, poised with muscles flexed, tracking her movement with its eyes.

'There's going to be a show for the children downstairs,' Muriel said, suddenly appearing next to her. 'I'd like to take him. I know he'd really enjoy it.'

Kaleb stirred in the corner of Mary's vision. His breathing became deeper and louder. Mary struggled to subdue her growing discontent at the thought of entertainment and laughter, but Muriel's soft smile tamed her thoughts. She leaned forward in the chair, her mouth slowly opening. 'I—'

'There's going to be magic and music,' Muriel interjected. 'It'll be good for him—a way to forget about this place for a while.'

Her voice was gentle yet strangely compelling. It reminded Mary of the sound of winter rain falling on the rooftop. On quiet days, she would often listen to Muriel's voice in the hallway and surrender herself to its soothing tone and rhythm. It would take her away from that place. Sometimes she was a little girl again, lying alone in her bed, listening to her mother's voice on the other side of her bedroom door, the thickly accented voice of her father accompanying it like a soft song. She would close her eyes and sink safely into the darkness.

'Okay,' Mary said. Beside her, Kaleb beamed.

With the aid of a nurse, Muriel prepared Kaleb for the trip. The nurses attached only a single condition to the journey: one of the medicine bottles would remain with him at all times. So while Mary carried him down the stairs, Muriel walked beside them, carrying the medicating system that consisted of a tall metal hanger, a bottle containing a clear, colorless liquid and a long delivery tube that terminated in a butterfly needle taped to his arm. When they reached the first-floor landing, Muriel took Kaleb.

'I'll take him from here,' Muriel said.

'I—thought I was coming with you.'

'You take some carefree time for yourself to do whatever you want to do, Mary. Think of it as a small but well-deserved treat.' Muriel rubbed her nose against Kaleb's. 'We're going to have a great time. Right, little monkey?' she said.

He nodded as he played with Muriel's hair, unwinding its length around his index finger. He placed his thumb in his mouth and smiled approvingly at his mother.

Mary returned to her son's room and stood within the unusual stillness, as if listening for the sounds that had vacated with her child. In a terrible moment, the silence seemed to foreshadow an inevitable loneliness that would soon fill her days, and she was struck with a powerful urge to go back downstairs after him. But the feeling soon dissipated as the ambient sounds of the hospital once again filled the corridors. Slowly, she moved to the leather chair and placed her hand on the Bible, but then abruptly turned and moved to the window. On the other side of the glass, the world stretched out invitingly. She inhaled deeply and closed her eyes. Placing her fingertips on the cool glass, she slowly exhaled. Her breath condensed against it instantly and evaporated into the invisible. The tiny droplets were not unlike people, she thought: from nothingness to substance, and then gone again. She gazed briefly at her reflection and then moved to the closet, retrieved a long, black cloak and left.

In the outer doorway of the hospital, Mary draped the travelling cloak over her shoulders. With her son in the trusted care of Muriel, she felt strangely unencumbered. As she stepped outside, the unusually cold air greeted her with an exhilarating wash and she drew it in. The nausea had receded like an unpredictable tide and she was now hungry.

Several small cafes and bistros dotted the street just to the east of the hospital. With no particular destination in mind, she started toward them and the setting sun, but after only a few steps she stopped and placed her hands into her pockets. They were empty. She sighed and had turned back toward the hospital when a glitter caught her eye, like the flash of a small silver fish darting through clear water.

Lying only a few feet away from her in a groove between the concrete walkway and the cobblestone road was the pendant. It seemed to shine up to her like a beacon for a passerby to find—and to *possess*. From the safety of the raised walkway, Mary stared at the wretched thing, almost expecting it to move. She bent over it, and with her hands on her knees she gazed down upon the manifestation of evil—an agent of misery, spawned from man's hatred of his own kind. Trembling, she took it into her hand. As she closed her fingers tightly around it, she briefly thought of how Kadesh had handled it the same way. With it once again casting its malignant rays into her flesh, she straightened up and headed toward home.

The huge oaks of her neighborhood were unmoving in the still air. They seemed aware of the malevolence clasped in her hand, and to watch her as she walked past the weeds and sleeping flowers of her home to a stone path that led to a narrow footpath through the woods. A sweet smell of undergrowth and damp soil lingered under the massive canopy of broad oak leaves, and she filled her lungs with it.

The short path led to a shallow and narrow river that flowed calmly over a rocky bottom. Mary followed the water's course northward for a short distance to a place where the river forked. There, not far from the shore near the junction of the two streams, a strange darkness lay in place of the mottled colors of the river bottom. Above the ten-foot diameter anomaly, the water was strangely still. She knew that from the aberrant darkness flowed highly mineralized groundwater heated deep within the earth. She and Aaron had frequented the spot to bathe in the warm and seemingly bottomless pool. Staring at the darkness in the water, she raised her hand, and with a quick arc of her arm she fed the silvery thing to it. One final flash of light reflected off the pendant as it descended into the unknown depths.

In the diamond-shaped space formed within Muriel's crossed legs, Kaleb sat attentively, listening to an old woman as she narrated a story about a young prince who had been given the gift of magic by his uncle. He watched, mesmerized, as actors portrayed colorful, animated characters and produced live birds and other wonderful things out of the sterile air. A small group of musicians highlighted the actor's movements with soft, playful music.

Kaleb leaned back against Muriel and toyed with her hair. She whispered almost continuously to him and squeezed him reassuringly during moments of excitement. At one point in the performance, the Prince sang about his special powers, but how empty his life remained without love.

'What would you do with such a gift, Kaleb?' Muriel said.

'I'd bring Puppa back,' he said without hesitation.

'Of course,' she said, stroking his head. 'What else would you do?'

'I'd sprinkle the magic dust on Mumma—to make her laugh again.'

'Yes, a beautiful face is such a waste without a smile upon it. Anything else?'

He thought for a moment and then whispered into the air, 'No.'

'Nothing?'

He shook his head.

'What about you, Kaleb? Isn't there anything in that bag of magic for you?'

Kaleb stared at the dark blue velvet sack and the golden rope coiled loosely around it. His head moved slowly from side to side.

'Kaleb,' she whispered into his ear. 'Your mother is very strong—you know that, don't you?'

'Mmm hmm. But she used to laugh all the time,' he said in a small voice. 'Now she's always sad. Sometimes I wish Puppa didn't die, because he used to make her laugh. Puppa could fix anything—even people. But he couldn't fix himself.'

'I'm sorry things haven't been easy for you, Kaleb. No one should have to go through what you've experienced. But you have—both you and your mother. You're a special boy. Do you know that?

'No,' he whispered.

'Well, you are. So you need to be strong like your mother.'

'I'm special?'

'Yes, you are.'

'How?'

'I'll tell you when you get better, all right?' she said, smiling into his searching eyes.

'Okay,' he said, slipping his thumb into his mouth.

He reached back and resumed toying with her hair. 'Your hair is just like Mumma's,' he said, looking up at her.

Muriel beamed.

More music played as the magic show continued and the echoes of song and delight filled the long halls. Surrounded by joy and nestled in the protective arms of Muriel, Kaleb soon fell asleep.

Mary stared at the glassy surface of the dark water. All around her, the gentle sounds of nature played: the voice-like trickle of water, the faint whistle of a soft breeze through the leaves, the soft touch of light rain upon damp soil. She closed her eyes and allowed the sounds to envelop her, dissolving into them. For a moment, she was the water and the air, and she moved with them. There was nothing else between them. Together, they were pure and undisturbed. As if summoned by the trickling voice of the river, she stepped forward and stood above the moving water. There in the darkness, looking up at her through the clear water was the vaguely familiar face of a once striking young woman. But that person was no longer she. Her innocence had been shed like an old skin, taking with it any trace of happiness. She was the metamorph: a new being formed from pain and despair.

Her foot moved over the water.

At that moment, a loud crack rang out from the woods behind her, splitting the serenity of the river like thunder. She wheeled around just as a massive limb of a huge oak fell from high above. It tumbled end over end to the forest floor, its branches thrashing at the surrounding trees as it descended. As Mary gazed into the scattered shadows of the woods, they suddenly appeared unfamiliar and looming.

Her hips complained bitterly as she climbed the soft soil of the riverbank toward the footpath that led home. The now-familiar ache radiated everywhere but seemed to originate from nowhere. On the grassy earth at the top of the riverbank she paused and stared toward her home, but then turned and followed the river downstream a short distance to another opening into the woods.

Wet, tangled shoots from the undergrowth and stiff branches that protruded into the meandering path brushed against her legs and thighs as she made her way through the forest. After a short while she arrived at a section of road about a quarter mile north of her home. There at the north-eastern part of the town, small businesses intermingled with homes. Their lights glowed from a distance. In other times, a warm, welcoming presence could be felt in the narrow, shaded streets that wound gently through the neighborhood, but that day she was alone.

She walked along the quiet road a short distance until she arrived at a well-lit house that stood at one corner. It was a small and humble wooden structure, surrounded by a wide porch and well-tended lengths of red and yellow rosebushes. A meticulously carved wooden sign with raised letters accented by brightly colored stains hung above the door:

Doctor's Office

Mary stared at the sign for a moment as though it were written in an unfamiliar language. She then stepped onto the narrow brick path, passing numerous small lanterns of clear, yellow glass that illuminated the way to the front door. A small bell suspended from the ceiling just inside the door announced her entry. As the sound trailed away, she stepped into the foyer and quietly closed the door behind her, sealing in an inviting warmth and the sweet scents of dried flowers and sterilizing alcohol.

'Hello,' came a voice to Mary's right. 'Can I help you?'

A middle-aged woman looked up at Mary from behind a large opening framed into the wall that separated the waiting room from the administrative area. Her grey hair was pulled back tightly and pinned into a small, braided bun at the back of her head. Behind the woman stood a large wall of colorfully labeled and meticulously ordered paper files. She stared at Mary with a mixed look of genuine surprise and mild disapproval.

'I'd like to see Doctor Côté, please,' Mary said.

The woman's chin dropped slightly. She eyed Mary from the top of her steel-rimmed spectacles. 'Do you have an appointment?'

Mary lowered her head. 'No.'

The woman glared at Mary as she surrendered her gaze to the countertop. With victory acknowledged, the receptionist sighed and began to flip through a large, leather-bound book that lay on the desk in front of her.

'I'll only take a few minutes of her time,' Mary said.

The receptionist placed her hand in the fold of the book and looked up at Mary. Her mouth had just opened when a woman called out from around the corner.

'Mary?'

A short, plain-faced woman rushed into the waiting area. Her shoulder-length, black hair was streaked with grey and tamed loosely at the top of her head with several large, wooden pins. Dark-rimmed spectacles framed ageless, steel-blue eyes. A short, navy jacket covered all but a narrow strip of the front of a light-blue blouse. Matching pants supported by a thin, black leather belt draped over her slender frame. Only the stethoscope that swung from her neck like a pendulum suggested that she was in the medical profession.

'Hello Adèle,' Mary said, moving toward her.

'Mary, where have you been?'

'I've—been with my son.'

Doctor Côté shook her head. 'Come with me,' she said, leading her down a narrow corridor. She stopped in front of a series of tightly arranged rooms.

'Come in, come in,' the doctor said, ushering Mary into one of the examination rooms. Mary stepped into the small, sparsely decorated space.

'Please sit down.' Doctor Côté gestured at a modest wooden chair that stood next to a stainless steel examination table. She stared at Mary with her arms folded, her head cocked slightly to one side.

'I've been expecting you for some time now, Mary. You had an appointment scheduled months ago.'

'I'm sorry. I was preoccupied.'

'I can understand that. Why didn't you reschedule?'

'I—guess I haven't been thinking much about it.'

Doctor Côté slid a wooden stool out from under a small desk opposite the examination table and sat down across from Mary. A flat expression of dissatisfaction was fixed firmly upon her face.

'How is your son?'

Mary's gaze lowered. 'He hasn't responded well to the treatments,' she whispered.

'I'm sorry, Mary,' the doctor sighed sympathetically. 'I can't imagine how you're coping with all of this. How are you feeling?'

'I'm fine,' Mary said in a distant voice.

'Then what brings you here?'

'I just wanted to talk with you.'

The doctor waited for more, but Mary just sat with her head bowed, hair hanging across her face.

'Mary, the results from your tests arrived some time ago.'

Mary avoided the doctor's stare, alternating her gaze between the floor and the doctor's flat-soled, brown leather shoes.

'Are you experiencing any nausea?'

'Not right now. I don't eat regularly. Sometimes I get hunger sickness.'

Doctor Côté moved her stool closer to Mary and leaned forward. She took Mary's face into her hands and gently lifted it. The whites of Mary's eyes were distinctly yellowed. The doctor sat back and sighed softly.

'My hips are bothering me,' Mary breathed.

'How are they bothering you?'

'They—ache.'

The doctor placed her hands on her lap. 'Much?'

'Sometimes. But it doesn't stay for long.'

'When did this start happening?'

'About a couple of months ago.'

'Any coughing?'

'Just a little. Not much.'

Doctor Côté appeared to collect her thoughts for a moment. In her eyes stirred a mix of stark frustration and sincere empathy.

'Mary, the tests confirmed that it's metastatic. It's spread to your left lung and your liver. Your liver is jaundiced and is probably the cause of your nausea. From your description of the pain in your hips, it sounds like it's also spread to the bones of your legs.'

A strange sea of incoherent sounds rose around Mary as the doctor spoke. She was engulfed by it, and taken down into a dark emptiness. There she sat, the creeping walls of despair closing in on her, waiting for the reassurance to come. It was always only a few breaths away. The voice of authority would offer hope again as it had so many times before, and Mary would rise into the light with it. But Doctor Côté remained silent and only watched Mary as she receded further into her seat.

'What do we do now?' Mary whispered.

The doctor's jaw muscles flexed; her breathing slowed. 'I could start another round of treatments,' she said, breaking eye contact. 'But I'm sure it'll only make you feel worse, and it won't help in the long run.'

A blunt finality resonated in the doctor's tone. Mary stared straight ahead, waiting for another option to be presented, but nothing emerged.

All doors were closed.

But there was no end, she thought. Her life would continue, with or without pain. It would continue as it always had. There was no other way.

'What do you mean?' Mary said.

'We failed to stop it, Mary. I'm so sorry.'

'There must be something else we can try.'

'We don't have anything else,' she said, her eyes glistening with sadness. 'I can only dull your pains and try to make you more comfortable.'

Mary searched the doctor's face for the slightest sign of hope—the trace of optimism that had always been there. But within the fine lines of experience etched into her ivory skin, there was nothing but grave sympathy. The two women sat unmoving through a growing silence, gazing at one another— no longer as doctor and patient, but as the living and the dying.

'Then—I'm finished,' Mary said.

The doctor bowed her head.

'How long do I have?'

'No one can say,' Doctor Côté replied, shaking her head. 'But I don't expect you have very long.'

Mary stared ahead as despair spilled over her like a cold sea, and she was claimed by it. The sounds around her became faint and distant, and she was alone again.

'It could be months, Mary—it could be days.'

'No,' Mary said rising suddenly. 'What about my son?'

'You've got to make preparations, Mary.'

'No,' she muttered and moved to the door.

'Mary, you've got to,' Doctor Côté said, following her. She placed her hand on Mary's shoulder. 'You need to think of your son. You've got to make preparations, just in case.'

The doctor's voice was lost behind Mary as she moved quickly through the office. The ticking sound of a grandfather clock came from somewhere nearby, as if marking her remaining time. She was suffocating. With the voice of Doctor Côté calling to her from somewhere far away, Mary burst through the front door and stumbled onto the brick path. Surfacing into the darkness, she drew the fresh air into her heaving lungs and started to run.

Nightfall had begun. The heavy grey clouds that loomed high above had lost what little twilight glow they had when she had arrived. The rain had stopped, but the air was still thick and damp. Majestic pines that bordered the narrow road seemed to conspire with the growing darkness, resembling tall, ominous shadows against the dusk sky.

Night birds stirred high above Mary under the cover of the approaching night, and seemed to take mild interest in her as she moved past glowing lanterns of various shapes and sizes that adorned the yards of the surrounding homes. The roughly textured road twinkled like a multitude of stars as the light of the lanterns danced upon its wet surface. Thoughts that ebbed through her mind dissolved instantly in the wetness as she moved further into the welcome embrace of night. All meaningful thought disappeared and she was left with only the most basic of instincts. One leg moved reflexively past the other. Her breaths followed the rhythm of her gait. Rain, which appeared black against the sky, descended again like cold tears from the heavens. Strong wind came too, howling like a banshee from the west. By the time she passed under the tireless gaze of the hospital's stone gargoyles, the icy rain fell almost horizontally, stinging her face like black flies.

As Mary passed through the grand doors of the stone sanctuary, a drone of voices met her like the hum of bees in a cave. Indiscernible shapes formed from weak light and dark shadow, moving all around her and flickering like strange candlelight. Quietly, she moved through the noise and ascended to the upper chamber, where the moving shapes were fewer and the sounds did not reach. There, bright yellow light was cast onto the walls and ceiling like a thin layer of honey. As she moved along the narrow passage that led deeper into the sections, more vague shapes approached, casting back the amber light from their forms, babbling imperceptibly as they passed. From the corner of her eye she saw something lying near—shiny and bright amongst other silvery objects: something useful. Something dangerous. She took it and slipped it into the pocket of her cloak.

Near the heart of the nest was the chamber in which the broken angel had taken refuge and now lay sleeping. She gazed upon it. Through its slow, labored breathing she could feel its pain. Its small chest rose and fell with impuissance, as if stoking a dying flame within. She alone had been charged with its care, but she had caused it to fall. And now it suffered.

Mercy, it silently pleaded with her.

She stepped toward it.

Mercy.

She reached over it and took a pillow into her hands.

Outside the wind howled like a tempest, throwing rain hard against the blurred glass. But the drops drizzled impotently to the stone sill. The light flickered around her as the helpless thing beckoned again to her.

Mercy, it pleaded.

She moved closer.

The wind slammed against the windowpane with a loud boom that echoed like thunder, but she heard nothing. She lifted the pillow to her chest and, holding it firmly, leaned over the suffering thing.

Kaleb opened his eyes.

'Mumma,' he breathed and looked at the pillow in Mary's hands. 'Are you going to sleep with me?'

With those words, the dark veil was lifted and Mary beheld her son: the strong spirit to whom she had given flesh. The inseparable life that had formed from within her and that with each breath was still a part of her. Behind the young and innocent eyes that gazed at her, a brightness prevailed—defiant as fire on water. And in those searching eyes she beheld the smallest ray of hope, and it moved her.

'Yes,' she breathed.

And as the wind and rain calmed outside, Mary lay next to her son and slept.

❧ CHAPTER SEVEN ❧

Judaea

Mary awoke to the pungent aromas of smoked meat and sharp cheese, and for a brief moment she was back at home, preparing an evening meal. She propped herself up, blinked away the sleep from her eyes and worked the present day into focus. Her son lay sleeping in his bed next to her, a wet thumb placed loosely in his open mouth. She wondered how long she'd been asleep, for she was unusually calm and well rested.

A ceramic cup covered with a small saucer sat on the table beside her. Next to it was a modest plate of food consisting of plain mashed potatoes, finely-diced boiled carrots mixed with peas and a piece of baked chicken breast—none of which appeared to have been disturbed. Only upon closer inspection did she notice that a tiny amount of each had been consumed. Next to the food was a smaller plate on which lay half a slice of banana and a quarter of a boiled peach in clear, light syrup. A sticky spoon resting in a cup of melted ice cream suggested where her son had focused most of his efforts.

As she reached for the larger plate she noticed a tray on another small table nearby. Over it was placed a large covered dish that didn't bear the familiar pattern of the hospital's ceramic kitchenware. Under it she found several kinds of smoked meats, some baked okra in a thick red sauce, a slice of dark rye bread, a small block of pungent white cheese, and several salted black olives. Preserved black figs in heavy syrup sat temptingly in a clear glass bowl. A familiar pinching developed under her tongue as her mouth began to water. For a moment she wondered whether the food was for someone else, but the persuasive reasoning of hunger prevailed. Sitting fully upright, she placed the tray on her lap and quickly consumed the meal, starting with the figs. Her hunger amplified the wonderful flavors. She could almost feel the food dissolving within in her and being drawn into her flesh, restoring her strength, her spirit.

When she was finished eating she slid off the bed, careful not to disturb her son, and moved to the window. Outside, tall gas street lamps provided the only illumination to the street below, which now lay under shadow. The rain had stopped, but the wet surfaces of the street glistened with the fire of the lamps. The shops across the street were dark except for the tavern, which was alive with consumption of food and drink, and the café next to it, where men still played backgammon or dominos.

Mary turned to her son and watched his chest rise and fall. She wondered what he dreamed of. Did the same beast that haunted her sleep torment him? Was it upon him now, with its talons sunk deep into his flesh? He never spoke of his dreams to her—except those of his father. As he lay innocent and helpless in a steel bed made for strangers, she thought of the silver malignancy she had placed around his neck and she shivered with anger.

It was impossible to imagine a link between the pendant and Kadesh's prisoner, but she couldn't help wondering whether there was. The man knew it was there around her neck, she was certain of that. It must have been the reason he reacted to her. But how could he know? She didn't want to see him again, but if he was somehow connected to the pendant or the people who made it, she needed to know. At that moment, two women passed by her door and she hurried after them.

'How was he?' Mary said, taking Muriel by the hand.

'Oh, Mary, he had a wonderful time. Thank you for letting me spend the time with him.'

'Thank you for taking him, Muriel.'

'He's so special. It's always a pleasure to be with him. Well, you look brighter. Did you eat your dinner?'

'Yes,' Mary said, moving closer to her. 'Where did it come from?'

'Muriel brought it for you,' a dark-skinned nurse smiling next to Muriel said in a deep, rich voice. '—Food for the soul.'

'Thank you, Muriel, it was just what I needed.'

'I'm glad. Daniel's mother brought you the preserves.'

Mary searched Muriel's eyes for a hint of jest, but there was none. 'Isabel?' she said, gazing down the hallway toward the other rooms.

'Yes,' she smiled. 'Some friends brought them for her and Daniel. I guess you made a good impression on her.' Sarcasm sparkled in her voice.

The food suddenly weighed heavily in Mary's stomach. Its residual taste rose again as she recalled with shame the tone of her unprovoked affront earlier that day.

'She still has family with them,' Muriel said. 'But I'm sure she'd enjoy your company later. You know, she's probably going through the same things you did when you first arrived.'

'I'll stop by later,' Mary said in a distant voice. 'Why are you here so late?'

'I'm working a night shift,' Muriel replied, smiling uncomfortably.

'I thought you only volunteered during the day.'

'I do, usually, but I wanted to work through the night tonight—something different.'

'Muriel thinks this is her last day,' the nurse said.

Mary stared incredulously at Muriel. Apart from a few days scattered throughout the months, Muriel had always been there with them. It was impossible to imagine life at the hospital without her.

'What?' Mary said.

'It's true,' Muriel said.

'But why? What about the children?'

'I'm sorry, Mary. It's time for me to go.'

She wanted to embrace Muriel—to beg her to stay—but pride kept her still. 'Where will you go?'

'Home,' she smiled.

Embarrassed by the obviousness of her answer, Mary dropped her gaze. She didn't know where home was for Muriel—she had never asked. *How could it be that after so many weeks I've never inquired about Muriel's life outside the hospital?* she wondered. Somehow during all those moments, it had never been appropriate to ask.

'Of course,' Mary breathed.

'Don't you worry now, Mary,' the dark-skinned nurse said in a bold voice. She placed a large, comforting hand on Mary's arm. 'I'll still be here to take care of you two.'

'Thank you, Amira,' Mary said, touching the nurse's hand. 'You've all been so good to us. I'll always be grateful for what you've done.' Mary turned her gaze to the hallway floor. 'Can I ask one more favor of you two tonight?'

'Of course,' Amira laughed. 'But I don't think you've ever asked a favor of me before.'

'I need to leave again—just for a short while. Would you please keep an eye on my son while I'm gone? He's sleeping now, but if he wakes up I don't want him to be alone.'

'Of course,' Amira said, squeezing Mary's hand.

'Go and do what you need to do,' Muriel said. 'Don't worry, we're here for him.'

'Are you going home?' Amira said.

'No,' Mary said, gazing down the hallway toward the stairs.

'Then where are you going—if you don't mind me asking?'

'I'm going to find some answers.'

The world seemed spent. The rain had stopped and the wind had slowed to an even, silent breeze. All was calm again.

Distracted by the unusual stillness, Mary looked all around her as she walked toward the industrial part of town. It was only when she was two-thirds of the way to the police station that she realized Kadesh had probably left for the evening. Most people would be home now with their families, gathered around the dinner table, laughing and talking across the remnants of their meals, their stomachs soothed with rich food and fresh, warm bread. Kadesh too would be among them, leaning back on his chair, his belly full and satisfied. Mary and his prisoner would be far from his thoughts. But she was determined to speak with his prisoner. If Kadesh had left for the evening, she would find someone else to arrange the meeting.

When Mary arrived at the police station she moved to the side of the building. With the falling of night, it had become draped in shadow. The only illumination in the narrow lane emanated from the small lamp that burned above the door, and dark, marbled clouds that loomed overhead and reflected the dim, scattered lights of the town back to the earth.

The black iron handle of the side door was cold and uninviting against the skin of her palm. It rotated freely, but the heavy wooden door wouldn't move. She rapped on the door and looked for any movement within the shadows of the alley. After a moment, she knocked again, rapping even harder, but still there was no sign of response on the other side.

As she stood alone in the dark lane, staring at the incompliant door, an icy feeling took hold. The skin of her arms and cheeks rose and tingled as the shadows around her seemed to shift.

'Kadesh!' she cried, slapping the palm of her hand against the door. She pressed her ear against it and to her relief, she could resolve the faint sound of approaching footsteps. She backed away from the door and stepped into the alley just as the lock bolt slid back. The door cracked open and warm amber light spilled out into the alley. Kadesh peered through the narrow opening.

'Mary!' Kadesh said and opened the door. 'This is a

wonderful surprise.'

'I was hoping I could ask your prisoner a few questions—if it's not too late,' she said, stepping into the light.

'Of course not, please come in.' He looked to the starless sky. 'It's unusually cold this evening.'

He ushered her into the hallway, which was marginally brighter than the alley. After a quick check of the lane, he closed the door and locked it.

'I am so happy to see you, Mary,' he whispered through the darkness. 'I have made you upset not just once, but twice in the same day. I have not had the opportunity to properly apologize for bringing you such terrible news, which has only added to your family's suffering.'

'You've explained some unanswered questions. For that I'm grateful to you.'

'Then we are still friends?' he smiled awkwardly.

Mary nodded and returned a slight smile.

'Good. And now you are here with more questions.'

'Yes. I'm sorry it's so late. I wasn't sure if you'd still be here. I realize you're probably getting ready to go home.'

'Unfortunately not,' he frowned. 'My work hours do not follow the sun.'

'I won't take up much of your time. I only have a few questions.'

'Ask all that you want to,' he said, moving close to her. 'But this time we must be more vigilant. I will endeavor to keep you out of harm's way, but you must also exercise caution. You will follow my instructions, precisely?'

'Yes,' she nodded.

'Good, then we can proceed.'

He turned down the hallway but took only a few steps.

'Eh, remember, Mary, if I see that he is becoming too anxious, I will stop the interview immediately.'

'Okay,' she said as a spidery shiver crawled up the back of her neck and over her scalp.

'Good,' he smiled.

He escorted her down the hallway to the unmarked door,

his feet shuffling loudly across the dusty floor. The door was closed but unlocked. Kadesh entered first, stopping briefly to look at a spot just outside of her field of view where his prisoner sat. Suddenly, all desire to speak with the man evaporated and she backed away from the door. But Kadesh's warm hand embraced hers and, like a guiding light, he led her calmly through the greyness.

Slowly, they moved to the wide table where the prisoner sat. The man's head was held down exactly as before and as they approached, he raised it. His black, expressionless eyes found hers and he stared at her, transfixed, tracking her path toward him with a slight movement of his head. Noticing that he was still unrestrained, Mary drew back.

'I will not let any harm come to you,' Kadesh whispered, tightening his grip on her hand. He gestured at a small wooden chair positioned directly across from the prisoner and dragged it several feet away from the table. 'Please, sit here.'

Trembling slightly from cold and fear, she sat down, her eyes locked on the prisoner. She was ready for anything.

'Well,' Kadesh said, clasping his hands together cheerfully. 'We had an awkward start earlier today, but it seems we are fortunate to have a second opportunity to talk. Mary, this is Judaea. Judaea, this is Mary. She is a psychiatrist.'

The man's stare moved to Kadesh.

'Hello,' Mary said, the word sticking at the back of her throat.

The man leaned forward. His pale, expressionless face seemed to glow softly in the dull light.

'Do not listen to his lies,' his raspy voice cut through the cool air.

Kadesh shrugged his shoulders and smiled at Mary, but she was wholly unaffected by his attempt to lighten the moment. As she prepared for her first question, the man's gaze moved to her chest; his head swayed mechanically as he surveyed her.

His stare weighed heavily upon her, the eyes probing her like fingers over Braille. She shifted uncomfortably and reflexively reached to where her pendant used to hang.

'Mister Judaea—' she began.

'Judaea.'

'Pardon me?'

The interrogation room hissed softly as the man drew the air into his lungs. Water trickled through a hidden pipe in the ceiling above them like the patter of running mice.

'I am Judaea,' he said. 'There is no more.'

'Okay. Judaea, why did you lunge at me when we met earlier today?'

He stared at her for a moment. 'The fire was upon you,' he said.

'You mean my pendant?'

He looked to Kadesh, as if expecting a response from him. 'It is not for man,' Judaea said. The words passed over her like an icy draft.

'I didn't know what it was,' Mary said. 'It was a gift from my husband. He didn't know what it was either. How is it that you knew?'

Judaea sat still as stone, staring through her question and into her eyes. Kadesh produced a small, leather-bound notebook from inside his jacket and laid it open in front of him. Into the deep fold between the pages, near the middle of the book, he placed an elegant, gold-plated fountain pen.

'Judaea,' Mary said. 'That's a very unusual name.'

Judaea offered nothing in response.

Kadesh sat motionless, his hands resting flat on his notebook. After a few moments of awkward silence, he removed the cap from his pen, laid it down on the table and began to write in his notebook.

Mary leaned toward the prisoner. 'Where does—'

The room filled again with the rasp of Judaea's breath. 'It was given to me,' he said.

There was no emotion in his tone. His voice was as empty and expressionless as his eyes.

'Of course,' Mary said. 'Where does it come from?'

Judaea turned to Kadesh. 'You have brought her here to do your bidding.'

Kadesh cleared his throat. 'She has come here of her own volition. The death of her husband has left her with a great emptiness. She is here only to find the answers with which to fill it.'

'My words will fill nothing,' Judaea said.

Mary's unease grew with the passage of each moment shared with the odd man. His movements were stiff and awkward, and suggested he was experiencing pain or discomfort. The rough sound that preceded most sentences brought upon her the urge to gasp for air. Yet the sound also invoked an unwelcome emotion: sympathy, which was quickly becoming curiosity—a personal luxury she could not afford.

'You called out a name as I left here,' she said. 'What was it?'

'It was not a name,' Kadesh interjected. 'It was a simple word: *tlitha*, which means *young girl*.'

'Why did you call me that?'

Judaea remained silent.

'What language is that?' But only unpleasant silence passed through the cool air between them over the moments that followed.

'Eh, it is an old dialect that is spoken in some parts of the Middle East,' Kadesh volunteered.

'Is that where you're from, Judaea?'

The man only gazed at her. The room was still and quiet again until Kadesh's chair squeaked beneath him. He leaned slightly toward Mary and placed his hand on her shoulder.

'Eh, perhaps we should focus our attentions on the reason you are here?' Kadesh said.

She moved forward on her seat and placed her hands on the edge of the table. 'Judaea, do you know anything about my pendant?'

His gaze moved again to her chest. 'It is no longer with you,' he said.

'That's right. It's gone. Do you know what it was?'

'Fire,' he said.

'Do you know who made it?'

'There is only one who does such things.'

She leaned toward him. 'Who?'

'Man.'

A telling bitterness carried in his tone. A subtle emotion, but so strong she could almost taste it. Kadesh cleared his throat.

'Eh, the story is told of widows who lost their families to war, and how they are recruited to shape the dangerous metal by hand into appealing forms: trinkets for the enemy,' he said. 'It is said that the women are completely unprotected from its effects. They toil, unconcerned about the metal's poison. It is a labor of revenge … and suicide. Their male co-conspirators stay clear of them for fear of their own lives—as though the women were lepers—venturing near them only to bring them food and supplies.'

As he spoke, Mary envisioned a dark and rank place full of sick women—young and old—covered in rashes, harboring malignant growths on and inside their bodies.

That was the birthplace of their illnesses, she thought—*the genesis of their disease.*

'Where are they made?' Mary said.

'It is of no matter to us,' Kadesh said.

'It matters to me.'

From the ceiling came the faint cracking sound of footsteps on old hardwood floorboards, and for a brief moment she was away from that place—at home in her kitchen, listening to the reassuring sounds of her husband moving in the bedroom above.

'The same will is everywhere,' Judaea said, his tone flat and even.

'That may be true, but I'm interested in the ones who hurt my family.'

'I know nothing of them.'

'But you knew of the pendant. How is that?'

Judaea turned to Kadesh, who sat frozen, listening to the unfolding dialog.

'I carried it around my neck for two years without knowing

what it was,' Mary said. 'But you recognized it the instant you saw it.'

Kadesh placed his hand on Mary's shoulder. 'I wonder if we could change the subject? I'm sure this discussion will lead nowhere.'

She glared at Judaea, her jaw muscles flexed. In the dark of her eyes, the solitary light of the room danced like a small fire far in the distance.

'This is all I've come to talk about,' she said.

As she watched him stare ahead—stoic and inanimate—she had a sudden appreciation of Kadesh's frustration. She briefly marveled at his success in deriving any material information from Judaea, especially in such a short time. She drew in a long, deep breath and relaxed as the cool air slowly filled her lungs, and dissolved the silence.

'What other languages do you speak?' she said.

Judaea made no attempt to respond. He remained statuesque and stared far beyond her through the concrete walls.

'Where do you come from?' she tried. Still there was nothing.

Mary leaned back in her chair and gazed at the man, who seemed to be asleep with his eyes open. But she sensed that behind his blank stare, he was taking it all in—collecting her words and actions into his thoughts. She passed her hand in front of his face. His head tracked her movement.

'Have you done something wrong, Judaea?'

'Eh, Mary,' Kadesh said, rising from his chair, 'could we speak privately for a moment?' He took her arm and led her to the farthest corner of the room.

'I am sorry, Mary,' Kadesh whispered. 'I should have prepared you better for the interview by giving you more history of this man. He was found in an abandoned building not far from here. I have reason to believe he had only been there for a few days. From the nature of the few possessions he had with him, it appears that he has traveled extensively.' Kadesh shifted from foot to foot as he spoke. 'Unfortunately, he seems to have few memories of his life, and those that have remained are broken into small pieces. I have good reason to believe that some of those fragments are very important pieces of knowledge that I most desperately need to assemble. If you can assist me with this endeavor, I would be forever grateful. I have only until tomorrow morning to accomplish this task.'

'What will happen then?'

'I am sorry, I cannot say.'

'Can't you tell me what it is that you need from him?'

'I am afraid I cannot tell you that, either. I ask that you trust that I must not.'

His pensive look convinced her that he was sincere.

'Mister Kadesh, how can you expect me to extract this *knowledge* if I don't know what I'm looking for?'

'I am not certain, but I believe it is possible—if you remain patient and do not allow his silence to frustrate you. Every word you speak affects him. I can see this. Also, understand that he may not have the answers for many of the questions you ask.'

'I don't have much time either,' she said, lowering her eyes. 'I have to get back to my son. Where do you suggest I start?'

'I cannot say. But I suggest you leave the topic of your pendant, for now.'

She returned to her seat across the table from Judaea. Moving her hands slowly along the smooth grain of the wooden surface, she collected her thoughts.

'Do you know why you're here, Judaea?'

'He brought me here,' Judaea said, referring to Kadesh.

'Do you know why he brought you here?'

'He believes I am someone that I am not.'

'Who does he think you are?'

Kadesh leaned slightly toward Judaea, like a spider at the edge of its web, moving toward an entangled prey. Judaea stared blankly ahead.

'Judaea,' Mary said. 'Why are you here?'

'He brought me here.'

'He brought you to this *building*. Why did you come to this town?'

The skin on the back of her arms prickled and rose as his dull black eyes looked into hers.

'Do you know where you are, Judaea?' she said.

There was only the soft scraping sound of the nib of Kadesh's fountain pen moving across the rough paper of his notebook. Noticing that her attention had turned to him, Kadesh looked up, smiled and gestured for her to continue.

'Where were you born?' Mary said.

Suddenly, across the dead space between them came a subtle, singular response. Even through his dispassionate gaze she could see that he was absorbed by the question, as if caught in a loop of impalpable thought. Behind his dark eyes, an inner struggle seemed to have ensued, a brief conflict that was resolved with the release of six words:

'I was born in a cave.'

❧ CHAPTER EIGHT ❧

Parturition

The man stepped out of the darkness and into the full light of the midday sun that peered menacingly through the sky like a burning eye. All around him the earth seemed to glow as if on fire, shrouding everything in a sea of blinding light. Shielding his eyes with a forearm, he waited for the light to recede, but it remained incessant. He stumbled over the uneven ground and fell to his hands and knees, his palms scraping along the rough, dusty surface. He turned his face away from the bright earth. Less than one hundred yards away, a small rocky hill stood, ominous, against the stark cityscape. Partially covering his face with his hands, he rose to his feet and turned his back to the malevolent sun.

From the other side of the hill came the faint sounds of approaching men. Dangling objects fastened to their bodies clattered as they walked. Laughter punctuated their voices. Peering through his fingers, the man could see the shadows of his legs cast in front of him like crooked stilts that moved with him across the rocky ground.

Not far from where he had awoken, the ground was in shadow. There, the darkened earth appeared softer and inviting to the raw soles of his bare feet, and from it sprang many strange forms in a wondrous array of shapes and bright colors. As he passed through the garden, the foliage brushed softly against his skin and moved gently with him. Under the thick, emerald leaves of a small tree he knelt down and endeavored to tame the flood of faded images that moved through his mind. Scattered and with no points of reference, they held no meaning.

All things seemed new and strange. Yet in the far reaches of his thoughts there lingered intangible familiarities: the shapes of the leaves, the brightness of the earth, the rocky hill in the distance. For several hours he remained in the shade of the small tree surrounded by asphodel, trying to assemble the images that passed into and out of his thoughts into cohesive and interpretable forms. But time passed and still he failed to extract any coherence from the disjointed memories.

Placing his hands above his brows, the man stood and surveyed the surrounding hills. He had no recollection of how he had come to be there. It was as though he had been spawned from the earth itself, like the various plants that surrounded him. Only the most basic of instincts now guided him from one moment to the next, and the one that spoke loudest was an encumbering desire to leave that place. But in the coolness of the vegetation he found a primal comfort that was equally powerful and difficult to abandon. So there he stood for many moments in the small refuge, staring into the growth like a statue, merging into the fragile serenity that surrounded him.

Suddenly, a veiled woman appeared at the edge of the garden. Black cloth that covered her from head to toe flowed behind her as she approached into a light wind. As he backed away from her, she was startled. She spoke to him in a quiet, gentle tone from behind her veil, but her words were like pieces of a clay pot scattered across the dusty ground and whose assembled shape was unknown.

Yet he was drawn to her soft voice and recognized her within some of the untamed images in his mind. He tried to gather them—to isolate them from the others—but try as he may, she remained an enigma. The more she spoke, the more confused he became.

The woman also seemed to become frustrated; her tone grew more and more emphatic as his silence continued. When she left him, he climbed onto higher ground and watched her hurry toward a tall stone wall and disappear through a large wooden gate. Somehow, he knew that like the rocky hill in the distance, he must not go there. He watched the gate for a few moments, waiting for her to re-emerge, and tried again to gather the memories that held her familiar image.

From where he stood, a sea of reddish-brown hills stretched far to the east. Beyond them stood a long mountain range partially obscured by a light haze. When the woman didn't reappear after some time had passed, he descended the rocks and headed toward the hills to the east.

Clusters of small evergreen trees and shrubs rose triumphantly from the dry land that stretched before the man—an appealing contrast of color against the barren earth. But traversing the hills was difficult, and periodically he needed to scale large rocky formations that blocked his way. Wherever possible he followed the folds between the hills, adjusting his course only to avoid encounters with ubiquitous travelers who dotted the hillside.

A multitude of small four-legged animals scurried over the stony surfaces, often presenting themselves with odd gestures and soft noises. Some had smooth, patterned skins. Others bore fur of a color that blended in with the surrounding earth. In and out of holes and through cracks between rocks they hurried, but for what purpose he did not know.

All around him winged creatures took to the sky in a dizzying array of movement. Some with smaller forms found temporary refuge in trees and shrubs nearby and called to him with strange, unintelligible sounds. He watched them as they hopped from branch to branch, fluttering their wings, moving with wondrous agility. Like the creatures that moved upon the earth, most bore the dull colors of the hills, but a few displayed unusual plumages of bright hues and dazzling patterns.

A continuous light wind moved hot air across his face. The ambient temperature gradually rose as he descended through the hills. When the town and the mountain range upon which it was built faded well into the distance, he took shelter in a shallow, triangular cave formed at the base of a massive stone hill. Just inside the entrance of the rocks, he gazed at the rising and falling land over which he had traveled. The wave-like depressions and contours held some inaccessible significance, hidden from him like the many creatures in the rocks. The hills further to the east seemed to beckon him into their folds. He would continue toward them later, but for now he would remain within the cool shadow of the rocks, sheltered from the sun.

In the darkest corner of the small refuge he had just begun to collect the scattered images that confounded his thoughts when a sudden movement caught his attention. He squatted and scanned the sandy cave floor, but in the dim light he could see nothing. Still as a stone he waited, staring at the dark sand with his hands laid flat on the ground. And then he saw it. Several feet away, a small pattern emerged from the cave floor. Slowly, it approached him on eight spindly legs, each one articulating in several places and operating with a complementary partner. The cryptic form moved in complete silence, holding up in front of it two appendages that terminated in long, V-shaped extensions. Its hard-shelled body looked as though it had been shaped from wax, its color uniform beige except for its dark grey back and its jointed tail, which curved over its back and terminated in a fine, black point. It appeared to have no head. He remained motionless as the creature approached and crawled onto the back of his hand. The tips of its legs lightly pinched his skin. As it moved up his arm, its jointed tail lay almost flat behind it. Fine, hair-like protrusions on the bottom of its tail brushed along his skin. He lifted his arm, bringing the animal several inches away from his face. Its tail rose threateningly toward him. It seemed to study him for a moment, then continued to ascend his arm and shoulder to the back of his neck. Just then, the light at the mouth of the shelter dimmed as the sun began to melt into the hills. As he turned to face the cave entrance, the scorpion fell to the cave floor with a click. It quickly righted itself and scurried into the darkness, dragging a bent leg to one side. In only a few seconds it was partially buried in the sand at the base of the rock wall.

The man moved to the cave entrance and watched the darkness approach from the east, drawing into it the fading colors of the surrounding land. Soon, he too was engulfed by it. Wrapped under the cloak of night, he left the shelter and headed away from where the burning eye had disappeared.

The moon also hid behind the shadow of the earth that night and so provided little illumination through the rough terrain. But the air was cooler now, and without the sun upon him the land was much easier to traverse. Instinctively, he knew the voices that occasionally came to him from across the hills would not find him in the darkness.

He followed the folds of the land for several more hours, accompanied by the soft sound of gentle winds moving through the rocks. With each step, the powdered earth rose around him in light clouds, covering his legs with a reddish-brown dust and claiming him as part of the desert.

The darkness yielded animals of different sorts than those that appeared in the daylight. Winged creatures appeared in multitudes from cracks in the earth, as though summoned to the blackened sky by some unseen presence, swooping and turning erratically above him. Only their silhouettes were visible against the vast emptiness above. He stared after them for some time, amazed at their skill. But then suddenly, as quickly as they had come, they disappeared into the thickness of night.

And then came the sounds of loud voices. He swiftly moved to a large rock on a slight embankment and hid behind it. There he listened closely as three or four distinctive voices echoed through the rocks. Slowly he ascended a nearby hill and from its peak spied the surrounding valley. About fifty yards ahead, a bright light flickered, as though the burning eye were watching him from a small mound on the earth. Four men were gathered around the bright light, holding long sticks over it. At the ends of the sticks were fixed the carcasses of small, skinned animals. Smoke rose from their shriveled and blackened forms.

Not far from the men stood a diminutive, unattended tent, a strange and aberrant silhouette set against the smooth curves of the desert landscape. From one side of the structure appeared the glow of two small, reddish lights that hovered close to one another a few feet above the ground. Together they vanished and reappeared again like fireflies. As he stared at the strange moving lights, slowly the face of a large, fox-like animal took shape around them, and then around it, the body of a jackal. The man watched the brazen animal as it searched the tent and the surrounding area, moving gracefully and silently, its long, bushy tail hanging down between its thin hind legs. Suddenly, the animal stopped and raised its head toward the man, its small, demonic eyes gleaming at him. Through the distance he could see the cups of its tall ears turn in all directions as it endeavored to gather his sounds. Slowly it moved toward him, its head moving from side to side as if sniffing the smoky air, and then it stopped, turned toward the blackness beyond the camp and with light, dance-like steps disappeared into the desert.

One of the men at the campfire rose to his feet. With the end of his stick he picked up a shiny hemispherical object and waved it insolently above the leaping flames. He raised and lowered it several times before placing it on his head. He jeered at the others, who laughed and groped for it across the flames. After a brief tussle, one of the other men gained possession of it and, laughing loudly, he tossed it into the fire, which threw glowing embers high into the air. The men burst into laughter and started to sing and drink from flasks that hung from their shoulders. One after the other, they unsheathed long decorated knives from their sides and waved them belligerently into the night air.

The man moved along the hilltop, keeping close watch of the men at the campfire. Gradually, the growing distance between them dampened their sounds, and he was comforted by it. But then suddenly their voices became silent and only the occasional pop of an ember could be heard through the darkness. He lay flat on his stomach at the same moment the men at the campfire turned their gaze toward him. One of the men reached for a long stick wrapped in cloth at one end and thrust it into the fire. Immediately, it was engulfed in flames. He raised the torch toward the hill, spreading his feet wide apart as he called out to the rocks. Another man also rose, swaggering, and called to the rocks. As the man lay still on his belly, those at the campfire listened into the stillness. But like the other night things of the desert, he remained silent and blended into the darkness. Soon, the men lost interest in the rocky hill and returned their attention to the fire and their flasks. As they laughed and drank, the man crawled down the side of the hill opposite their camp and headed toward the still blackness.

Uncertain when or if the burning eye would return, the man moved quickly along a flat stretch of land at the base of a large range. The stone formation appeared to have been scraped into the earth by a giant finger. Following its snaking course, he travelled through the hills, deeper into the desiccated land, wherever possible remaining on the path, leaving it only to climb to higher ground to survey his vast surroundings. About fifteen hours after he had left the coolness of the garden, the man climbed the side of a hill that rose steeply to the south. Although the stones of the rock side were sharp and loose, the grooved and roughly textured side of the hill made climbing much easier. At the top of the hill, almost four hundred feet from the valley floor, he stood and gazed at the land to the west, which rose majestically above him. Waves of heat rose from the coral-colored earth like an army of ghosts, distorting the view of the land beyond. There the hills disappeared as though they had been drawn back into the land, but farther into the distance they rose up again even higher into the mountains.

In the expanse between the coral-colored earth and the mountains to the east lay a vast flatness that extended eastward about ten miles and to the south as far as the eye could see. The brightness of the sun behaved differently on its surface— dancing across it like tiny sprites. There, a great body of water stretched at the base of the mountains, defiant of the parched lands surrounding it. Cautiously, he descended the hill and headed toward it.

As the hills disappeared into the distance, so too did the endless arrays of meandering valleys. There was a noticeable paucity of animals, whose presence he had become accustomed to. Animals of all kinds, furred and smooth, large and small, seemed to vanish from the sand and rock. Even the skin-winged animals of the night appeared to have abandoned him.

After a few more hours of walking, the folds of the hills disappeared behind him and he stood before an expanse of land with vein-like depressions: vestiges of ancient tributaries whose bases were considerably flatter than the surrounding terrain. He entered into one of the veins and followed its meandering course along the bedrock, which led to the edge of the great body of water.

Small, hardy plants grew along the muddy shore. Nearby, white sponge-like crystalline rocks sat glittering in the early morning light. Shrouded in a pale mist, the water seemed to speak to him as it lapped softly upon its shores. Slowly he entered the deep blue water until it reached his thighs, then knelt into it. Almost floating in the dense liquid, he placed his face into its coolness, drawing it over him, washing away the sand and earth. With the water streaming down his body and dripping from the ends of his hair, he emerged into a pale pink-blue morning light as it unveiled a spectacular view of the hills through which he had travelled.

The heat of the day quickly gathered strength and he sensed that the burning eye would soon return. To the southwest stood a large stone ridge at the edge of the hills. He took refuge there under a large rock overhang that provided shelter from above and on one side. The darkness was incomplete, but as the burning eye ascended over the mountains it did not find him there. Nearby, the jackal followed just out of view, weaving in and out of small clumps of tall papyrus reeds, sniffing and snorting at the warm, unpalatable salt water of the sea.

❧ CHAPTER NINE ❧

The Secret

'I know you,' Judaea said in his flat, expressionless tone.

'I don't think so,' Mary said and looked to Kadesh, who smiled at her with nervous surprise. And then the silence again settled between them like cold, heavy air.

In spite of what Kadesh had said earlier, she couldn't help feeling that his silence was not because he couldn't answer her rudimentary questions, but because he wouldn't.

'How is it that you know me?' Mary said.

'I see you in my thoughts.'

She shivered. Where could she feature in the mind of this unshaven and unwashed man? *He was found in an abandoned building not far from here*, Kadesh had told her. He could have ventured anywhere in the town. She imagined him watching her from a distance, hidden in the shadows of her neighborhood, and she shuddered again.

'What am I doing in your thoughts?' she said, measuring her response.

'Many things.'

'Such as?'

'You are smiling. Sometimes you are weeping.'

'Why am I crying?'

He paused for a moment and seemed to consider her question. 'I do not know,' he said.

'Do you know when you saw me?'

'No.'

'Where did you see me?'

'At a place where the sun burns bright.'

'At a beach?'

'No.'

'You're sure it was me?'

'It was you, but you are not the same way.'

'What do you mean?'

'Your skin is darker. Your hair is longer. Your clothes are not the same.'

The level of detail gave an unexpected legitimacy to his claim. But what did it mean? Were his memories from a distant past when she was much younger? That could explain his vague familiarity to her. But as intriguing as the thought was, too much had passed since she had left her son, and she had none left with which to probe deeper into this. She needed to quickly return to the issue of the pendant—to the reason why she was there.

'Have you travelled to the Middle East?' she said.

'Yes.'

'Why were you there?'

'There was no reason.'

'You were just *there*?'

'Yes.'

'Is that where home is?'

'No.'

'Where is your home?'

He paused for a moment. 'Here,' he said.

'This town?'

'Here.'

'This room?'

Mary studied the small room, almost expecting to see makeshift sleeping and washing areas. But there was no sign of habitation—not even a cup of water.

'Yes,' he said.

'Where were you living before he brought you here?'

'I have been through many lands.'

'Could you name a few?'

There was a long pause, during which he seemed to consider her request. 'No,' he said finally.

'Do you know the name of this town?'

Again he seemed to ponder the question. 'No,' he said.

Mary sat back in her chair, which creaked beneath her. Kadesh looked up briefly from his notebook and then resumed his writing.

'Judaea, do you not remember, or is it that you won't tell me?'

'I do not know the names.'

'Do you know where you are now?'

'Yes.'

'Where are you?'

'I am here.'

Mary laughed silently and without smiling. He could only be having fun with her, although he displayed no perceptible emotion.

'Do you know how old you are?'

'No.'

'Do you know where you were born?'

'I was born in a cave.'

It was a mistake to come here, she thought, bowing her head. She knew that she could go around and around this loop of questioning for hours without making progress. She inhaled deeply and held her breath for a few seconds before slowly releasing the air through her nose. Kadesh was still preoccupied with his notebook as she leaned over to him and whispered, 'Do you know what time it is?'

'Yes,' Kadesh said, slightly startled. He closed his notebook and produced a pocket watch from his vest pocket. 'It has just passed the ninth hour.'

'I'm sorry,' she said, standing, 'I can't stay any longer. I have to return to my son.'

'Of course,' Kadesh said, also rising. He stared at his pocket watch for a moment, closed the golden cover and dropped it back into his pocket. 'I understand—you have your priorities,' he replied, but made little effort to hide his disappointment.

Across the table, Judaea appeared to show the mildest interest in her.

'Do you have a family, Judaea?' Mary said.

His eyes seemed to brighten, but only for an instant.

'In my thoughts,' Judaea said, 'there is a boy.'

'Your son?'

'He was.' He looked to Kadesh.

The hair on Mary's arms stood on end. 'He died?' she said.

'In my thoughts, he is alive. I see him as I see you. But he is no more,' Judaea spoke into the solitary light of the room.

Mary gazed at the strange man sitting across from her and surrendered a brief moment of pity for him. 'I'm sorry," she said. She watched him for a moment longer, then turned to Kadesh. 'I have to go now.'

'Of course,' he repeated. He took Mary's arm and escorted her to the door.

'Why didn't you tell me about the child?' Mary whispered.

'Eh, it is not material,' he said, waving her question away. 'It did not occur to me to mention it.'

'It seems important to him. It may not be linked to what you're looking for, but I think it would be useful for you to explore it further.'

'You may be right,' he said, blushing. 'But I am not convinced that he had a child. His mind is full of holes. I think he has filled some of them with his own ideas.'

'Why do you say that?'

'You will remember that I have information which I cannot share with you. I can only say that I accept he *believes* he had a child. But we should work with the assumption that he did not.'

'If he doesn't know the difference between truth and fiction, how did you expect me to distinguish between them—

without your *information?*'

'My role here is to separate fact from fiction and to translate fiction into fact. It is not necessary for you to know which is which. At least, it is not required for me to achieve my goal. You need only to ask him questions. I will do the rest.'

'That seems like a strange method of interrogation.'

'Yes, but this is not a typical interrogation.'

'I still don't know why you need me. It sounds like you made a lot of progress without me.'

'I have, but progress has slowed lately. I am hoping that you can accelerate the process. Remember, my time is very limited. Please know that your presence here is helping greatly. I can see that it is.'

'I don't know why you think I'm helping. He's hardly said anything.'

'Ah, but I see his reactions to your questions. We *are* making progress.'

Kadesh touched her arm. 'If you could just speak with him a little more, Mary, I would be very grateful.'

At that moment she was gripped with a strange sense of urgency to return to the table. But the expanding length of time that now lay between her and her son was becoming increasingly difficult to accept, and with each passing moment guilt pressed harder upon her. Still, something seemed to bind her to that room. Perhaps it was the link to her pendant—or just a fascination with Kadesh's prisoner. And then suddenly her responsibilities faded again far into the recesses of her mind, where they could not reach her. She looked across the table to Judaea and listened for the rasp of his breath, but there was no sound. He sat unmoving, like a machine at rest, responding only when queried.

Mary moved to Judaea. 'How old is the boy in your thoughts?' she said.

'He is small.'

'Do you know his age?'

'No.'

'Would you like to remember more, Judaea? —About the boy?'

'No.'

'Why not?'

'In time, all things left in the desert are buried under the sands.'

'But they don't need to remain buried. Some things—important things—thought to be lost can be found again. Will you let me help you find these things?'

'No.'

'Why not, Judaea? Have you done something you shouldn't have?' She sat in the seat across from him; a lump formed at the back of her throat.

'Did you hurt the boy?' she said.

The scraping sound of Kadesh's writing stopped.

'All is as it should be.'

'Nothing is as it should be,' she whispered under her breath.

'I do not have the answers you seek.'

She leaned toward him. 'Why does Kadesh think you're dangerous?'

'He has many lies.'

'Why would he lie about you?' Mary said.

At that moment the door shook. Kadesh wheeled around and stared at it wild-eyed, as if at any moment something terrible might pass through it. A hard knocking ensued and the handle rattled violently, but Kadesh remained fixed in his seat. Mary felt her face flush as the tension became palpable.

And then the sounds stopped.

Mary's attention moved from Kadesh to the door as she tried to understand his strange reaction. Suddenly a key rattled triumphantly in the lock.

Kadesh sprang to his feet and hurried to the door. 'Please stay there!' he said, holding out his arm to Mary.

The door had opened only a few inches when Kadesh reached it. He slid his foot to the bottom of the door, stopping it from swinging inward any further. At that same moment, the flame of the oil lantern flickered and the room seemed to shake with the fading light. Mary's chest tightened at the thought of losing their only source of light. As the light danced threateningly, a woman's voice came from the other side of the door. But her English was too broken and the voice too soft for Mary to understand her. Kadesh responded to the voice, speaking fluently in a language unfamiliar to Mary.

Many tense moments passed as an emphatic conversation developed at the door—moments made more uncomfortable by Judaea's incessant stare. Mary distracted herself by surveying the small interrogation room. It was then that she for the first time noticed many strange details: deep, extensive cracking in the stone floor tiles and concrete walls, the inappropriate lighting provided by the single lamp, the weak ventilation. Even the furniture was of surprisingly poor quality and impractical for its intended use, although what bothered her most were the mismatched chairs. There was also no residual trace of food or drink anywhere, nor any other sign that the room had been occupied for any length of time. Eventually, her gaze fell upon Kadesh's notebook, lying open only a few feet away. One of the pages was filled with meticulous fine writing, but from where she sat she couldn't quite make out the small, tightly formed letters. She was surprised that any information had been noted from their brief conversation, and became suddenly curious to know what Kadesh had extracted from it.

At the door, the hushed conversation continued. Kadesh's voice lowered as the woman's tone became increasingly emphatic. Seemingly in response to the finality in the woman's unintelligible words, he quickly moved into the hallway, keeping the door slightly ajar behind him. The woman remained out of Mary's view.

As the theatre continued nearby, Judaea remained still, his dull, glassy eyes still fixed on Mary, seemingly infinitely content with his silence. It seemed to her that if she never spoke to him again, he would remain in his stoic state indefinitely. He seemed fundamentally void of any curiosity and lacking any initiative. She tried to recall whether he had asked a single question since her arrival. Running her damp hands along the tops of her thighs, she listened for a resolution of the conversation in the hallway. His stare was becoming intolerable, as was the passage of time, which began to weigh heavily upon her again. But she could not bring herself to interrupt Kadesh's discussion, which had become increasingly animated. She was desperate for a distraction. Again she looked to Kadesh's notebook, which sprawled invitingly beside her. After a quick glance at the door, she leaned over and read:

Mary had a little lamb …

She stared at the fine black lines that formed the meticulously printed words, reading them over and over again without comprehension. As Judaea sat staring, mutely watching her, she flipped through the thin, crisp pages of the notebook. But there was nothing but the twenty-four-line nursery rhyme. A fury welled within her as she sat back into her chair. She looked to Judaea in disbelief as the sound of his breath filled the room.

'Now you see his lies,' he said.

Her mind filled with thoughts of her son, left at the hospital, and she shook with rage. She was a fool. Sensing tears coming, she quickly turned away from Judaea.

'You have come here for nothing,' he said.

With those words, he unleashed her anger upon him. She plunged her hand into the pocket of her dress and withdrew the worn piece of heavy paper on which was the image of her son. Her hand trembling with rage, she held it out to him only inches from his face.

'This is why I'm here!'

His gaze locked onto the image. As he stared at it, something terrible stirred in the blackness of his eyes. Something behind them had been disturbed, or awoken. Slowly, he leaned toward the image.

Intrigued by the profound effect the photograph had on

him, Mary moved closer and watched as it worked upon him. All other thoughts dissolved away as she gazed at Judaea's intangible familiarity and wondered what memory had been roused.

And then it happened.

Judaea's body seized. His arms dropped to his sides, his head cocked backward as though he had been struck with a strong electric current. In his open mouth, poorly aged and yellowed teeth protruded from pale grey gums. His waxy and lifeless face gazed upward. In his dull eyes was reflected the solitary light of the room. The rough sound of air coursing through his lungs had ceased. He was completely still. After a few moments, she slowly reached across the table and placed her index and middle fingers upon his outstretched neck, just in front of his ear. Beneath his long, rough whiskers, where a pulse should be perceptible, his skin was cold and still.

'Kadesh!' she called.

Kadesh peered into the room through the door opening, muttered something to the woman and quickly slipped back into the room, slamming the door shut behind him. 'Do not touch him!' he cried, fumbling at one of the locks that bordered the door.

'His heart has stopped,' Mary said. 'He needs a doctor.'

'I instructed you not to touch him! Why did you touch him!?'

Kadesh's eyes were wild as they danced between Mary and Judaea. He moved quickly toward her, no longer resembling the meek, unassuming man she had known until now. In an instant, he had become something more formidable, and frightening. He only glanced at Judaea. Her heart pounded as the walls of the interrogation room seemed to close in. She felt suddenly cold and isolated.

'I'll go,' she said, backing slowly toward the door.

'No,' he said, gripping her arm.

'He'll die if we don't get help soon. Look at him!'

Kadesh turned to his prisoner, whose incapacitated body remained seized. But he showed no sign of compassion.

Instead he exuded anger, disappointment. As the moments passed, he seemed to grow nervous, staring flustered at the moribund man.

Mary scanned the room, her senses charged with fear. But there was little she could do. His grip was firm and unyielding. He was much stronger than he appeared. And then suddenly, as though a cold hand had been laid upon the back of her neck, she remembered how she had entered the building through the side door—not the front entrance. Her mind raced as she recalled how Kadesh had checked the lane after her. Not even the woman in the hallway had seen her—he had denied her entry and blocked her view into the room.

No one knew she was there.

Terrible thoughts flooded her mind. Her son would wake up alone, wondering where his mother was. As the days passed without her return, he would come to believe that she had abandoned him.

The color in her face faded as she stood between the dying prisoner and the locked door behind Kadesh—the door, she suddenly realized, that was locked from the inside. The locks were there not to prevent a prisoner from leaving the room, but to prevent someone from entering. The air became thick and moved like water through her lungs. Her chest rose and fell, but she couldn't catch her breath. She groped for the memory of Kadesh locking the door only moments earlier, but nothing was clear. Her thoughts were cluttered with horrible images that swooped in and out like bats from a cave. One after the other, they flashed and disappeared an instant later, leaving nothing tangible in their wake. For only a brief moment she heard it: the sound of a single lock being engaged—only one of the many. If she could get past Kadesh, she would need to guess the right lock on her first attempt. There would be no second chance. Her muscles tensed.

'It is much too late for him,' Kadesh said, moving between her and the door. 'He is beyond the help of medicines.'

He paused for a moment, his brow furrowed. 'You must go back to the hospital, Mary. Forget what has happened here.'

'I will,' she breathed.

But Kadesh did not move. He remained between her and the exit. They faced one another, each appearing uncertain of the next move. Mary searched for something to say, but nothing came. She knew he could sense her fear and it seemed to intensify his frustration. Just as she was about to try to pull free, he bowed his head and relaxed his grip on her arm.

'I am sorry,' he said. 'I never wished for you to become involved in this. Please do not be afraid. It causes me great pain to see you so fearful.'

'Then I can go?' she said while drawing her arm away.

'Of course you may go,' he said, moving aside. 'But there are things you need to know before you leave.'

'I should just go now.'

Trembling, she quickly moved to the door and tried one of the locks. The door wouldn't open. She tried each lock, one after the other, but the door was unyielding. As she stood staring at the final untested lock, she realized that even if she fled now, she could not escape what had happened there. One day she would need to reconcile the events that had unfolded in that room and until that was accomplished, she would be haunted by the memory. She turned and faced Kadesh.

'Good,' he said and listened for sounds from the other side of the door. But there was only silence. He stepped toward her.

'I felt very strongly that the things I am about to tell you should not be disclosed to you. But I am afraid now that given the circumstances, I have no other choice but to trust in you. Can I trust in you?'

'I—yes.'

'Good. I know you can be trusted. That is one reason why I came to you for help. I am a very good judge of character,' he smiled briefly.

'When he was found, I made the decision that no one else should know that I had him—so I brought him here. As I am sure you have noticed,' he said sweeping his hand in the air, 'this is not an interrogation room.'

The gentle tone in his voice was reassuring and it comforted her. The wildness in his eyes had disappeared and he was once again the man she had first met, relieved to be sharing the information with her.

'It was of great importance that no one else should know of him,' he said. 'You were not to be an exception. But now this has happened and I am left with a terrible dilemma.'

'Please don't tell me any more,' she whispered. 'I don't know what I've seen here. Really, I don't.'

'But you do. We both know.' A weak smile moved across his face as he looked past Mary and toward his prisoner. 'You know just as I know that he is deceased. But what you do not know is that he is watching you right now. Turn around Mary and see...'

Even before she turned her head, she could feel the unmistakable weight of Judaea's stare upon her, chilling her spine like cold running water. She gasped when she saw him sitting upright at the table, gazing blankly at her. Slowly, she moved to the table and stopped directly across from him.

He was still as stone.

'Judaea,' she said. But there was no response.

She took several deep breaths and reached over the table. She placed her index and middle fingers onto his neck and waited for the pulse from beneath his skin, but there was nothing. Like a wax statue, his dull unblinking eyes stared lifelessly into nothingness and she knew he was dead. And then Judaea's mouth dropped opened, and the room hissed with his breath.

'Do not listen to his lies,' he exhaled.

The skin on her arms tingled and rose as though thousands of tiny insects crawled just beneath the surface. Nausea took her as she pulled her arm away, and she collapsed to her hands and knees, fighting hard against her stomach as it wretched. But there was no stopping the powerful cascade of involuntary reflexes that were set into motion. As the convulsions came, she fought hard against them, swallowing the acidic liquid back into her gut. The burning in her throat brought tears to her eyes. When her struggle was over she turned to Kadesh, shivering and exhausted.

'Why did you bring me here?' she said, wiping her eyes.

Kadesh kneeled beside her and placed his hand on her shoulders. 'Come, Mary,' he said. 'I will tell you.'

❧ CHAPTER TEN ❦

Father

Muriel stood just inside the doorway to Kaleb's room, gazing at the young boy as he slept. Tears rolled down the gentle contour of her cheeks and under the curve of her jaw. Small splashes dotted the tops of her soft leather shoes.

'I put the kettle on,' Amira whispered to her as she passed. 'What's wrong, girl?' she said, placing her hand on Muriel's arm.

'It's as if he was meant to suffer—and no one can ever change that,' she spoke in a faraway voice.

'We're all born into suffering, Muriel. Some just more than others.'

'It's not right. *This* is not right.'

'No, it's not. That's why we're here—to make things better for them.'

Amira looked upon the boy's small body as he shifted in his sleep. 'He is very young,' she said, 'but he's part of our Lord's plan.'

Muriel crossed her arms and turned her gaze to her shoes. 'You believe that?' she murmured.

'If I didn't, I couldn't work here—not with the children.'

'He wouldn't make him suffer like this.'

Amira cupped Muriel's face in her hands. '*And He will wipe away every tear from their eyes,*' she said, wiping Muriel's tears with her thumbs, '*—and there will no longer be any death, there will no longer be any mourning, or crying, or pain.*'

'You believe He is coming?' Muriel smiled.

'No, girl. I know He's already here, working through each one of us at the hospital. We are here for those who are in need. We dull their pains and show them love. And when their bodies finally surrender, we are there to hold their hand and to show them that through the darkness, there is light.'

Amira took her by the hand and led her into the hallway under a flickering lamp.

'Are you sure you can't stay just a little while longer?' Amira said. 'I've seen the pattern many times before. He doesn't have long now.'

Muriel nodded.

'I don't understand, girl. What could be more important than this?'

Muriel slowly raised her head. 'Nothing,' she breathed.

At that moment, McLeary appeared down the hallway, approaching quickly, carrying a large cloth handbag. A long brown coat covered her nurse's gown. Thin leather gloves were being drawn with difficulty over her thick fingers as she walked.

'It's cold out there,' McLeary announced in a bold voice. She shivered emphatically. 'I don't recall it ever being so cold at this time of year.'

Noticing Muriel's state, she moved to her. 'Oh dear,' she sighed. 'Having separation anxieties are we?'

Before Muriel could answer, McLeary turned toward Kaleb's bed. 'Oh no,' she said. 'He's awake.'

The women moved to Kaleb's bed, where he sat upright, staring at the far wall.

'Puppa,' he spoke in a thin voice. His eyes were wide and glassy.

'No, lad,' McLeary said, taking hold of his hand. 'It's only us.'

'Puppa,' he whispered.

'What is it, little potato?' Amira said stroking his head. But he remained focused on something in the infinite distance, deeply absorbed in his exclusive experience.

'Call to him, Kaleb,' Muriel said, moving to his side. 'Call for him.'

McLeary wheeled toward her. Taking firm hold of Muriel's arm, she led her quickly into the hallway.

'What are you saying, Muriel?' she whispered into Muriel's face. 'Why would you encourage him? You know his father isn't alive.'

'His time has almost run out.'

'—And there's nothing that boy can do about it. You know that.'

Muriel's reddened eyes darted from side to side. 'He has to do something.'

'The only thing he needs to do is to go back to sleep. And you, young lady—you need to pull yourself together right away because other than his mother, you're the only person who can properly deal with him in this state. You know you're like a sister to him. I've always relied on your sensibility in these matters. Don't let me down now.'

She wiped the remnants of Muriel's tears away with her coat sleeve and raised her chin. 'Now,' McLeary whispered, 'do you think you can get him back to sleep without any more shenanigans?'

'Yes,' Muriel breathed and looked into McLeary's eyes.

The head nurse turned ghostly pale. Muriel's face seemed to dissolve before her, becoming ethereal, faded. For an instant, the young woman seemed to take on another form: that of McLeary's deceased niece—a young girl whose memory had become comfortably buried under years of distraction. The large woman swayed and her legs buckled beneath her but before she collapsed, Muriel embraced her.

'Betty!' Amira called and ran to the nurse's side.

Under the support of Muriel's arms, McLeary fought to regain her composure. She placed her hand on the wall and leaned her weight against it. Blinking hard, she ran her tongue over her dry lips.

'What happened, Betty?' Amira said, placing her palm on McLeary's forehead.

'Nothing,' she mumbled. 'I just felt dizzy for a moment.'

Muriel released her hold of McLeary and went to Kaleb's side. McLeary stood dazed, watching Muriel as she knelt next to Kaleb and began to stroke his hair.

'Betty you're white as a ghost,' Amira said, taking hold of McLeary's arm. 'Do you have any chest pains?'

'No,' she murmured.

'All right. Let's go to the supply station and get some food into you,' she said, pulling on McLeary's arm. But the large woman wouldn't budge. She was transfixed on Muriel. Slowly, she moved toward the doorway, but Amira held firmly onto her.

'Amira, what's wrong with you?!' McLeary demanded, and with a heavy downward thrust of her arm, she broke Amira's grip.

'Nothing's wrong with me,' she said, folding her arms defiantly. 'Have you eaten anything today?'

'How should I remember? I'm running around all day, trying to keep this place in a shape that loosely resembles some kind of order. I don't know if I'm coming or going half the time.'

'Well then, I'm sure some food will do you good.'

'Now don't you play nurse with me, Amira. I know what I need and it's not food. Do I look like I need more food?' She placed her hands on her ample hips.

'You're pale as dry bone under a hot sun,' Amira insisted.

'Now you're repeating yourself,' McLeary said, shaking her head. 'Right, I'm in early tomorrow. If I let you keep me here any longer, I may as well not go home tonight.'

And with that, McLeary turned on her heels and hurried down the hallway.

Amira folded her arms across her chest and called after her as McLeary headed down the stairs. 'You'd better eat something when you get home!'

'Kaleb,' Muriel whispered. 'Do you still see him?'

'No,' he said.

'Don't be afraid, I'm here with you.'

'Muriel, why are you crying?'

'I was sad—that's all,' she said, wiping her tears.

'Why?' he said and embraced her.

'I'll tell you some other time—when you're better,' she whispered into his ear.

'Where's Mumma?'

'She had to step out for a short while. She asked Amira and me to take care of you.'

'Did she have to go?'

'Yes. She had to do something important. She'll be back very soon.'

His bottom lip trembled. 'Are you sure?'

'I'm sure,' she said, sliding under the tubes and wires that surrounded him. She took him into her arms.

'She'll be very back soon. Don't you worry.'

'I want her to come back now so she can see him when he comes back.'

'I don't think she can see him, Kaleb. Only you can.' She rested her chin on the top of his head.

'Did you see him, Muriel?'

'No.'

'How come?'

'He must come here just for you.'

The young boy stared into the silence as Muriel stroked his head.

'Kaleb,' Muriel whispered. 'The next time you see him, I want you to ask him to help you.'

'But he's a ghost.'

'Will you do it anyway? —For me?'

He slowly shook his head. 'What if he's still mad at me?'

'Why would he be mad at you?'

His breathing became deeper and louder. 'Because I lost his picture,' he said, fidgeting with his hands.

'You didn't lose it, silly monkey. You told me that when you were here the first time, it dropped from your bedside table and was swept away. It wasn't your fault. Remember?'

He shook his head.

'Well, I do,' she said. 'And I also know that your father would *never* be angry with you.'

At that moment, Amira entered the room holding a wooden tray, on which was a small ceramic cup filled with steaming liquid.

'Someone's going to be very tired tomorrow if they don't get some sleep,' she said, resting the tray on the bedside table.

'I made you some tea. It'll help you fall back to sleep. It's very hot, so I'm going to let it cool down for a bit.'

As she blew across the surface of the liquid, Kaleb stared into the expanse in front of him. 'He's still gone,' he said.

Amira passed Muriel a concerned look and sat down on the bed.

'You know, Kaleb, the mind is a very wonderful and mysterious thing. Sometimes it plays games with us when we're tired or when we're sleeping.'

Muriel gently rocked him and ran her fingers through his fine hair.

'I think what you need is a story,' Amira said. 'Don't you think so, Muriel?'

'I think you're right. That's just what he needs.'

'I haven't told you a story in a long time, have I?'

Kaleb shook his head and smiled brightly.

'Just as I thought,' she laughed. 'Hmm, now let me think… Your favorite animals are butterflies, right?'

He shook his head.

'No? Pink, prancing ponies is it?'

'No,' he giggled.

'No? I thought for sure that was you. That must be the boy in three-twenty down the hall. Now what was it? Let's see…'

He hissed softly.

'Ah, yes, now I remember. You like *snakes*.'

Amira gave an exaggerated shudder as Kaleb nodded enthusiastically.

'Well, this story was told to me when I was a little girl. It's about how the snake lost its legs.'

After an emphatic pause, she leaned over him and whispered, 'And don't look so surprised to hear that I was once a little girl.'

He smiled.

'Did you know that snakes had legs a long time ago?'

He shook his head.

'Well child, then you're about to hear something new.'

Kaleb watched, mesmerized, as Amira narrated the story, animating the plot with the pale palms of her hands and the bright whites of her eyes, which created a captivating contrast against the dark chocolate-colored skin of her face.

'A long time ago, the moon saw that the land was drying,' she began in her deepest, richest voice. 'So he told a special person named Mantis to tell all the animals to find new homes before the land turned to desert. All of the animals listened and left that place except for the snake, who was lazy and at that time had legs—just like a lizard.'

Kaleb's eyes widened.

'*I'll stay here and take my chances*, the snake said. But when it didn't rain for many days, all the grasses dried up and there were no more frogs for the snake to eat. Soon, the snake became very hungry and skinny. He tried to follow the other animals, but the land had become a desert and he couldn't walk in the hot sand. *Please save me*, the snake cried to the moon. Well, the moon felt sorry for the poor snake and, using powerful magic, he made its legs shrink away. With no legs, the snake easily moved across the hot sand, slithering on its shiny skin. Eventually it found a new land where it could live. That's why even today, snakes don't have legs.'

'Is that true?' he whispered.

'It's just an old story, little potato,' Amira smiled. 'But it teaches us something important about ourselves. That's why we tell it to our children. You see, the snake wanted something, but it got what it *needed* instead.'

Kaleb tugged on his sheets and stared blankly at her.

'Love is the most powerful thing there is. Evil can only destroy, but love has the power to create. Your love for your father is still so strong that your mind created an image of him. That image is so clear to you that you thought he was actually here in the room.'

He slunk down in Muriel's arms. 'I don't have the picture anymore—it got swept away.'

'Yes, I remember,' Amira said. 'When your mother gets back, we'll ask her to bring you another picture of him. We'll put it right here where you can see it.' She placed her hand on the bedside table and then took the cup and held it to her mouth. Her thick brown lips puckered and she blew over the liquid.

'Drink some,' Amira said, bringing the cup to his lips.

He inspected the golden-yellow liquid and breathed in its aroma. 'It smells like apples,' he said.

'It's made from chamomile flowers. They're very special. They do wonderful things for us. Some people even think they're magical.'

'Magical flowers?' he breathed.

'Yes,' Amira smiled, tilting the cup toward him. He took a small sip.

'Good?'

'It's sweet,' he nodded.

'I put a little honey in it. Soon, you'll feel right as rain.'

'Mumma says Puppa could fix anything—even people. If he was here, he'd fix us, too. Can we save some?'

'Of course. But who shall we save it for?'

'Mumma,' he said, taking another sip.

'Why would she need some tea?'

'She's sick,' he whispered into the cup.

Amira threw Muriel a questioning glance, but she responded with a blank look.

'How is she sick?' Amira said, taking the cup from him.

Kaleb shrugged.

'Did she tell you that?'

'No.'

'Then why would you think that, little potato?'

He shrugged his shoulders and bit down on his lower lip. Carefully, Amira placed the cup on the tray as Kaleb stared into the still liquid.

'Well, we'll make sure she gets a cup as soon as she gets back and she'll be just fine. You don't need to worry about her. Okay?'

'Okay.'

'But right now, I want you to drink some more of this magic tea.'

'Is it really magic?'

'If you believe it's magic, it's magic.'

'What will it do?'

'Well, let's see now,' she said, furrowing her brow. 'Dried chamomile flowers mixed in hot water and just a drop of wild honey... Ah, yes. It'll make you sleepy.'

'Really?'

'Oh yes, *very* sleepy.'

As Amira spoke, Muriel continued to stroke his head. Soon, his eyes became heavy, his stare distant and relaxed.

'Have just a little more,' Amira said, lifting the cup to his lips.

'I'm full,' he breathed into it.

'Good,' she said, placing the cup on the tray.

Suddenly, Kaleb's eyes filled with tears. 'Are you sure she'll come back?'

'Of course she'll come back, silly monkey,' Muriel said. 'She'll be back very soon.'

'Are you sure?'

'I'm absolutely sure.'

Amira rose from the bed and affirmed what Muriel said with a slight nod and a smile.

'The potion is having its effect now,' Muriel whispered in his ear.

Gazing placidly ahead, his eyes heavy and unfocussed, Kaleb lay fully immersed in the calm that now embraced him. Even the unsettled air outside seemed to accommodate him with a gentler wind and lighter rain. Soon, his chest began to rise and fall in the rhythm of sleep, and the women knew he was once again untethered from that place—free again to play like other children: without sickness, without pain.

'Come to Me, all who are weary and heavy-laden, and I will give you rest,' Amira whispered to him.

Carefully, Muriel slid out from underneath him and laid his head down upon his feather pillow. She kissed him on the forehead and folded the covers over him as Amira adjusted the drip rate of one of the clear tubes that led into his forearm. Staring at the soft curves of his face, she shook her head.

'Where is she?' Amira said. 'What could be more important than this?'

'Nothing,' Muriel breathed.

Amira moved to the tall window and gazed into the empty street below. Cold, heavy air tumbled down her face and along the front of her white uniform. Dark clouds bloated with precipitation loomed threateningly as far as the eye could see. As Muriel dimmed the light, Amira placed her fingertips on the cool window pane and whispered to the night, 'Mary, where are you?'

❧ CHAPTER ELEVEN ❧

Confession

Mary's legs trembled as Kadesh helped her to her feet. Her lips were pale and dry. She would not look at Judaea, but she could still feel his stare upon her.

'Don't be afraid, Mary,' Kadesh said taking her hands into his. 'You are safe.'

Safe. A simple word that in that dimly lit stone hollow she occupied with an unliving man should resonate emptily within her, but instead it carried a strange reassurance. The genuine sympathy that warmed Kadesh's tone was deeply comforting, and her desire to flee dissipated like smoke in a gentle breeze.

'Please come with me,' Kadesh said.

Mary followed him down the hallway, which seemed to narrow with each step into the poor light. He stopped in front of another unmarked door on the opposite side of the hallway, pushed it open and reached for a small lamp suspended on the wall just beyond the door. In only a few moments, warm light filled a small, windowless room packed with assorted clutter. The smell of damp, old books hung thickly in the air and reminded her of an old school library.

'Please,' Kadesh said, gesturing for her to carefully enter.

'Where are we?' Mary said, stepping between stacks of old

books.

'This is a simple storage room—similar to the one where Judaea is. I moved most of the items from the other room into here. As you can see, it is now a little crowded. My apologies for the poor accommodations.'

How could I have so easily accepted the façade? Mary wondered.

It seemed as though she had lost all capacity for sound judgment. Standing in that cramped storeroom with a man she hardly knew, she realized she could no longer rely on her instincts. Like a small child lost in an unfamiliar place, she suddenly felt exposed and vulnerable.

'Perhaps you can now understand why I brought him here,' Kadesh said, creating a small clearing within several stacks of books. He placed two decrepit wooden chairs into the space and sat heavily onto each of them in turn. 'Please,' he said, gesturing at the more stable of the two.

The chair complained beneath her as she slowly sat upon it. When she was satisfied that it would support her weight, she gazed around the room. Several bundles of old paintings mounted in cracked wooden frames lay stacked precariously near the far wall: colorful images of servicemen sitting tall upon large, handsome horses; portraits of unsmiling men with large mustaches; landscapes and architectural renderings of old buildings and other unidentifiable structures.

'How to begin?' Kadesh said, sitting across from her. He stared for a moment at the concrete floor directly in front of him, his hands flat on his knees.

'Man is very unpredictable,' he sighed. 'But one thing you can always be certain of is that he will exploit anything and everything as it suits his purpose. He will mortgage friendships to achieve power, and enslave his brothers to gain freedom. In many ways he possesses the reckless spirit of a child, except that the consequences of his actions can be much more severe.'

He raised his eyes to meet hers.

'Sometimes one must intercede without consultation of others—for the better good,' he said. 'Judaea is a threat to mankind, and mankind is a threat to Judaea. Therefore, he must be isolated. This is why I have not been completely forthright with you. And I apologize for this. But now that you know of his existence, I am afraid that you are in danger.'

Kadesh leaned toward her. 'You must never disclose his existence, to *anyone*.'

The cool air seemed to suddenly thicken. Soft ambient sounds that trickled incessantly around her became noticeably louder. She was ensnared like an animal, caught in a trap set for someone else: Kadesh's collateral issue that now needed to be addressed discreetly. A strong current of fear coursed through her, and she was taken by a powerful desire to say or do anything that would erase what she now knew or to go back in time—if only to the moment just before she had met Kadesh.

'Does anyone else know about him?' Mary said.

'No,' Kadesh said, slowly shaking his head.

'Are you sure?'

'Very.'

Her gaze dropped to the smooth concrete beneath her feet as various options raced through her mind. Soon, she realized that her only power lay in destroying the secret—by disclosing it. In that instant, it would disappear forever and so release her from its grip. But with this realization came a bitter shame that settled in like an unwelcome visitor, and the thought dissolved away in disappointment. For a moment, she allowed herself the rare luxury of self-indulgence and wallowed in silent acquiescence.

'Do not worry, Mary,' Kadesh whispered. 'He is my responsibility, not yours.'

There was nothing to say but she spoke anyway, if only for the comfort of her own voice. 'How did you find him?'

'I would like to tell you. I truly would. But I cannot.'

'Why not?'

'I am sorry. You must simply accept that I cannot.'

'When did you find him?'

'Eh, some weeks ago.'

'You've kept him hidden down here all that time? How did you prevent him from being discovered?'

'It has not been easy. My secret was nearly discovered today when the custodian stumbled upon my keep.'

'What did you say to her?'

'Among many other things, I told her I was conducting highly sensitive and important business, and she should not concern herself with the room until further notice. But she is new to this place and does not know me. I believe she was dissatisfied with my explanation. It appears she had other, conflicting instructions. I expect she will return tomorrow—perhaps with others.'

'You don't seem too concerned.'

'I must conclude this business tonight. What happens tomorrow is not important.'

She shuddered at the thought of being alone in that room all night with the unliving man. Her guilt was made worse for wanting so desperately to abandon him to his seemingly insurmountable task. Somehow in the following hours he would need to succeed in accomplishing that which he had failed to do over weeks. But Kadesh was right: it was his responsibility, not hers.

'It has been a very slow process,' Kadesh said, gazing into the clutter. 'You have seen his response to pressure. Under stress, he recedes into himself to evade that which he cannot—or will not—deal with. He becomes unresponsive, sometimes remaining that way for hours. This has greatly hindered my progress.'

'Why did he react like that to a picture of my son?'

'Eh, I do not know,' he said, rubbing his palms along his lap.

The muscles of Mary's back and shoulders tightened; her skin tingled and prickled.

'He doesn't know him,' she said.

Kadesh was silent.

'He couldn't have recognized him. He's never seen him before. Right?'

'I found Judaea very soon after he arrived in this town,' he said, waving his hands in the air. 'I am certain he has never been here before. So they could not have met.'

'Why did he come to this place?'

'Eh, that I cannot say.'

'Do you mean—?'

'I would like to tell you, but I must not.'

The macabre scene in the interrogation room flashed in her mind: Judaea's body bent awkwardly backwards, his mouth and eyes open wide. Like a figure of wax, his lifeless, unyielding stare was chilling and unnatural. She could still hear the hiss of air as it passed into him—air needed not for breath, but for speech only. The familiar squeeze of nausea set in again and the world shifted around her. Gripping the edge of her seat, she closed her eyes, swallowed hard and waited for the misery to pass.

'Are you all right, Mary?'

'I'm fine,' she said, passing her tongue over her dry lips. The back of her throat burned where the residual stomach acids still worked.

'Please forgive my rudeness. I will get you some water.'

'No—thank you,' she said, clenching her teeth. 'Does he eat?'

'I beg your pardon?'

'Does he eat—food?'

'No, he does not. Nor does he sleep. He has few of the requirements of the living.'

'His door locks from the inside only. He never tries to leave?'

'You are very perceptive. Why would he leave? He has nowhere to go. He has everything he needs. Here, his exposure to others is minimal—except me, of course,' he laughed. 'This is how he prefers to be ... alone.'

His brow furrowed as Mary licked her lips again. 'Please, allow me to get you some water.'

'I'm fine, thank you. So what role was I supposed to play in this?'

'I have asked you here for the purpose I already stated: to help him remember. Nothing more. I need only this from you.'

'To help him remember what?'

'Who he is—or who he *was*.'

'Who was he?'

'I am sorry, I cannot tell you.'

'Why is it important that he remember?'

'I believe that if he remembers, the problematic situation which has brought us together will be resolved.'

'And you thought I would help him without discovering your secret, or his?'

'I had hoped, perhaps naïvely, that this could be possible. I am sorry, Mary, but I felt it necessary to take the chance. I am solely responsible for the predicament we find ourselves in.'

As Kadesh lowered his head, she resolved that she would never again accept what he said as simple truth. It was clear now that the facts lay buried under layers of façade and half-truths fabricated to serve his unknown purpose. He would tell her only that which would placate her, satiate her.

'I now understand why you recruited me,' she said. 'It doesn't really matter what I discover here. Does it? You know I won't live long enough to reveal your secrets.'

'No, Mary,' he said shaking his head. 'That is not true.'

'But then, how would you know?' she whispered. A dark conspiracy unfolded in her thoughts like a sequence of images from an old movie film, animating its story to her frame by frame.

'You've searched through the hospital records,' she whispered. '—And you found my file. You know I'm dying.'

'It is not true.'

'But it is true. Soon, everything I know—my memories, my thoughts—everything I learn here will be lost forever.'

'You must not believe such a thing. This thought has never occurred to me—not for a moment. And who can say what is lost or not lost in the afterlife? Did you not believe less than an hour ago that Judaea could not exist? Yet he exists!'

'I don't know what he is. I don't know anything about

him.'

'But you know enough. He is an enigma, a man who has been reduced to little more than the shell of his former self, with only a scattering of residual memories of his life. He is a ghost of solid form, who walks amongst us without purpose or understanding of who or what he is.'

'Why did you believe my discussion with him would change things?'

Kadesh pursed his lips, took a deep breath and exhaled slowly. 'Do you believe in destiny?'

She turned the cliché over in her mind. 'I don't believe in anything.'

'I see,' he sighed. Kadesh rose, supporting himself with the leg of a nearby chair that was stacked upside down. 'I see things from a slightly different perspective. Could it be that more than chance has assembled the components of this story together? —That you have more significance in this matter than you realize? Ask yourself this: How could it be that from our chance encounter at a gathering some time ago, you would be so relevant to me now? You can help him. You have already seen the effect you have on him.'

'I don't think that's much of a coincidence.'

'No? I believe that our paths were always meant to join here, at this place and at this time. I know you can help this man—if you are willing.'

It still seemed to Mary that between each of his words, there was a tiny gap: a void that remained after extraction of a small fact, a small but vital element necessary for her to understand the truth.

'Why does he seem familiar to me?'

'Eh, I cannot say.'

'I need to know, Mr. Kadesh. Do I know him?'

'I can honestly say *no*. How could you?' He leaned in close. 'Mary, I too am seeking answers. That is why I came to you.'

'I thought you wanted his *knowledge*.'

'Yes, but of course I have questions, too.'

'Then why didn't you give me the questions you want

answered?'

'My questions,' he said, smiling, 'are of a completely different context. There is no need for you to ask them or any others. By simply speaking with him as you have been, I believe you are helping.'

'How can I help Judaea when I can't even help the living?'

'You are what he needs to help him remember.'

'Can he help *me*? He knew about the pendant. Does he know anything more about it, or about Aaron's death?'

A thick silence settled between them as he closed his eyes and stroked back his silvery hair.

'Mary, I assure you that he cannot provide any insight into the circumstances of your husband's death.'

She stared silently at him, unconsciously stroking the smooth underside of her chair with her fingertips.

'I know that the pendant is the reason you are here, but he is in no way associated with the cause of your suffering. Do not make him the focal point of your anger, for this will only lead to frustration and disappointment.'

She bowed her head and covered her face with her hands.

'Judaea is not truly of the flesh. He does not see things in the same way as you or I. His references are altogether different. We can only imagine the context with which he perceives things around him. I am certain that he saw the Mukkadesh atesh for the poison that it was—even hidden beneath your clothing.'

'Mr. Kadesh,' she whispered from behind her hands. 'A very sick child is waiting for me back at the hospital. I need to believe he's still sleeping and not awake, wondering where I am. If Judaea doesn't have any information about my husband or our pendants, then I shouldn't be here.'

'I understand. But you are the only one who can help prevent his recessions, and help him accept that which he rejects. You have seen how he responds to you. He is comfortable in your presence.'

Kadesh fidgeted incessantly as he spoke, seemingly searching for something with which to occupy his hands. After sliding along the length of his lap several times, his hands finally found solace there, like golden moths resting against the bark of a tree.

'I have one more question, Mr. Kadesh.'

'Please.'

'Why did he come here?'

'That,' he breathed, 'is a very good question.'

Mary waited for a moment, as if he might provide the answer that she knew he had. But when the moment passed and nothing followed, she rose from her chair and moved into the hallway. Kadesh followed closely behind.

'I know that I can trust you to keep my secret,' he said, touching her shoulder. 'I also hope you will remember that I have only until morning to resolve this matter.'

'I remember. But I also have an important matter to attend to.'

'Of course. I understand the difficulty you are going through, and I appreciate what you have already done for me.'

For the first time since her arrival, she became aware of activity in another area of the building. Muffled sounds radiated through the low ceiling like strange angelic voices whispering to one another just beyond the threshold of her comprehension. She stopped in front of the makeshift interrogation room. It would be difficult to leave so many unanswered questions behind, but she knew that crossing the threshold back into the deep realm of infinite questions would only lead her farther away from her son, and that path was Kadesh's to follow, not hers.

'Is there something you wish to ask him?' Kadesh said as she listened to the familiar silence that hung ominously on the other side of the door.

'No,' she said and moved swiftly down the hallway.

Mary unlocked the outer door and stepped out into the cold air. As she peered back down the dark hallway toward the interrogation room, she envisioned the door slowly opening. Gripping its edge was a crooked hand, its flesh dangling from the narrow bones of its thin fingers. A single eye peered through the crack.

'Goodbye,' she said, backing into the alley.

'Goodbye, Mary,' he whispered and closed the outer door.

Kadesh stood facing the door, his hands running along the deep cracks of its surface. He remained there for a few moments, staring at its worn painted surface before returning to the interrogation room. With a quick twist of his key, the door opened and he entered. The two men looked at one another, neither of them making a sound. And then something caught Kadesh's attention. He moved toward the table, knelt down and picked up the photograph from the floor. He turned it over, carefully brushed away the dust from the glossy image and smiled.

'Now you see,' he said, holding it out to Judaea, '—the boy *lives*.'

❧ CHAPTER TWELVE ❧

Visions

Mary peered into the veil of grey shadow that cloaked the small hospital room and reduced the sparse contents to colorless shapes. It took a few moments for her eyes to adjust to the dim light and resolve the tubes that normally terminated in her son, dangling from their bottles like arms of a limp octopus. A sinking feeling came over her as she scanned the room for him.

'Welcome back,' said a hushed voice from down the hallway.

Muriel approached, carrying Kaleb in her arms. His back was to Mary, but his smiling face was turned toward her. He stretched out his arms and Mary rushed to him.

'Kabe,' Mary said, embracing him. 'Where were you?'

'I'm sorry I worried you,' Muriel said, stroking the back of Kaleb's head. 'He was awake, so I thought we'd go for a walk. I hope you don't mind.'

'Of course not, Muriel. Thank you for watching over him.' She squeezed Kaleb and brushed the hair from his forehead. 'I'm so happy to see you, Kabe. I'm sorry Mumma wasn't here when you woke up. I had something important to do, but I'm finished now.'

'We've only been out a short while,' Muriel said. 'He just woke up.'

Mary reached through an opening in the front of Kaleb's gown and touched the thin, clear tubes taped flat against his narrow chest.

'Amira took them off. She said it would be okay. He's between medications.'

'Did you walk?' Mary said, kissing Kaleb on the forehead.

'I tried,' he said, looking down at his thin legs, 'but they still won't wake up.'

'Well it's no wonder,' Mary said. 'It's very late. I'm surprised the rest of you isn't asleep, too. Let's get you back to bed.'

'But I just woke up.'

'Aren't you sleepy?'

'No, that's why I woke up—'cause I wasn't sleepy anymore.'

'Well then, let's get you back to bed and I'll lie down with you for a while.'

She placed him on his bed and lay next to him on her side, her right arm tucked under his neck. With a gentle back and forth motion, she rubbed the palm of his hand with her thumb. His eyes turned to hers.

'Where did you go, Mumma?'

'Not far away, angel.'

'Why did you have to go?'

'I needed to do something important. I knew it wouldn't take long and that Amira and Muriel would be here if you woke up before I got back—just like you did, silly angel.' She tickled him under his arm.

'Did you go home?' he said.

'No. Why would I go home?'

'I need another picture of Puppa. Remember?'

He lay his hand palm up on the table where the picture of their family used to stand, his fingers opening and closing as if endeavoring to summon it from the air.

'I remember. I'll get another one for you the next time I go home.' She turned his face toward her. 'We have more pictures at home—even better ones. I'll bring one tomorrow. I promise.'

He frowned into his mother's eyes. 'You promised you wouldn't leave me.'

'I know, angel,' she said brushing away the hair from his forehead. 'I'm sorry. I needed to go out for just a little while. I thought you'd be sleeping and you wouldn't miss me because I'd get back before you woke up. But I guess I took too long. What made you wake up?'

'I thought you'd never come back.'

'Kabe, that would *never* happen. I'll always be here for you, for as long as you need me.'

'I need you forever, Mumma.'

'Then I'll be with you forever.'

Kaleb scanned her face, as if searching it for the unspoken truth. In his eyes she could see the inherent understanding that she could never keep her promise. But he remained silent, touching her cheek with the tips of his fingers.

'When did you grow up?' she whispered.

'One day I'll be just like Puppa.'

'You already are, angel. You have his courage, his wisdom and his wonderful smile. I know he's so proud of you, just like I am.'

He smiled.

'Have you had any more bad dreams?'

'No,' he said, stroking her cheek.

'Good. Then close your eyes and I'll lie with you while you fall asleep.'

'I feel better,' he said, closing his eyes. His sweet, warm breath touched her face. 'I had magic tea.'

'Magic tea? Where did you get that?'

'Mira made it for us. It has flowers in it. We saved you some.'

'Mmm, it sounds wonderful. I'll have some later.'

'I'll ask her to bring you some now,' he said attempting to get up.

'Lie still,' she smiled, placing her hand on his chest.

'You should have some.'

'I will, angel. I'll get some later.'

'You should have some now.'

'Why should I have some now? What's wrong, Kabe?'

He gazed at the wool blanket draped over his bed. With his index finger he played with a loose thread, winding it around his knuckle.

'Kabe, why should I have some?'

'I don't know,' he said. 'It's magic.'

She leaned in close and took his face in her hands. 'There's nothing wrong with me, angel. I don't need any magic, no matter what anyone's told you. If it makes you feel better, I'll have some. I promise. But right now you need your sleep. It's very important. Will you try to fall asleep—for me?'

'Okay. Can you sing me that song?'

'What song?'

'The one you used to sing when we lived in our house—before we came here.'

She shuddered at the thought of her voice travelling through the hallways. Very few voices carried a tune on that ward. Only the rich sound of Amira's song occasionally moved throughout the rooms.

'Angel, I can't sing right now. It's too late.'

'But you never sing anymore.'

The young boy's gentle words awoke in her a profound guilt that slept only lightly when she was with him. It reminded her of the many childhood experiences that he'd been denied by his long illness. She too had been alienated from the joys of motherhood and often felt the great emptiness left in its stead. As she gazed upon her son, Mary bathed in the innocence that radiated from him. She closed her eyes and for a moment disappeared to the kitchen of her home, the bright light of the afternoon sun streaming in through the window, warming her face. In a soft voice she sang:

When it's time for sleep

I close my eyes
I hear the sounds around me
And though I can't see Puppa
In the garden below
I know
There's peace beyond my window

And when I still can't sleep
Although I try
I smell bread baking
And though I can't see Mumma
In the kitchen below
I know
I'm safe behind my window.

As she sang the verses, Kaleb's breathing slowed to a shallow, steady rhythm. Soon his eyes danced behind their lids. Resting her head on the pillow next to him, she gazed upon his soft, angelic face and watched his chest rise and fall defiantly against his disease.

'It's true then,' Amira said, leaning against the door frame, '—you do have a beautiful voice.'

In her hands she held a small bundle of medical equipment. A large rubber bulb swung at the end of a smooth, black rubber tube.

'He's told me about your singing many times, but I'm sure I never heard you before.'

Mary blushed and got up from the bed.

'I hear you used to sing all the time,' Amira said, moving toward the bed.

'That wouldn't have been me.'

'He must have been talking about his other mother, then,' she whispered. A deep dimple formed on each cheek as a broad smile stretched across Amira's face. Carefully, she lifted the boy's arm and wrapped the cuff of the device around it. She placed the earpieces of her stethoscope into her ears and held its broad end against his inner elbow while squeezing the rubber bulb. The cuff quickly expanded and became taught, then the air softly hissed as she slowly deflated it with a small needle valve.

'Were you able to do the things you wanted to do tonight, Mary?' she asked while listening into the stethoscope.

'Not everything.'

'That's too bad.'

Amira released the remaining air in the cuff. She removed the device, wrapped the rubber tube around it and tucked it under her arm. 'This one's been a little rascal tonight,' she grinned. 'He just doesn't seem to want to sleep.'

'I know he's exhausted. I guess he was worried.'

'Hmm. He's a fighter.'

Mary nodded, smiling sadly.

'The Family Room is ready for you, Mary. You should get some sleep.'

'Thank you, Amira. I think I could use some rest.'

Amira blushed, staving off a wide grin as she tucked the blanket under the mattress. 'You've got a companion tonight,' she announced.

'What do you mean?' Mary said.

'Now don't get excited,' Amira laughed. 'It's not a *man*.' She took Mary's arm and led her into the hallway.

'Daniel's mother is staying overnight. This is his first night.'

As they walked down the wing that led to the Family Room, Mary was haunted by the memory of the overwhelming helplessness she had felt on her first night at the hospital. She remembered the much-needed comfort the nurses had provided during that terrible time; then she recalled the way she had treated Isabelle earlier that day.

When they reached the end of the hallway, Amira placed her hand on Mary's arm. 'I don't want to upset you, Mary, but I think you should know something.'

'What is it?' she said, moving closer.

'Earlier tonight, Kaleb said he was seeing things that weren't there.'

'He was hallucinating?'

'I think so.'

The uncharacteristic concern in Amira's voice frightened Mary. She had become dependent on Amira's perpetual optimism and omnipresent smile—bright lights that led her through the darkest times. Now her thoughts wandered to another desolate place where she was met by a terrible sadness that knew her well. She wanted to stay at that place in her thoughts, to suffer more—to be like her son. But a light squeeze of her arm brought her quickly back.

'I'd like to tell you that it's all right for him to have these experiences, Mary. But I'm a little worried. I think you should stay near him for the next while.'

'Why? He's feeling better. He told me so.'

'I know, Mary. It's a strange thing, but it's usually not a good sign at this late stage.'

Amira led her into the darkness of the Family Room to a small bed at the far side. She directed her to a stack of linens, a hospital gown and a pair of lambskin slippers placed at the foot of the bed. To her right lay the smooth curves of her companion, nestled under a thin woolen blanket.

'Thank you,' Mary whispered to Amira, whose dark face was hidden in the shadows.

Amira touched Mary's hand and whispered goodbye, then closed the door behind her, sealing the room in darkness.

Embraced by near-complete silence, Mary closed her eyes and drew in the cool, still air.

At one corner of the room stood a door that led to a tiny washroom, just large enough for a small washbasin and a toilet. Quietly, Mary moved into the washroom. She stood before a framed mirror that hung above a plain white porcelain sink, and gazed at her tired reflection. Even in the dim light, the yellowing of her eyes was visible, accented by the sinking flesh of her cheeks.

How could I not have noticed it earlier? Mary wondered.

As though cast at her from her reflection, a strong wave of nausea struck. She wavered and grasped onto the sink; its rusty metal stand squealed as she bore her slight weight upon it.

Staring at the worn surface of the sink, she waited for the nausea to overcome her and bring about the indignity she so bitterly despised. But the sensation mercifully subsided. She turned her gaze back to her reflection, which stared disapprovingly at her.

It serves you right, it seemed to say. *Did you eat today?*

Yes, but I nearly left it with Kadesh, she thought, almost laughing out loud.

And drink? it jeered, moving slowly in and out of focus, as though taunting her from behind the thin glass.

'No,' she breathed.

'He neither drinks nor eats,' she heard Kadesh say from behind the mirror.

You're like him and he's like you … just like you, her reflection said.

'I'm not like him,' she whispered.

Then you soon will be.

'No.'

Your suffering won't ease your son's pain.

She turned away from the image and silenced it, but the words still haunted her: *Your son's pain*—one of the many things that were not under her control. She was powerless against it. With a deep breath she removed her shoes and climbed into the unoccupied bed.

The crisp smell of starch and bleach covered her as she drew up the sheets. Her eyes adjusted to the new light while she gazed at the multitude of unfamiliar shadows that surrounded her.

No light reaches the belly of the snake, she thought.

'Is everything all right, Mary?' Isabelle's dimly glowing face smiled from the bed next to her.

'I'm sorry, Isabelle,' Mary whispered. 'Did I wake you?'

'No. I've been drifting in and out of sleep for a while,' Isabelle said in a soft voice. 'Is everything all right?'

Mary swallowed hard. Her tongue passed along the back of her dry throat. 'Everything's fine,' she said, wrapping the covers tightly around her. 'I'm sorry for how I treated you earlier today,' Mary spoke to the disembodied voice in the shadows. In that small sanctuary cloaked under a veil of darkness, words seemed to escape unencumbered.

'There's no need to apologize, Mary. I can only imagine the pain you've been living with.'

Mary's emotions surged. Tears pressed almost beyond her control and for a brief moment, she was nearly willing to accept her own suffering. But that moment was only fleeting, and she would not let it in. She thought of her son bound to his bed, never sharing his pain with anyone—not even with her. Somehow his young spirit had remained strong and uncorrupted through all that he endured—and she revered him.

'Your son is Daniel?'

'Yes, he's eight. He's a bit big for his age,' she beamed proudly.

Mary reflected on the disease that had seized their children, and its seemingly infinite power to macerate even the strongest and fullest of bodies. She knew that in a short while, Isabelle's son would also yield to the adamant power of the faceless malevolence, and he too would be reduced to a smaller, more humble child. Unconsciously, she drew her hands over her face.

'You mustn't despair, Mary. The Lord hasn't abandoned us. He still watches over us. It's His love that carries us through these difficult times.'

'I don't believe,' she whispered.

'Believe what, Mary?'

'Anything.'

'I see. We all start out life not believing. But that changes—for everyone. When your heart is ready, you'll accept Him, and He will be your salvation and guide you out of suffering, and you will feel joy again. *I have come as light into the world, that whoever believes in me may not remain in darkness.*'

'I guess I haven't gotten there yet. That might explain a few things.'

'You've been reading the Holy Book?'

135

'Some of it.'

'Then let it give you strength and guidance in these difficult times.'

Mary gazed at Isabelle whose eyes glittered through the darkness between them.

'Do you know what it says about death?' Mary whispered.

'That's one of its most important messages. *He who believes in me, though he die, yet shall he live, and whoever lives and believes in me shall never die.*'

'Does it say anything about the dead walking the earth?' Mary swallowed against a dry lump at the back of her throat.

'Oh my,' Isabelle breathed, placing her hands over her mouth. 'Why would you ask such a thing?'

'I know it's a strange question, but I need to know.'

'That's not anyone's destiny, Mary—certainly not that of our children.'

'It's not about them. I'd just like to know what it says.'

As silence settled between them, Mary wondered what poor opinion Isabelle had formed of her, and she was ashamed.

'There is the story of Lazarus,' Isabelle said, '—whom Jesus raised from the dead.'

'What does it say?'

Isabelle cleared her throat. 'Lazarus was a friend of Jesus who became ill and died. When Jesus learned of his death, He took His disciples to see him. Lazarus had been dead for several days, but when Jesus called for him, he emerged from the burial cave.'

'I was born in a cave,' Judaea's voice rang in Mary's thoughts.

'How old was he?'

'Lazarus?'

'Yes.'

'I—don't know. I'm not sure the Holy Book says how old he was. I imagine he was probably in his twenties or thirties.'

'What happened?'

'I don't know what you mean.'

'What happened to him after he was brought back to life?'

'I believe the chief priests plotted to kill him, but I don't know if they ever carried out their plan.'

'It doesn't say how he dies? Or if he dies?'

'I really don't remember. It's so late. The Book implies that he was the same as he was before his death, so I imagine he lived the rest of his life like anyone else at that time. Mary, it was a singular miracle performed by our Lord a long time ago. It has no relevance to us, except that it demonstrates the power of God working through our lord Jesus.'

'I understand,' Mary said, sitting upright. 'You don't need to worry, I'm still of sound mind. But I'd like to know more about him.'

'About Lazarus?'

'Yes.'

'*Now?*'

'Please, Isabelle.'

'Well, I don't know much more than what I've already told you. The miracle of Lazarus is told in the gospel of John.'

Mary reached over to the small wooden table that stood between the two beds and drew open the drawer. She reached into it, removed a leather-bound copy of the Bible and rose from her bed like a bird of prey carrying food in its talons.

'Are you really going to read now, Mary?'

'Just for a little while,' Mary said, moving toward the washroom.

'Maybe I can remember a few more details. Please don't read in there at this hour.'

'I'll be okay. I don't want to bother you anymore.'

'You're not bothering me. Please, come back to your bed.'

Mary hesitated for a moment, then returned. She felt like a young girl again, lying comfortably in her bed while Isabelle recited the story of the man from Bethany whom Jesus had befriended. Isabelle spoke wraithlike into the darkness as she revealed it was that miracle that turned the spiritual leaders against Jesus and sealed His fate.

'Thank you,' Mary whispered.

'I don't know why you feel this is important, Mary, but this isn't the sort of thing you should be thinking about. There are many other stories that are more appropriate.'

But as the silence settled again around them, Mary considered each detail of the story and wondered whether it fit with the little she knew about Judaea.

If it was him, how did he lose his identity? she wondered. *And why did he react so strongly to the picture of my son?*

As those and many other questions occupied her thoughts, her world dissolved away. Just at the moment when sleep finally took her, Isabelle whispered. 'I do remember one other thing. Lazarus had two sisters: Martha and Mary.'

The sounds of anxious voices filled the room. Mary quickly rose and moved to the door, quietly passing Isabelle, who was asleep—somehow oblivious to the commotion just outside. Strong light streamed in from the narrow space under the door and onto her bare toes, which glowed from the light like burning embers. As she opened the door she was met by a wave of warm, dry air that carried on it fine clay dust and the sweet scent of large animals. Outside her door a crowd of people was gathered, their bodies fully covered under layers of plain cloth garments and headdresses. Some of the women spoke from behind veils. Upon noticing her, they drew away, whispering to one another.

The bright yellow sun that shone from high above compelled her to turn her eyes to the rocky clay soil that lay beneath her feet. She made her way through the crowd and started to run in the direction of her son's room, but she could see through the distance that it was no longer there. Instead, there stood a modest dwelling built of sun-bleached stones. An orange-red clay pot that nested a hardy shrub sat perched on a ledge below a glassless window opening. A narrow, stone staircase at the side of the home led to a flat roof where several men stood talking and gesticulating. Thick grape vines that trellised just above her reached from one home to another. She stepped under the arched entrance of the stone home and pushed open a worn wooden door. Inside, half a dozen men and women stood talking. The women were weeping.

'Where is my son?' Mary said in another tongue.

The youngest of the women removed her hood and ran to Mary. 'Oh Maryam,' she said, embracing her. 'They took him!'

'Where?' she implored. But the young woman was too distraught to answer. Mary held her at arm's length. The woman's face was red and swollen from crying, but Mary knew well the curves of her round face.

'I'm so sorry,' the woman said, shaking her head. 'There was nothing we could do.'

'Where is he?' Mary demanded, gripping her by her shoulders. 'Where did they take him?!'

Trembling, the woman embraced Mary again. With her warm tears soaking into the rough fabric on Mary's shoulder, the woman cried, 'They took him to the Place of the Skull!'

❧ CHAPTER THIRTEEN ❧

Bakr & Ghassan

The man stood at the mouth of the shallow cave, gazing out over the crests of the falling hills. Bright pastel hues of pink and blue blanketed the reddish-brown face of the mountains to the east, which appeared as faded shadows through the morning mist that hung over the sea. Just beyond the cave, the earth effused a surreal yellow-orange glow that slowly brightened, as if waking with the rising sun. A light wind passed over the jade sea, which shimmered like trembling pieces of glass. He watched the sun ascend over the grand rock formation near the southern tip of the sea, as if it were scanning the rocks for him. He retreated into the darkness of the cave.

For five nights he had traveled south along the sea's western shore, occasionally soaking in its buoyant salt water. During the heat of the day he found shelter among the caves and large rock formations that were in abundant supply. The great sea seemed to speak to him, its lapping and rolling forming strange words that carried softly in a light breeze. Its voice became as constant and dependable as the appearance of the sun each day. But just beyond the land outside the cave, the sea abruptly ended. There he remained for three days within the shadows of the rocks, as though waiting for the sea to extend like a hand over the cracked earth and guide him away.

Crouching near the back of the cave, he placed his hands palms down onto the cave floor and spread his fingers into the soft, powdery soil. Opening and closing his hands, he observed their strange intricacy: how they terminated in ten digits, each with multiple points of articulation, flexing and extending like the eight legs and two arms of the scorpion.

Out of the corner of his vision he noticed a subtle change in the pattern of light and shadow. He turned toward the movement as two human figures rose over the crest of a sandy hill. Their bodies appeared to float ghost-like up the steep rise. Large beasts, each a different shade of the desert, emerged beneath the riders, carrying the figures high upon their humped backs. The long, slender legs of the beasts seemed to split at their ends, forming eight separate feet that glided confidently over the uneven terrain.

The two figures perched tall upon the dromedaries like Magi draped in long robes of dark cloth. Their heads and faces were wrapped in the same dark fabric. Through a narrow slot above the veils their eyes peered, any emotion cloaked. From wide cloth belts wrapped loosely around their waists hung several small satchels, and amulets of rounded metal plates and brightly colored stones. Over the backs of the beasts were draped long, intricately patterned blankets, their once vivid colors now faded from exposure to the sun and dusty winds. Frayed tassels dangled from the edges of the blankets. A variety of leather and cloth pouches also hung from the animals, which appeared wholly indifferent to their burden.

The man watched as the figures swayed in synchrony with the rhythmic gait of the animals, when suddenly a silhouette moved into the narrow cave opening. Only a few yards away stood the jackal, hunched over, its broad tail tucked between its hind legs. Its short brown fur clung tightly to its ribs and legs. The soiled hair on its back was raised. The man stood to his full height and towered above the animal, but it was unperturbed. Slowly, it advanced toward him, growling and baring its teeth.

'Look,' one of the riders spoke in an ancient tongue, pulling gently on the leather reigns. He gestured toward a hole in the rocky cliff. 'The jackal has found something. See how he moves.'

The older rider stopped his camel and faced the cliff. He squinted at the bright morning light that reflected off the rock formation, and shaded his eyes with his hand.

'Let it be,' he spoke in a low, seasoned voice as the younger man started toward the cliff.

Small bells that hung from the camel's neck jingled as it approached the cave, carrying the younger man upon it. The older man followed and stopped near the cave opening as the younger man grasped the shaft of a long, decorated spear sheathed to the right side of the camel.

'Leave the poor creature,' the older man said, taking hold of the spear.

'It is not for the jackal, father. It is for that which interests him so. Look,' he said, pointing at the cave with the spear. 'It is prey he has found, not carrion.'

As if performing a strange dance, the jackal plunged into the cave and quickly re-emerged, scurrying backwards with its head low and tail tucked down. The aggression was repeated over and over again, almost rhythmically. Its low growl could be heard through the distance. As the riders approached, the animal took notice of them and stiffened.

'I have never yet seen a jackal this aggressive,' the older man said as the animal growled at them and bared its teeth. 'He must truly be hungry.'

Upon their signals, the legs of both beasts slowly folded beneath them until the animals were lying flat on their bellies. The younger man dismounted and gathered a few stones from around the cave entrance as the older man carefully lowered himself to the sand.

As if anticipating the theatre about to unfold, the camels looked to the cliff. With a swift arc of his arm, the man threw a stone at the jackal and struck it on the darker fur of its back, just above its tail. With a sharp yelp, it hopped a few steps and rounded toward them. The camels rose from the sand and stepped back as the younger man ran toward the jackal, waving his arms in the air. 'Fsshhht!' he called and threw another stone, this time striking a shoulder.

The jackal whined and licked its lips. It glared into the cave for a few moments, turned its back to them and disappeared into the surrounding hills.

The men slowly approached the cave, led from a short distance by the pointed end of the younger man's spear. He held out his arm and gestured for the older man to stay back, but his companion protested. When they reached the cave mouth, they stared into the unfamiliar rock and waited for their eyes to adjust to the darkness within.

Slowly, a figure became visible from amongst the shadows. About ten yards away in the farthest corner of the cave, the man stood bent under a rock overhang. Long dark hair hung lank over his forehead and brows, and a thick beard of similar color covered most of his face. The whites of his eyes peered at them through the darkness.

The older man lowered his son's spear and stepped into the cave. 'Peace be with you,' he said, removing his veil.

He drew in the strong botanical fragrance within the cave through his wide nostrils. Heavy lines that marked the dark brown skin around his eyes and under his cheeks darkened as he smiled. A long silvery beard and mustache clung thick and full to his leathery face.

The man in the cave looked toward the jackal's scattered prints.

'It is gone,' the older man said. 'And if it returns, the pointed end of my son's stick will surely find him.'

'Father, he may be a leper,' the younger man whispered, holding his veil against his face. The older man drew back. His eyes swept over the man's still form, looking for the gruesome signs of the wasting disease: sunken facial features and horribly receded digits.

'Are you hurt?' the older man said, holding his veil over his face.

The man shook his head.

'Father, do not go close,' the younger man urged, then motioned for the camels, which obediently moved toward the cave.

'Look at him, Ghassan,' his father whispered. 'His body is good. His arms and legs are full and strong. Have you not seen a leper, that you would speak thus?'

The man seemed oblivious to the passionate discussion of which he was the subject. Instead, he appeared captivated by the beasts that stirred at the mouth of the cave. Their seemingly smiling faces bathed majestically in the diffuse morning light. Bushy eyebrows and long eyelashes gave them a friendly, strangely humanoid appearance. On the top of their snouts, slot-like nostrils were shut tight against the warm desert wind.

'A thousand apologies for our rudeness,' the older man said, bowing down. He removed his veil again. 'I am Bakr, son of Hamid, and this is my son, Ghassan. We are merchants of all manner of spice who have traveled here from Qer Harreseth.'

The man stared expressionlessly at the camels. After a few moments of silence, Bakr moved toward him. 'And what is the name your mother and father have given you?'

The man slowly shook his head, still fixated with the beasts. Bakr turned to his son, who wore a stern look of disapproval.

'Do you wish not to tell us, or is it that you have been given no name?' Bakr laughed lightly.

The man moved slowly toward the camels. Ghassan took their reigns and backed them away from the cave.

'You like our camels?' Bakr said. 'They are fine animals. Bring them closer, Ghassan. Where are you taking them?'

'Father, this place has been used as a tomb. The scent of death that lingers here has brought the jackal. Let us make haste and be off.'

'Yes, I too recognize the distinctive aroma of our wares,' Bakr said, breathing in the sweet air. 'Pray you, lower your veil, so that our friend who has been given no name will not be so suspicious of us.'

Ghassan slowly removed his veil. On his face, a thick dark beard grew high upon his cheeks so that very little facial definition was visible. His narrow eyes scanned the inside of the cave. 'We have no time for this strangeness, Father.'

'Was it not you who hastened us to this place?' Bakr laughed. 'Is our time so precious that we have none to spare for this man?'

Ghassan glowered. With his eyes fixed on the stranger, he whistled for the camels and made a slight motion with his hand. Immediately, they moved toward him and stretched out their long necks into the cave. As he stroked the short fur of their necks, he spoke to them with soft clicks of his tongue.

'I apologize for my son. He is a good and loving man, but the quenching of age has not yet tempered his impatience. God has vouchsafed our travels together for many years, but my son has not learned that if one is not careful, the desert will take one's manners—and whatever else it can.' Bakr smiled. 'Tell me, have you been in its grasp for so long that it has taken your voice?'

'No,' the man croaked.

'Ah, then will you tell me how it is that you have come to this unseemly place, without clothing, or even shoes on your feet?'

The man stared at the mouth of the cave, as though it were a great jaw of rock that might open wider and speak for him. With slow, even steps he moved closer to the dromedaries, which reared from him as he approached. Ghassan endeavored to calm the animals, but they dissented and dragged him away from the cave. Leaning against the reigns, he fought to bring them under control, calling to them in his unusual dialect.

'Where have you come from?' Bakr said.

The man gazed at the bright light that streamed into the

front of the cave, illuminating the fine, dust-like powder of the cave floor that had become airborne with the men's movements and now tumbled through the air. Bakr watched the man stare at the sparkling dust.

As the man moved toward the swirling light at the front of the cave, his impressive height was noticeable for the first time. Bakr looked beyond the cave mouth to the sun that was nearly completely obscured by white and grey cotton-like clouds suspended over the eastern mountains. Rays of light streamed through narrow breaks in the clouds, like long white spears dipping into the sea.

'Look, Father,' Ghassan whispered as the man stepped to the mouth of the cave.

The man's hair and skin sparkled as the sun's rays refracted through the countless tiny crystals of sea salt that covered his body. Dark marks—signs of recent injury—enhanced by sand and dirt contrasted against his shimmering skin in places. When he reached the edge of the cave, the man inhaled and stretched out his arm northward.

'There,' he said.

Bakr looked to the range of barren hills that rose northward along the west side of the sea. Even partly engulfed in shadows, they appeared arid and baleful. His brow furrowed.

'From Masada?' Bakr said.

The man slowly shook his head.

'There is nothing else there,' Ghassan said. 'Only spiders and snakes dwell in those hills.'

'My son speaks the truth. Perhaps you have been delivered to us from the earth itself, like Adam, and you are made of rock and clay?' Bakr smiled and peered into the cave. There were no sacs of food or clothing visible. No water flasks or supplies of any kind. It was also void of the special plants that would explain the sweet fragrances that emanated from the cave. Except for rocks and powdery sand, it was empty.

'Where are your supplies?' Ghassan said.

The man retreated into the shadows of the cave. An

unsettling hiss echoed off the rocks as the cool air filled his lungs. 'There is only me.'

Ghassan took his father's arm. 'Come, let us leave this place now. We have no business here.'

'Ghassan, this man is bereft of food. He has no clothing or supplies to survive here. What would become of him?' Bakr rested his hands on his son's shoulders. 'It is by the will of God and His infinite mercy that we have found this man.'

'He has come here on his own. He has had no need for us this far.'

'It is not by chance that the jackal led us here. It is because of God that we are here. Have you forgotten that we will be judged in the afterlife by our deeds in this life?'

Even under the shadows of the cave, the blush in Ghassan's cheeks was obvious.

'Come, we are hungry,' Bakr gestured to the man, leading him to the cave opening. 'You will break bread with us this glorious morning.'

As they approached the edge of the shadows, the man inhaled deeply. 'The burning eye still searches,' he said, peering at the sun that was partially hidden behind thick white clouds.

'Burning eye?' Bakr laughed. 'I have never yet heard such a thing! You need not fear the sun, stranger. You need only to respect it. Like us, it is a servant of God. As is proper unto Him, it gives us light so that we may find our way, and brings us warmth so that we should not suffer the cold.'

Bakr leaned over and whispered to his son, who then proceeded to his camel. There he moved aside a colorful blanket, exposing a large beige bag made from rough fabric. He withdrew a bundle of neatly folded cream-white cloth and presented it to his father. Bakr separated a long length of the cloth and draped it over his shoulder. He held up the remainder of the bundle, which unfolded by its own weight into a long robe with sleeves.

'You shall wear this, that you shall be hidden from the sun during the day and be given comfort by it during the night,' Bakr said.

At that moment the sun peered out from behind the clouds. A long ray of yellow light touched the earth in front of the cave and shone back to the heavens. Holding his hands palms out in front of his face, the man backed into the cave.

'If you will trust me,' Bakr said, pursuing the man, 'you will see that the sun will not find you under these clothes. They are made of cotton reaped from the fertile soil of Egypt. Neither light nor sand can penetrate its fine weave.'

Bakr held out the robe and smiled, caressing it, gesturing for the man to touch it. The man brushed the palm of his hand along the soft fabric, which became soiled from his touch. Bakr respectfully brushed off the dirt and draped the robe over the man.

'It could be longer,' Bakr said, gauging the fit, '—but it will serve its purpose.'

Bakr removed the long strip of cloth from his shoulder and folded it lengthwise several times. Carefully, he wrapped the cloth around the man's head, winding it methodically and evenly around him, ensuring that no part of it touched the dusty ground. As he wrapped, he pulled on the cloth, tucking parts of it under the forming shape until only a short length remained.

'With this veil,' he smiled, placing the remaining length across the man's face, 'God Himself could not find you.'

Bakr led the man to the cave opening and stepped back to admire his work. With the garments of bright white covering all but a small strip of skin above the bridge of his nose, the man blended into the brightening desert like a proper element of the wilderness.

'Good?' Bakr said.

The man nodded.

'Ah, then these magnificent clothes are our presents to you. But every child of God must have a name.'

Bakr placed his hand to his chin, his brow furrowed in thought. 'You say that you come from the northern hills,' he said, looking toward the barren land, '—from the Judaean Wilderness.' He paused and reflected at the great expanse before him. A wide smile slowly stretched across his face.

'Well then,' he said, placing a thick hand upon the man's shoulder, 'you must be Judaea!'

❧ CHAPTER FOURTEEN ❧

Nexus

Mary stood in the sedate darkness of her son's room with tears cooling upon her face. She could still feel the rough texture of the young woman's headscarf touching her cheek, and the itch of fine dust lingering in the back of her nose. The distinctive smells of the small village also seemed to prevail: the scents of animals, the dull smell of dry clay, the sweet aromas of wild herbs drying in the warmth of the still morning air.

'What's happening to me?' she breathed into the stillness as fresh tears streamed down her cheeks. She sank to her knees, placed her elbows on her son's bed and folded her hands together.

'Please help me, Aaron,' she whispered. 'I can't go any farther.'

Her son shifted restlessly as she wept next to him, his eyes dancing under their lids as he dreamt. As she leaned over to kiss him, his eyes opened.

'Puppa,' he said.

His face was waxy, his lips pale and cracked.

'No, Kaleb—it's Mumma.'

He lay absolutely still, as if listening to sounds cloaked

within the silence.

'No one else is here, angel,' Mary whispered, stroking his hair. 'It's just me and you.'

'Puppa,' he mouthed.

'There's no one else here, Kabe. You were dreaming.'

He slowly raised his arm and pointed over her shoulder.

As Mary turned toward the empty space behind her, a strong wave of nausea passed through her. She quickly placed her hand over her mouth and closed her eyes, hoping for it to pass without incident.

'There's no one there, Kabe,' Mary spoke into her hand.

'There, Mumma.'

But Mary's thoughts were torn away at that moment to an isolated place where she struggled alone, staving off the terrible sensation that coursed through her gut like a poisonous tide. Her palm began to sweat against her face. Her tongue was dry and sticky. She closed her eyes and waited for the misery to pass as it always had, but now it seemed determined to stay. A few moments had passed when a small hand touched her shoulder and the wretchedness dissolved into the ether.

'Mumma, what's wrong?' Kaleb whispered.

'Nothing, angel, I'm just tired.'

The young boy surveyed his mother, watching for signs of distress. 'He's still angry at me,' he said.

Mary brushed the hair away from his forehead. 'Kabe, Puppa would never be angry with you. *Never.*'

'Are you angry at me?'

'Of course not. Why would I be angry with you?'

'For tricking you.' His bottom lip quivered.

Her lips parted but before she could speak, Kaleb shuddered.

'What is it, Kabe?'

'Did you hear him?'

Mary turned to the stillness behind her, but there was nothing.

'Hear what?' she said.

'Puppa.'

'No, Kabe. There's no one here. You're still waking up.'

'No, Mumma. He said something to me.'

'Kabe—'

'No, Mumma.'

'Okay. What did he say?'

His eyes fixed on hers. 'He said … *I'm a dream.*'

She embraced him. As she pressed her lips against his forehead, her heart emptied onto him.

'You are not a dream,' she said. 'You are everything that's real. You are the sun and the moon, the earth and the seas. You've got to fight these, Kabe. I know they may seem real to you, but they're only dreams. That's all. Your mind is playing pretend. It does that sometimes when we're not feeling well. But you mustn't believe it's real, because it's not.'

'But he's here. I can see him,' he said, pointing again behind her.

As he extended his arm again toward the stillness behind her, a chill crawled like a large spider down the back of her neck. This time, as she gazed into the shadows beyond her son's outstretched hand, she almost expected a figure to emerge from the darkness, ghost-like and ethereal.

'There's no one there,' she said in a weak voice.

'Maybe he's somewhere else.'

'What do you mean, angel?'

'I see him, but I don't see anything else around him.'

'Kabe,' she said, cupping his face in her hands. 'Puppa's not here anymore. He's in heaven, where he belongs. We need to make these dreams stop. We can do it if you help.'

'But I don't want him to go away.'

'Mumma doesn't like it when you do this. It scares me. Will you try to make it stop—for me?'

'I don't know how. I see him even when I close my eyes.'

'You can, sweetheart. If you remember that he's not real and that he's only there in your imagination.'

'How do you know, if you can't see him?'

'I just know.'

152

'Are you sure?'

'Yes, I'm sure. And I'll show you how I know. I want you to do something for me. I want you to try to talk to him. Will you do that?'

'Why should I do that?'

'It'll show you that he's not really there.'

'What should I say?'

'Ask him where he is.'

The young boy stared into the darkness, listening into the silence, as if speaking without sound or movement.

'He doesn't know,' he whispered. 'He's in a strange place.'

This development caught her off guard, and she was taken aback by his answer.

'He's in heaven?' Mary said.

'I don't know.'

She wondered for a moment if she was heading down the wrong path. But curiosity had become a rare quality, and she could not ignore it.

'Ask him if he's in heaven, Kabe.'

After another moment of silent staring, he looked to her questioningly. 'He doesn't know. But he doesn't like it there.'

'Why doesn't he like it?'

'I don't know.'

'Can you ask him why?'

After another moment of enigmatic conversation he turned to her. 'He says it never changes there. It's always the same.'

'Kabe, does he know who you are?'

He looked into the darkness and smiled lightly. 'He says I'm his son.'

Mary returned the smile gratuitously, softly rubbing the palms of his hands with her thumbs. 'He said that?'

He nodded.

With his searching gaze moving across her face, she felt guilty about wanting to end his experience. Imaginary or not, he believed that he was able to see and speak with his father, distant memories of whom had all but vanished from the young boy's mind. She knew the vision was born from his illness, and it pained her to participate in his delirium, but a small part of her wanted him to savor the sweetness of the experience that they missed so dearly and could never have again.

'Does he see me?' Mary said.

He shook his head.

A twinge of jealousy rang unexpectedly in her. She thought of the implication of this exclusion and how with his response, Kaleb's private vision took on the slightest breath of legitimacy.

'I want you to tell him to stop talking with you,' Mary said.

'Why?'

'Puppa's in a special place now. You shouldn't be talking to him like this.'

Tears welled in his eyes. 'No, Mumma.'

'I know you miss him, angel,' she whispered in his ear. 'Your father loved you so much, but this isn't the way he'd want you to remember him.'

'Why?'

'It just isn't right, Kabe. You need to trust me.'

'How does he want me to remember him?'

She pressed her lips against his forehead. 'I'll help you remember him in other ways. I promise.'

'Will God get angry with him if he talks with me?'

'Of course not, sweetheart. God loves all his children,' she said, reciting Isabelle's words.

'But Puppa's not a child.'

She smiled down at him. 'He is to God.'

Sensing the unusually light moment, Kaleb smiled. He seemed to want to say something.

'What is it, Kabe?'

'I think there must be a garden in heaven, just like at home.'

'Why do you think that?'

'Puppa's—dirty.'

'Dirty? What do you mean?'

'He's not like I got when I used to play outside. He's dirty like grown-ups get.'

'How do grown-ups get?'

'Well, you know. You can't really see the dirt on their clothes. They're just dark all over.'

Mary sat up on the edge of his bed and searched his face for an explanation for this strange detail. But in his eyes there was no hint of lie or jest, only the same glow of wonder and concern as in hers.

'Kabe, can you describe him to me?'

'Don't you remember what Puppa looked like?'

'Yes, angel, but I'd like to know how he looks now.'

'Well, he has brown hair and eyes—just like me. He let hair grow on his face.' He smiled up at her.

Her heart sank. Kaleb's olive complexion and dark features were indisputably hers. Aaron's skin was fair—the kind that easily burned under a bright sun. His hair was very light brown. Although he was almost completely void of vanity, her husband had never allowed more than a few days' growth of facial hair to accumulate, as he was sensitive to his mild affliction of facial alopecia.

'Kabe, what is he—'

'He says he's sorry.'

'Why is he sorry?'

Kaleb focused far into the distance. His breathing accelerated; his complexion paled.

'He says he's sorry ... because he let me die.'

'Kabe, Puppa would never say that,' she said, cradling his face in her hands. 'Those words were made up by your own mind because you're not feeling well. Don't you believe them, angel.'

'But I can hear him. I can see him.'

'No, Kabe. You *think* you hear him. Puppa's gone to heaven. He can't talk to us from there. Nobody can. You just think he can. Do you remember when we used to go to the place where he's buried? You knew exactly where his gravestone was, so when we got there you'd run straight to it. You'd run your fingers along the words carved into it. We would bring flowers and you'd place them on the grass. Once, you started to gather flowers for me from another grave, but I wouldn't let you and you got upset. Do you remember?'

He shook his head and started to weep.

'Okay, Kabe. Tell him Mumma's here with you and that you're okay. He doesn't need to feel sorry about anything.'

As she spoke to him, the silvery pendants that had destroyed their lives suddenly entered her mind. She willed the thought away.

'None of this is his fault,' she said, shaking her head. Tears welled in her eyes. 'Tell him I forgive him, angel. Tell him I was angry before, but I'm not angry anymore. Will you do that for Mumma?'

Kaleb's wet face slid up and down against her cheek.

'Tell him now, Kabe.'

He pulled away from her and gazed again into the darkness, remaining still as he carried out her request in silence.

'Did you tell him?' Mary whispered.

'Yes, but he didn't say anything.'

'Okay. Now I want you to tell him that Mumma's looking after you, so you don't need him to visit you anymore.'

'No, Mumma,' he pleaded.

'I need you to do this, Kabe. Only you can do it. Tell him that you love him, but you have to say goodbye.'

'No, I can't. Don't you love him, Mumma?'

'Of course I do, but we need to do this so Puppa can go back to where he should be.'

His eyes swept through the darkness, as if searching for reassurance within the emptiness. Again, Mary felt an unnerving chill like a cool breath passing across her face. She drew her hand through the air in front of them.

'What's wrong, Mumma?'

'Nothing, angel,' she whispered. 'I'm just tired.'

She wiped the tears from his face and laid him back against his pillow. He closed his eyes.

'Can we go home tomorrow?' Kaleb said in a thin voice.

Mary turned away just as tears ran down her cheeks. They

fell silently onto his nightgown, which drew them into its fabric like raindrops into parched earth.

'Don't cry, Mumma.'

'I'm not crying, angel.'

'He said he saw you.'

'What do you mean?' she said, wiping away her tears with the backs of her hand. 'I thought you said he couldn't see me.'

'He said he saw you before, and you looked like you did when you were young.'

'Where did he see me?'

He was silent for a moment as he listened to the stillness.

'He doesn't know,' he said.

'Kabe, how could he see me if I couldn't see him?'

'You did see him, Mumma. You asked him some questions.'

'Questions? When did I ask him questions?'

'Today.'

Icy cold hands seemed to reach out from the darkness and rest upon her shoulders, drawing out all warmth from her body. She shivered, staring wide-eyed at Kaleb, incapable of accepting what she had just heard. Kaleb reached up and touched her face.

'Mumma?'

'Kabe,' she said, her tongue moving awkwardly in her dry mouth, 'what is he wearing?'

Kaleb described Judaea's clothing in elaborate detail, including the extensive fraying at the ends of his sleeves and the heavily soiled area around his neck.

'He has something here,' he said, touching the skin above his right eyebrow.

'What is it?' Mary whispered, recalling a prominent unhealed wound above Judaea's right eye. 'What does he have?'

'A cut,' he said, drawing his finger along his eyebrow.

Her heart unleashed itself within her chest and palpitated wildly against her ribs.

'Kabe, ask him what his name is.'

'Why?' he breathed.

'Please, do it for Mumma.'

Again Kaleb stared into the emptiness. After a moment, he turned to his mother.

'It's not true,' he whispered. 'Puppa must have forgotten.'

'What did he say, Kabe?'

'He said his name is *Judaea*.'

Mother and son stared at one another, each struggling in silence with their interpretation of the revelation. Mary could hear his tiny voice echo in her thoughts.

His name is Judaea.

It was impossible.

And then she heard Kadesh say: *Did you not believe … that Judaea could not exist?*

'Kaleb,' Mary said, touching his shoulders, 'he's *not* Puppa.'

'Yes, he is.'

'No, Kabe. That man is someone else.'

'No, Mumma.'

'He's not Puppa. You have to trust me.'

'Who is he, then?'

'He's a stranger—someone who should be in heaven with Puppa. He's a bad man.'

Kaleb's grip on the sheets tightened; his breathing quickened.

'No, Mumma.'

'Don't be afraid, angel. He'll never hurt you.'

'How do you know?'

'I just know.'

'Are you sure?'

'I'm very sure. He's confused, that's all.'

'Is that why he isn't in heaven? —Because he's lost?'

'That's right. He shouldn't be doing this with you. He's confused.'

'Why does he think he's Puppa?'

'I don't know. I think he had a child who looked like you, but something happened. He might think you're his son.'

'What happened to him?'

'I don't know, Kabe.'

'Did he hurt him?'

'No—I don't think so,' she said, recalling the incident in the interrogation room.

'Will he come here?'

'No!' she jumped, startling Kaleb. 'I don't want you to talk with him. There's nothing you can do for him. Only a grown-up can help him. Someone's already trying to help him, and I'm sure he wouldn't want you to be talking to him like this.'

'Who's helping him?'

'A policeman—a detective. He helps people who're in trouble.'

'Why? Is he in trouble?'

'No, he's just confused. Kabe, you can also help him if you don't see him or talk with him anymore. Okay?'

'I can't help it, he's just there.'

'He's not there, Kabe. He's just in your mind. Mumma can't see him. You need to stop it from happening anymore. It's very important.'

'Why?'

'It just is.' Mary paused for a moment. 'Do you see him now?'

Kaleb blinked and slowly nodded.

Anger swelled within her, pressing against her chest like her heart was expanding. She was certain Kadesh knew of the link between Judaea and Kaleb.

Was that was why he came for my help? she wondered. *Is this really about Kaleb?*

She shook as she recalled the writing in Kadesh's notebook: *Mary had a little lamb…*

'Kabe, I want you to tell him: *My name is Kaleb. I am not your son.*'

'But Mumma…'

'You have to do this. Do it for Mumma.'

'Are you sure?'

'Yes, I'm sure. Do it now, angel.'

He lowered his head and reluctantly surrendered to his

mother's request. After a moment passed, he whispered to her.

'He said that I *am* his son.'

For the briefest instant, it seemed to Mary that she was looking at Kaleb through someone else's eyes, and in that same moment he too was someone else. Like the boy she had been seeking in her dream, he was her son, but not Kaleb. And she was frightened of him. Frightened of his power. She closed her eyes and tried to push the thought away with several deep breaths.

They took him to the Place of the Skull.

The ring of those words had invoked in her a terror unlike anything she had ever experienced: a raw, primal fear that attached itself to her most fundamental vulnerability and drained her of all power. She was ashamed to have dreamt such a thing. The image of the woman in the village was clear in her mind, and although in the dream she had known who she was, here the context of her face was lost.

'Mumma, don't go to sleep,' Kaleb said, touching her arm. His empathic eyes searched hers for reassurance.

'I'm not going to sleep, Kabe.'

'Can you bring him here?'

'No,' Mary insisted, shaking her head. She shivered at the thought of Judaea speaking to her son.

'But if he sees me, maybe he'll know who I am.'

'He's not allowed to come here. The policeman won't let him leave where he is.'

'He can't go out?'

'That's right, Kabe. He's not allowed to go anywhere. He has to stay where he is.'

'Never?'

'Not for a while.'

'Oh,' he frowned. 'Mumma, are you *sure* he's not Puppa?'

'I'm very sure, angel.'

She looked to where the picture of Aaron used to sit on the bedside table.

It's been so long since you've seen him, you've forgotten what he looked like, she thought.

'I'll bring you another picture tomorrow and then you'll remember how Puppa looked.'

'Okay. But maybe he looks different now. Maybe it's really him.'

'No, Kabe. He wouldn't change like that. When I was away earlier today, I did speak with that man—and he isn't anything at all like Puppa.'

'Why were you talking to him?'

'I thought he might have known Puppa,' she said, bowing her head, '—but he didn't. He doesn't know anything at all. He can't help us, Kabe. Do you know what he wants from you?'

He shook his head.

Kadesh knows, she thought. *Judaea was his find. He knew about the link between them. But even if he knew, how did he find us?*

'Did he ask you for anything? —or to do something?' she said.

'No. He didn't say anything before. Are you sure he's a bad man?'

'No. I—don't know, angel. I know very little about him. No one knows much about him. We don't know why he's not in heaven. Kabe, there must be a reason why he comes to you like this. Can you think of a reason why?'

He was silent again as he searched his thoughts, but Mary knew he was too young to understand. Much too young.

'I think he's sad,' he said. 'He doesn't smile. Maybe he's lonely and he needs someone to keep him company.'

'Maybe,' she nodded, 'but that someone isn't you. You're just a little boy.'

'I'm five and a half.'

Mary smiled and brushed the hair away from his forehead. 'I know, angel. I can't believe how quickly you've grown. Sometimes I think of you as a grown-up—just like your father. But I need to be careful of things that I don't understand. That's why I want you to stop this, until I find out why this is happening. Will you do that for me?'

'What do you want me to do?'

'I want you to shut him out.'

'But I don't know how. He's just there sometimes.'

She thought for a moment. 'Well, you can talk to him, right?'

'Mmm hmm,' he nodded.

'Then I don't want you to talk to him anymore—even if he speaks to you. I know it'll feel strange to not answer him, but I want you to do it anyway. Will you do it for Mumma?'

'Okay,' he said finally.

'Promise.'

They brought the tips of their right index fingers together, and without a word their agreement was sealed. Mary tucked him snugly into his bed, drawing the cotton sheets up to his chin.

'Go to sleep now, okay?'

'Okay. Mumma, are you *sure* he's not Puppa?'

She leaned over and kissed him on his forehead. 'As sure as I'm your mother.'

'What if he finds out what you told me to do and he gets angry at you?'

'Well, first of all, he's a prisoner. Do you know what that means?'

'He's in jail?'

'It means that he can't get away from where he is. So he can't hurt me or anyone else—even if he wanted to. And second, he won't know why you're not talking to him. Right?'

'I won't tell him. I promise.'

Again they touched the tips of their fingers together.

'Good,' she said and knelt at the side of his bed. She took hold of his hand and they gazed at each other until his eyes closed and his thoughts drifted to a place far away. As his small chest rose and fell in that familiar rhythm of sleep, her thoughts turned to Judaea, whose breath was needed only to produce sound, and whose defiant existence seemed to mock life.

She moved into the hallway and looked back at her son through the thin window in the door. She wondered whether Judaea was again whispering to him through their singular nexus.

Will he do what I asked of him? she wondered. *Does he have the strength, or the will, to shun the man who he believed was his father?*

Suddenly, she recalled a moment in the mock interrogation room, staring at Judaea's unresponsive form, his head cocked back.

Was it during those events that he communicated with my son? Is that where he retreated?

Her son had had at least one vision that day, around the same time that Judaea slipped into his altered state. *But why does this link exist?* she wondered.

On the way back to her room at the end of the long hallway she stopped, closed her eyes and tried to release her many unwanted thoughts into the still night air.

❧ CHAPTER FIFTEEN ❧

Muriel

'M uriel, what's wrong?'
   The young woman raised her head from between her knees and squinted at the tall shape standing a few feet away.

'Rosemary?' Muriel said in a soft, listless voice.

Taken slightly aback by the unusual informality, Mrs. Timble drew an involuntary breath and blushed. She paused for a brief moment then stepped toward Muriel, endeavoring to hide a slight loss of dignity with a smile.

'Why are you huddled in the corner like that, dear?' Mrs. Timble said.

Muriel mumbled something unintelligible into the calmness. Her eyes were glassy and puffy, the thin nostrils of her modest nose red and flared. Shoulder-length brown hair that normally fell elegantly along the side of her smooth face was now wet and clumped at its ends.

The wall opposite the alcove in which Muriel had taken refuge encased a full-length window of beveled glass, partitioned into four sections by a brass t-shaped frame. In the daytime it admitted much-needed light into an otherwise grey and lifeless section of the building. Now, with the night sky behind, and the single lamp in that area darkened, it acted like a mirror, creating a double of the young woman crouched before it in semi-darkness.

'Good heavens, dear,' the old woman said, brushing her long white hair over her shoulder. 'You shouldn't be huddled here like this, all alone. You're in a hospital, dear. There are so many people here who can help you.'

'There's no one here who can help.'

'Don't say such things, child.' Mrs. Timble said, shuffling closer.

The brushing sound of the old woman's slippers sliding across the linoleum floor carried down the hallway like a strange whisper.

'What's happened, dear?' Mrs. Timble said.

Muriel gazed up at the old woman. 'Rosemary,' she breathed. 'Why are you here? It's so late.'

'Oh, I don't sleep much anymore. No need for an old woman like me. I usually do my rounds at this hour, wandering the halls like an old ghost. It relaxes me. Clears my mind.' Mrs. Timble smiled and peered down the empty hallway. 'There's always a certain peace at this hour. Even in this place,' she sighed.

'There's no peace tonight,' Muriel whispered.

'Good heavens, dear. Won't you tell me what's happened?'

Muriel stared through the old woman to a place deep in her thoughts.

Steadying herself against the wall, Mrs. Timble bent over, wincing as her back curved toward Muriel.

'Have you done something?' she said, placing a bony white hand on Muriel's shoulder.

'No. It's what I *haven't* done.'

'What haven't you done, child?'

Muriel wrapped her arms around her legs and once more lowered her face between her knees.

'Please, won't you tell me what's wrong, Muriel? Did someone get hurt?'

'No,' Muriel breathed.

Mrs. Timble pulled back suddenly; her eyes were wide and grave.

'Are all the children—all right?' she whispered, placing her fingers over her mouth as though a curse had slipped past her lips.

Muriel slowly nodded.

With the support of the adjacent wall, the old woman took a deep breath and straightened up, a gracious smile stretched awkwardly across her face as she rose. Her head shook involuntarily from Parkinson's as she peered down the hallway toward the nurse station. Except for the soft sound of shuffling paper that drifted periodically from around the far corner of the corridor, the halls were silent.

'I'm going to find Amira,' she said.

'No,' Muriel said, taking hold of the old woman's nightgown.

'You can't stay here like this, dear. You need someone to help you.'

'Don't,' she pleaded.

Mrs. Timble gazed at the folded form of the young woman as she sat, forlorn and quiescent, like a wilted flower.

'Muriel, why are you still here?'

Muriel mused at her dress, running her fingers slowly across the soft pleated fabric that covered her knees. 'Tonight is the last night,' she whispered.

'Oh, yes. This was your last day. I forgot. I'm so sorry to see you go, Muriel. The children are going to miss you so much. And I will, too, of course. Now I understand why you're so upset. But don't you think you should be in the company of a friend at a time like this, dear?'

Muriel remained silent, resigned to the shadows of the alcove. Mrs. Timble stepped forward and placed her hand on Muriel's head.

'I'll get Amira,' she breathed.

Muriel turned her gaze up to the old woman. A strange, unnerving look of anger and despair was frozen within her eyes.

'*No*,' Muriel said, her voice resonating with strong yet indiscernible emotion.

The old woman stumbled backward into the hallway. She placed one hand over her mouth and groped for the wall with the other as Muriel again lowered her head between her knees.

'No,' Muriel repeated, her voice muffled within the heavy fabric of her dress.

Mrs. Timble shuffled down the hallway, glancing back at Muriel only once. From a distance, it appeared as though the young woman had fallen asleep, tucked into herself.

The hallway was still and calm again, resuming the détente that nightfall usually brought, but only for a moment. For just as the light above her flickered back to life, Muriel sprang to her feet and raced down the empty hallway.

Mary moved lightly across the floor toward her bed and lowered herself onto the stiff mattress, lifting her legs slowly so as to stave off the imminent creaking of the old metal bed frame. Staring up at the white textured ceiling that appeared like the rough terrain of some dark and unknown land, she slowed her breathing and waited for sleep to come. But her mind raced over the events of the day. Unencumbered by the many distractions that daylight invited, she was enveloped by the cool darkness, which normally harbored within it a soothing calm, and it became a canvas upon which her imagination spread. Many images filled her thoughts: the dark interrogation room, Judaea's seized body and upward stare into nothingness, Kadesh's notes:

Mary had a little lamb...

Mary looked toward Isabelle and watched the young woman as she slept, hoping that her stare would be enough to awaken her companion. But Isabelle's breathing remained slow and even. Mary sighed, reached over to the small table next to her and took the Bible. Holding it open in the palms of her hands she tilted it in all directions, searching for enough ambient light with which to read. But even with her eyes fully adjusted to the low light, the letters remained elusive in the darkness of the pages. She glanced again at her sleeping companion, rose from her bed and moved into the washroom. Lowering herself cross-legged onto the cold linoleum floor, she laid the book open across her thighs and began to read.

The chill of the cold floor slowly dissolved beneath her as she swept through the Bible's many verses. Starting with the gospel of John and the story of Lazarus, she scanned the verses for anything that might explain the existence of Judaea, and the strange link between him and her son.

Muriel surveyed the area outside Kaleb's room and then slipped inside. Very carefully, she closed the door behind her, preventing the latch from making any sound. The plastic tethers that the young boy had been freed of earlier that night had been reinstated. They glistened with the moonlight, making him appear to be entangled in a giant spider's web. Slowly, Muriel moved to his bed and placed her hand upon the bottles that dangled from the tall metal stands. She looked upon the boy as he lay sleeping, immersed in his innocence. Then she closed her eyes, leaned over him and whispered into his ear, 'Please forgive me.'

Moving swiftly through the empty hallway, Muriel soon arrived at Mary's room and stopped just outside. She closed her eyes and placed her hand upon the painted white door. After a moment, she pushed it open.

A broad fan of soft light followed Muriel as she moved across the floor. The door slowly closed behind her, extinguishing the light from the hallway, leaving her standing in the darkness, ghost-like and faded, gazing at the amber light that escaped from under the washroom door. She scanned the room, pausing only briefly at Isabelle's sleeping form. As she took a step toward a closet at the far corner of the room, the faint light from under the washroom door suddenly disappeared and the door opened. With the speed and agility of a cat, Muriel dropped to the floor and disappeared among the shadows underneath Mary's bed.

Her arm outstretched into the darkness, Mary found the top drawer of the bedside table and placed the book inside. Staring into the silent void between her and her sleeping companion, she allowed it to draw out all of her remaining energy. Then she closed her eyes and surrendered to exhaustion.

Not long after she fell asleep she was back in the village, standing in the midst of a frenzied crowd that was moving quickly through a narrow lane. People spilled out of nearby homes and shops, filling the streets leading out of the city with a churning sea of people. Her head pounded as she stumbled over the rocky ground; her knees complained bitterly with each step.

But this experience was unlike any other. Everything was crystal clear and lacked ambiguity. Her senses were at their highest acuity. Yet it was a strange experience, completely out of her control. It was as though she were a mere observer gazing through someone else's eyes.

A woman's voice called to her from within the mob. 'Maryam!' But the voice was swallowed by the crowd, and as she tried to locate its source, she was swept along with the rush of people. Frightened by the power of the moving mass, she was trying to reach the stone border of the lane when her legs became entangled with another's and she fell hard into a cloud of dust.

Fine particles of clay filled Mary's lungs and she coughed into the dry earth. Panting on her hands and knees, with the sting of dust pricking in her chest, she waited for the imminent crush of feet. But the wide stream of people passed quickly by, and the crowd thinned to a trickle. Soon, individual voices became discernible and the one familiar voice rang out again.

'Maryam!'

A young woman emerged from the dust and embraced Mary. It was the same woman from the house in the village, someone she knew well.

'I'm not hurt,' Mary said, rising to her feet with the woman's help.

Mary watched the mob as it moved into the distant landscape, like a swarm of ants following an invisible trail. Just outside the village walls, the people converged upon a small hill: a dry, barren mound that at first glance seemed unworthy of attracting such attention.

And then she saw it.

On a steep, cliff-like side of the hill the pale rocks took on a strange and terrible shape: that of a large, pale skull. And at that place, a horror was unfolding.

Mary cried softly in her sleep as the woman in her dream tried to comfort her, while hidden in the shadows beneath her bed, Muriel wept silently with her.

❧ CHAPTER SIXTEEN ❧

Cerberus

Mary awoke suddenly, her gut clenched tight like a fist. The bed creaked loudly as she threw off the covers and slipped on her shoes.

'Where are you going?' Isabelle muttered.

'To get help,' Mary said and ran from the room.

Her legs seemed heavy and unresponsive as she ran down the hallway toward the stairs. She stopped only briefly at her son's darkened room to retrieve her cloak, which hung near the door. Flying down the two flights of stairs several steps at a time, she threw the cloak around her, then raced through the foyer to the outside doors and launched herself into the darkened world.

As the brisk cold of the night air met her face and chest, she was struck with a profound feeling that something was wrong. Her gaze turned to the sky, where thick clouds now blanketed the town, glowing dimly from its lights. A strange hush encompassed her, as though the town, like a living thing, was also aware that something was amiss. But there was no time for wonderment. With her cloak fluttering wildly behind her, she raced down the walkway toward the police station.

As if born from the phenomenon above, an eerie stillness

permeated the streets and between each brick and stone building that bordered her way through the night. Mary had never felt so alone. Not a single soul moved through the streets at that late hour. Only she disturbed the night. Had it not been for the heat that rose beneath her cloak, she would have felt the shiver of fear that trickled down her neck.

He knows, Mary thought as she rounded the corner of the police station and ran into the alley. He knows the secret of Judaea. He was guarding it from me. But now I know.

Mary froze.

In the shadows behind the police station, only nine or ten yards away, lurked the silhouette of a large, four-legged beast. Warm, wet breath streaming from its nostrils formed white mist in the cold air. It lumbered through the narrow lane, its massive, jet-black head, nearly twice the size of hers, hanging languorously from a short, thick neck. Startled by her sudden appearance, the animal tensed and shifted its weight slightly to its hind legs. They stared at one another under a veil of shadow, each of them still as the night air. As Mary gazed upon the animal, the fullness of its body took shape and the markings on its fur became slowly visible.

'Cerberus,' Mary breathed.

The huge mastiff raised its head. Its jaws opened slightly; its tongue lolled to one side. Long jowls drooped almost to the bottom of its lower jaw. In every way the animal was identical to the notorious dog from her childhood, which stood three feet tall at the shoulder and stretched nearly eight feet from the tip of its snout to the end of its tail. Even the signature band of light-colored fur was visible, wrapping around its neck like a thick brown collar.

The jet-black head and the mottled fur that covered most of his body had given Cerberus a profoundly imposing appearance for his breed. Even with the encouragement of his owner, a large man whose dark hair and full beard gave him an uncanny resemblance to his dog, few people had the courage to venture within the fenced boundary of his yard. Incessantly bound and isolated from other living things, the dog's true temperament became the subject of myth. And so it remained for many years until the day Mary and a friend found the beast in his yard, tethered to a steel stake, standing over the body of a young girl's cat.

The images from that day nearly twenty years ago still remained with her, as clear and vivid as her memories of yesterday. No one could separate Cerberus from his prey, not even his master. As she stared at the massive animal in the alley, she could almost see the large man fighting with the beast, striking him with the back of his hand as he tried in vain to snatch away the body of the cat. She and the other neighbors who had gathered there looked on in horror as the mastiff consumed the cat—even the head, which slid down his throat in a single gulp. That same night, the owner shot the nearly three-hundred-pound animal that had been his only companion for more than a decade. And then he turned the rifle upon himself.

She knew she couldn't outrun the beast in the alley. Even with its cumbersome size, its long strides would quickly overtake her. Her heart pounding, Mary scanned the alley for anything that could be quickly scaled, but there was nothing. Adrenaline coursed through every vein; her muscles were taught. She had to run. But just as she was about to bolt, she saw them: thin streams of light radiating from around the side door. It had been left ajar. Yet with the beast standing so near to it, eyes fixed on her, the door seemed a thousand miles away. For a brief moment she indulged in the cruel irony that only a few hours earlier she had been devising a plan to escape from the building.

Noticing her interest in the door, the mastiff turned its stare to the bands of bright light. Without the slightest hesitation, she seized the opportunity and ran for the door. As she heaved on it with all her strength she could hear the animal's breath behind her. To her relief, the door swung freely on its hinges, and she slipped into the building and locked the door behind her.

Light blinded her as she turned toward the empty hallway

that in the daytime had seemed so dim. As her eyes adjusted to the new light, she suddenly felt alone and vulnerable. In that makeshift space within the belly of the stone building, the row of unmarked doors seemed to conceal unknown terrors.

'Hello,' she spoke into the empty hallway.

There was no reply.

Slowly, she approached the door to the interrogation room and stood in front of it. Just like the outside door, it too had been left open. As she gazed at the opening, she wondered what could have caused Kadesh to leave both doors open and unattended. Had Judaea been moved? Her gut tightened and heart pounded as she peered through the opening.

Judaea was seated at the table exactly as she had left him hours earlier. His chilling stare was upon her. At that moment, she heard the lock on the outside door move. She looked down the hallway just as Kadesh slipped into the building.

'Mary!' Kadesh said, catching his breath. He moved quickly toward her, a broad grin stretched across his face.

'I know who he is,' she said.

Kadesh's smile evaporated.

'Why didn't you tell me?' Mary said.

'Eh, it is not what you think.'

'Isn't it?' she said, backing into the interrogation room.

'Mary!' Kadesh cried.

Judaea's dark eyes tracked Mary as she rushed to him. His blank expression remained unchanged as she reached across the table, took hold of his right hand and turned it palm up. His hand was blackened with filth. With her other hand, she drew up his sleeve...

❧ CHAPTER SEVENTEEN ❧

Fallen

Bakr gathered the leftover dried meat from the evening meal and placed it in a soft leather sack. He drew the leather strings woven through the skin, wrapped them tightly around the top and tied them with a simple knot. A large ivy-wood bowl sat on the sandy ground in front of him, empty except for a small amount of salty broth pooled at the bottom. Next to it, a small loaf of unleavened bread sat upon a row of sticks laid out like a mat. Bakr inhaled a light wind that passed over the small camp and savored the sweet aromas that escaped from the bowl. He broke off a large piece of the bread and wiped it along the bottom of the bowl, soaking it with the remaining broth, then popped the bread into his mouth and turned toward a modest campfire that burned a few yards away. Behind him stood a large olive tree, the base of which was comprised of three trunks that wound together like a massive wooden braid. Upwind of the fire and smoke, a black goat fur tent stood erect and defiant against the elements.

From a small clay ewer, Ghassan poured a scant amount of water into his hands and rubbed them vigorously together. When he finished shaking off the last drops, Bakr presented his own hands, palms up. His son obliged by pouring water sparingly over them. Bakr rubbed his hands together and shook off the excess water into the sand. He broke off another piece of bread, placed it into his mouth and peered over his shoulder, chewing slowly. On a small, distant hill to the east, Judaea's silhouette stood tall and unmoving against the orange glow of a darkening sky.

'He follows us still,' Ghassan said, casually throwing a stick into the fire, which erupted into a brilliant array of red and orange embers.

'Yes,' Bakr replied, turning his attention to the flames.

'It seems he enjoys our company but not our conversation.'

Bakr smiled into the fire. The red and orange mosaic light of the embers reflected dully off his worn and yellowed teeth. 'Truly,' he said. 'It also seems that his strange manner still rankles with you.'

'We travelled a great distance today. I did not think it possible that he would catch up with us this night, but he has the persistence of a hunter. I pray you, stop giving him our food, that he may leave us and go on his way.'

Bakr laughed. 'Two days have I brought to him bread and water, but neither has he accepted from me.'

'Perhaps, then, he is a hunter.'

Bakr's brow furrowed. 'Ghassan, you cannot really believe he is stalking us—that he means to make an end of us.'

'How would I know? We know not whither he comes from or who he is, except that he is a wayfarer. His words are few and without meaning.'

'He has told us that he is lost. Are we to not believe him?'

'Father, I do not know. How should he come to be lost?'

'For what purpose would he lie to us? We have offered him what we have, but from us he takes nothing.'

'I do not know, but this is a very strange thing.'

'Truly it is.'

Bakr reached for an olive branch that lay nearby on the clay soil. With a slight flick of his wrist it flew into the fire, hissing and popping as the flames consumed the narrow green leaves.

'I wonder, Ghassan,' he said, speaking into the glowing

embers, 'what misfortunes must befall a man for him to lose all that he has?'

'This I also do not know. But to this question I hope never to know the answer.'

'I would like to know,' Bakr muttered under his breath.

Ghassan squatted next to his father and rested his forearms on his knees.

'He is a stranger to us. Why do you fawn upon him?'

Bakr snuffed into the air and turned toward the still silhouette in the distance.

'He is like you in years. When I look at him, I am reminded that he was once someone's son. Perhaps he is someone's father. I cannot help but feel that somewhere, someone is wondering if he is safe, while there he stands in this dangerous place alone, surrounded by sand and sky—like a stone.'

Ghassan rested his hand on his father's shoulder and smiled.

'Do not worry over him, old man. Your excellent son is here with you, safe and sound under your care.'

'Truly,' Bakr said, touching his son's arm. 'For many things I am thankful.'

'And blessed is a son who has the company of such a father on his travels, to care for him—and for strangers. Go to him, then, and bring him food and drink, that your worries may be settled.' Ghassan gestured toward the hill. 'Soon we will cross into Egypt and conduct our business. Surely then he will leave us.'

With the satchel of dried meat in hand, Bakr walked to his camel, retrieved a goatskin flask that hung from its side and slung it over his shoulder. From another bag, he removed a small loaf of unleavened bread and placed it and the satchel into a small pouch suspended from his belt. As Ghassan fed more wood to the fire, Bakr climbed the gentle slopes of burnt orange earth that stretched eastward toward Judaea.

'Again I bring you food, Judah.'

With a reassuring smile, Bakr presented the bread and meat. But Judaea looked only briefly at the smooth skin cloth and slowly shook his head.

'It is good,' Bakr said, opening the satchel. He tore off a small piece of meat and popped it into his mouth, imparting its fine flavor with a satisfied grin.

Judaea glanced at the meat and looked away. Bakr offered him the water flask, but again he refused.

'With the mercy of God a man can live many days without food,' Bakr said, 'but only three without drink. For two days you have followed us, and each day I have presented you with our excellent food and clean water but you have partaken nothing. And yet you have no supplies of your own. Are you not pressed by hunger? Or is your belly full with manna that has been offered to you from God?' Bakr laughed.

'I desire nothing.'

'All men hunger and thirst—unless they have sickness,' Bakr said, placing the food into his pouch. 'Tell me now, have you taken ill?'

'No.'

'Then take this, I pray thee,' he said, handing the flask to Judaea. The old man's face was tired and drawn. His eyes pleaded with Judaea from within deep depressions lined with dark and wrinkled skin.

After a few tempting shakes of the flask, Judaea cupped his hands together and presented them to Bakr. The old man smiled and poured a small amount of water into his hands. Judaea spread the water over his lips, smearing dirt over his mouth and cheek.

'You must wash your hands first,' Bakr said.

Again, Judaea cupped his hands as Bakr poured water over them.

'Bring your hands together like this,' Bakr demonstrated enthusiastically. 'One hand washes the other.'

As the water drizzled over Judaea's hands, he rubbed them back and forth until the light brown skin of his palms was visible.

'Good,' Bakr smiled. 'Now you can drink.'

Again Bakr poured a small amount of water into Judaea's hands, but again he spread the liquid over his lips, allowing it to run down his chin and taking none into his mouth.

'Have you found other water?' Bakr sighed.

'No.'

'If you are not stricken with sickness, pray tell me what troubles you?'

'There is nothing.'

'Your mind, it is still empty?'

'In my mind there are many things.'

Bakr raised his eyebrows. 'What dwells there?'

'Many things. I see many faces.'

'This is indeed good. What manner of people? Are there women?' Bakr smiled. 'Perhaps a fair wife?'

'There are men. Men in great numbers.'

The smile faded slightly from Bakr's leathery face. 'The eyes of a soldier bear witness to many things—some of them unspeakable and best forgotten. Perhaps in your desire to forget some hardship, your mind has forsaken everything.' The old man placed his hand upon Judaea's shoulder. 'Judah, look into the faces of the people who gather in your thoughts. Maybe in them you will find the thorn whose poison distresses your mind.'

Judaea stared at the darkening horizon. He stood tall and majestic in his long robe of cream-white, appearing vastly different than the man whom Bakr had discovered naked in the cave only a few days earlier. There now appeared about him a commanding presence. A certain stoic elegance.

Bakr cleared his throat. 'Even through your silence I can see that you carry a heavy burden, one that may not be easily cast down.' He looked to the camels that were grazing on dry, rough brush at the edge of camp. 'They too carry heavy burdens, but their burdens are of the flesh. We should envy them. Their lives are simple, so when sleep is shed over their eyes they rest peacefully. And when they awaken, they have only to think how to fill their bellies. But the children of God carry their burdens in here—and here,' he said, tapping his head and chest. 'They are with us from sunset to sunset.'

The old man gazed at the deepening colors of the evening sky, as if reflecting on his own tribulations.

'Through His infinite generosity God has given us dominion over all the animals, but in return He has cursed us with the burden of intelligence, and we suffer greatly for it. But enough talk!' Bakr again placed a hand on Judaea's shoulder. 'End this obstinacy. I beseech you. Come and join our camp this good night. Tomorrow we shall cross into Egypt and conduct our business. Will you ease an old man's mind?'

Judaea slowly shook his head.

'Why? Are you to stay here in the desert alone? Solitude cannot help you, Judah. It can only help to settle those problems that dwell in thought, not those which are lost deep within.'

'I have made this solitude for myself,' Judaea said, gazing at his hands and flexing his fingers. 'This I know.'

'All men sin Judah. It is our nature. No man can say even after washing his hands a thousand times that they are truly clean. But judgment is reserved for God only. Do not condemn yourself, for you have not the right.'

Bakr's eyes twinkled through the dark skin of his face, which appeared more leathery with the coming of night.

'I do not know of whom you speak,' Judaea said.

'Lo, then you do not know of He who has dominion over all things: the Creator of the lands and the seas and everything within and upon them. But it matters not, for He knows of you.'

Judaea looked toward the barren lands that stretched as far as the eye could see. 'I have been through the hills and along the shore of the great water,' he said. 'Yet I have seen nothing of Him. How does He know of me?'

A warm wind whistled gently through the dense leaves of a nearby carob tree.

'He cannot be seen,' Bakr laughed. 'He is of spirit only. But be assured in your heart, Judah, He knows very well of our miseries and afflictions, and He is with you—even now.'

The sun began its descent behind the western hills as Ghassan prepared their tent. The heat of the day no longer lingered within the bestial scent of the goat hair fabric that formed its walls. But as Ghassan toiled within the tent, outside the fragile stillness of the desert was disturbed, as two thin figures cloaked in black moved silently into the camp. The camels stirred and called for their masters, pulling hard against the long leather tethers that bound them to the trunk of a large olive tree.

Hearing the cry of his animals, Ghassan seized his knife and rushed from the tent. The dark figures had worked quickly to unbind the camels, so when Ghassan reached his animals they had already been mounted and were turning wildly in dissent.

'No!' he cried, slipping his knife under his belt. He seized both reigns, one in each hand. 'You shall not take them!'

The animals reared, but Ghassan put his full weight against the reigns and drew the animals moaning toward the ground.

'Fool,' hissed one of the figures, beating Ghassan's forearms with a long stick.

But Ghassan held tightly onto the reigns and leaned heavily upon them. Following the will of their master, the animals complied and knelt into the sand.

The dark figures slid in unison from the backs of the kneeling beasts. For a brief moment the air seemed to hold a pulse of elation, but it vanished in an instant. The figures moved quickly upon Ghassan, and he was stricken to the ground with a heavy blow to the head. He rolled over in the sand and reached for his blade, but he had barely touched the smooth white ivory of its handle when a knife came down upon him and pierced his chest. He issued only a slight moan as it sank into him. From the other figure came another blade. Except for the damped thuds of the blades plunging into his upper body, the camp was quiet. When Ghassan no longer resisted, the figures moved silently into the tent, like dark shadows cast by a moving sun.

Judaea stared past Bakr toward the camp, his face still smeared with a light mud. Intrigued by Judaea's uncharacteristic display of interest, Bakr fixed his gaze in the same direction.

'What is it that you see?' Bakr squinted, barely able to discern the dark shape of the tent in the distance.

'Ghassan has fallen.'

'Eh? How has he fallen? Where?'

'There,' Judaea said, raising a long finger toward the camp.

The color drained from the old man's face. 'Where is he?'

'Near the animals.'

Bakr ran toward the camp, moving awkwardly over the soft, shifting sand. As he neared the campfire he resolved the crumpled form of his son lying in the sand like a dark mound of discarded cloth. When he reached Ghassan's side, he collapsed to his knees and embraced the bloodied body. Tears ran along the deep wrinkles of his face as the camels grazed on thin grass around the olive tree.

'Why?!' Bakr cried.

Like demons summoned to a host, the figures emerged from the tent and moved swiftly toward Bakr. The old man faced them as they came, his eyes wide with rage.

'Marauders!' he cried. 'May you suffer for eternity in the afterlife!'

As they descended upon him, Bakr remained fixed on Ghassan, holding his body against his chest, barely reacting as the sting of their blades came again and again.

Judaea squatted next to Bakr and placed his hand upon the thickening crimson flow that oozed from the old man's chest.

'No, Judah,' Bakr murmured. 'A father should join his only son in death.'

With an expressionless gaze, Judaea looked down upon the

old man, as if searching his body for an answer to an unspoken question. Bakr's bloodied hand reached up and touched his shoulder.

'Quickly, you must leave here. They may return and find you. I bid you, take for yourself whatever supplies are left.'

Judaea faced the fading light of the sky as the dusty air hissed through him. 'I saw them come,' he said, his voice thick and heavy as Bakr's blood, which coagulated at his feet, '—in my thoughts. Yet I knew not what to do.'

The old man took Judaea's hand, his eyes welling with tears. 'Alas, how are you to survive in this harsh land with the body of a man but the mind of a child?'

Judaea stared at Bakr through flat, unblinking eyes, and as he did so a strange sensation passed over Bakr. Even as his body succumbed to his wounds, Bakr could feel the unnatural cold of Judaea's hand trickle like ice water onto his palm. He drew Judaea's arm toward him and in doing so, he exposed a large dark bruise that surrounded Judaea's wrist. Near the center of it was a deep oval-shaped wound. The old man stared at it for a moment and slowly rotated his arm. The terrible wound appeared to extend through the back of his wrist to the base of his palm. Carefully, Bakr moved away the other sleeve and saw that the other arm had the same affliction. He grasped Judaea's robe and struggled to raise his head. Judaea reached under the old man's shoulders and sat him upright. Cringing with pain, the old man moved aside the bottom of Judaea's robe. His feet were darkened with fine sand and earth, like old stone carvings set upon the sand, but underneath the thin coating, the flesh was horribly torn about halfway up on one of his feet and slightly to one side on the other. Bakr searched Judaea's face, but there was only the familiar stare through blank, expressionless eyes.

'I saw you fall,' Judaea said, 'and it passed through me like fire from the burning eye. I trembled with it, and it shook with me. There were great cries of suffering, but I would not stop it as it consumed them.'

Again the old man looked at the torn flesh around the

holes on Judaea's feet. 'What mischief is this?' he said.

But Bakr had seen the distinctive wounds before. They were made by long nails driven through the wrists and feet, and lengthened by the weight of the body as it hung on the spikes high above the ground.

'This cannot be,' Bakr said.

His body writhed and seized as Judaea looked on. Again Bakr reached for Judaea's arm. It was icy cold against his cooling skin.

'The jaws of death have closed upon you,' Bakr spluttered. 'Yet God has forsaken you.'

Judaea stared unblinking at the old man.

'You know not what has befallen you. Like a new babe, you gaze upon me without understanding. But you must find the reason for this cruel mischief before others find you. For if they discover what you are, they will become afraid. Do you understand?'

Judaea was silent.

'They will destroy you, Judah! They will feed you to the burning eye!'

Judaea looked to the vanishing sun, shielding his eyes with his hands.

With a long sigh, Bakr lowered himself to the sandy ground. 'Make haste, Judah. Night comes like an old friend to hide you from your enemies. May God be with you.'

With those words, Bakr closed his eyes and the air slowly left him, as though he were parting with a final, imperceptible whisper. Judaea placed his hand on Bakr's forehead and moved his head from side to side, but there was no response. He sat back, squatting on his heels, and gazed upon the old man.

As night covered the camp, Judaea remained with the bodies, as though waiting for them to awaken. But neither man stirred. The hours passed and another day emerged from the darkness, once again spreading light over the still bodies. Judaea stood over them and held his hands out in front of him, musing at the dark marks on his wrists. He looked again briefly at the body of Bakr before turning his back to the camp and to the sun that slowly rose above the eastern hills.

The camels grazed untethered on a thorny bush, their loads still fixed ghostly upon their humped backs. Nearby, two other figures lay crumpled in the sand, silent and still like blackened rocks. Soundless screams were frozen within their open mouths; milky-white eyes gazed skyward without seeing. The skin of their faces was peeled away—seared free from the purplish flesh beneath. Flies buzzed in and out of their mouths and nostrils, busy feeding and laying eggs. Not far away, the jackal approached, moving quickly but cautiously toward the fresh carrion. High above, scavenger birds circled against the broken colors of the sky, and as Judaea moved westward toward Egypt, they began to descend.

☙ CHAPTER EIGHTEEN ❧

Purgatory

Mary gazed at the horrible wound on Judaea's wrist: an elongated hole of soiled, dry flesh that showed little sign of decay. Even the extensive deep purple and black bruising around its fringes suggested it had been only recently inflicted. She looked to Judaea, but his stare was blank and impassive as always. As she reached for Judaea's other wrist, Kadesh placed his hand on hers.

'The other is the same,' he said.

'I'd like to see for myself.'

She pushed up the other sleeve of Judaea's age-yellowed tunic and exposed another wound of similar size and shape. Carefully, she rotated his arm, as though it might still cause him pain, and confirmed that the wound extended to the other side.

'You should not touch him, Mary,' Kadesh said.

Judaea withdrew his hands and placed them on his lap, hidden from her view.

'And your feet,' Mary said, '—are they the same way?'

'They are the same,' Kadesh said.

'They are as they have always been,' Judaea exhaled.

'How long has *always* been, Judaea?' Mary said.

He looked beyond her for a moment, still and silent. 'Since I was born,' he hissed into the cool air.

'Yes,' she said, sitting across from him. 'You said you were born in a cave. But it wasn't a cave. It was a *tomb*. Your name is not Judaea.'

For the first time, Judaea seemed to display the slightest expression of interest. But it was a fleeting response, for as she continued to watch him she could see no trace of emotion. Once again, he was completely unanimated and appeared wholly indifferent to her presence.

'There was a garden near the tomb.' Mary said. 'You encountered your friend, Mary Magdalene, but she didn't recognize you. Do you remember her?'

As she spoke, the orange flame of the lantern danced in the blackness of his eyes, like the heat of a living forge working her words into some unimaginable form that would fit within his singular perception of reality.

'There was a woman,' Judaea said.

'I know what happened, Judaea. *He* knows what happened,' she said, looking to Kadesh.

'Then you have fallen under his lies.'

'I haven't fallen under anything,' she said, wondering whether the anxious trembling that had developed in her hands was perceptible. 'It's the truth.'

But her words rang out ludicrously. It was a ridiculous assertion that the man across from her was the same man who had performed miracles and delivered messages of hope so very long ago. His stare was cold, his eyes dark and dispassionate. His aura was markedly unpleasant and seemed to cast about him a sensation of imminent danger. She recalled Kadesh's warnings to her.

'I know the truth,' she insisted. 'I want to help you remember.'

'I need no help,' he said. 'I have many memories. None are lost to me. You have come here not to help me, but to help yourself. Disappointment is all you will find here.'

As his disheartening retort echoed around her, Mary now

understood Kadesh's frustration. She found a new respect for his enduring calm and seemingly endless patience. But Judaea was right. Her reason for being there was self-serving.

'You *can* help,' she said, blushing. 'You weren't always Judaea. You were once someone very different. Someone very important.'

He stared at his hands as they slowly opened and closed upon his lap. 'I am like you,' he said.

'Mary,' Kadesh said, touching her arm. 'May I have a word with you?'

'You look like us,' she continued, 'but you're not like us. You're not alive anymore. A long time ago, you were empowered to do great things so people would believe in you and your purpose.'

'I have no purpose.'

'You do—or you did. You were born to take away sin. To protect us from evil.'

The familiar hiss filled the room.

'Evil,' Judaea breathed. 'I know of this. It is a cloak behind which man conducts his deeds.'

Her head slowly moved from side to side.

Kadesh rose from his seat and took her arm. 'Please, come with me,' he said and led her to the farthest corner of the room. Under the flickering light of the lantern, he appeared unusually fatigued and distressed.

'Mary, I am not comfortable with the nature of this conversation. I see that you are upset, but this is not how it is supposed to be.'

'Then tell me how it's supposed to be.'

'I, eh—'

'I know who he is, Kadesh. I've seen the proof.'

Kadesh fidgeted, running his fingers along the grey concrete wall beside him, clearly struggling to find the appropriate words with which to respond. His gaze turned away from Mary and toward the reliable comfort of the concrete floor.

'Crucifixion was once a common method of execution,'

Kadesh said. 'There were many such deaths—'

'No,' she said, throwing him an icy look. 'No more half-lies and twisted truths. Your talk won't distract me from the truth anymore.'

While Kadesh again fixed his gaze on the cracks in the floor, she approached Judaea.

'You were a teacher once. You taught the will of God to the people and preached that there would be everlasting life for those who believed in you.'

'I say to you that I am not that man.'

'But you are! I saw the soldiers take you to Golgotha. I saw what they did to you—how they inflicted the wounds to your hands and feet.'

Kadesh shuffled to her. 'How have you seen this, Mary?' he said.

'I saw it as I lay in my bed tonight.'

'Oh,' he smirked. 'Have you now begun to believe in dreams?'

'It wasn't a dream. I was there. I saw the faces of the people in the mob. I felt the warmth of the sun on my face that morning. I breathed in the scents of garden lilies and flowering grapevines. And I witnessed with these eyes what they did to him on the hill that day. I don't know how, but I was there then, just as I'm here now.'

Kadesh turned away from her. His disheveled hair only partly obscured his face, which screwed into a disconcerting look of frustration and anger.

'No more secrets, Mr. Kadesh.'

He looked on as Mary moved to Judaea and brushed aside the tangled hair from his forehead. Just below his hairline was a staggered array of dark puncture wounds, barely visible under a thick film of dirt.

'Tell me, Kadesh,' Mary said. 'How many condemned men wore a crown of thorns?'

She sat down again across from Judaea. 'I know what happened to you. I know who you are. I want to help you remember, so we can help each other.'

He stared long at her, like a wax statue long neglected in the bowels of a dusty museum. 'No,' Judaea exhaled.

'Why don't you want to remember?'

'You have fallen under his lies.'

'No, Judaea. You were put here to help us. There's so much suffering,' she whispered to herself. 'Don't you care?'

'I have no pity for them.'

'Then what do you have?'

His stillness fixed uneasily upon her. 'Hate,' he spoke into the coolness.

She swallowed into the great distance that had suddenly formed between her and the man she was convinced he was.

Hate. The word seemed to ring around them, echoing off the walls and their bodies before dissipating into the air. Her mind raced.

'You were betrayed,' Mary said, taking his hands in hers. She rotated his palms up. 'Look, you still bear the scars.'

A barely perceptible shudder suddenly passed over Judaea, and his body seized. And in that instant he went once again into the catatonic state, fully immersed within the incomprehensible.

The soft sound of shuffling feet drew Mary's attention away from the macabre spectacle and toward Kadesh, who was peering up at a narrow window that lay horizontally just below the ceiling.

Thickly coated in cobwebs, the textured glass of the window allowed only amorphic shapes of dull colors to pass through. Heavy iron bars shaped into a cross-work pattern and mounted into the concrete wall divided the glass into eight small sections.

'What are you looking at?' Mary said.

'Eh, it is nothing,' Kadesh said, turning to Judaea. 'We don't have much time, Mary. We must avoid these episodes at all cost.'

'You know who he is. Why wouldn't you tell me?'

'I—eh, realize that as a result of my poor judgment you have developed distrust in me, and for that I am truly sorry.

But I still hope you will appreciate that I have asked for your assistance at the eleventh hour, only after I felt that there were no other options available to me.'

He rested on the chair next to Mary, his knees cracking as they bent.

'I am a willing participant in this,' Kadesh continued. 'My role has been voluntary, and so I accept full responsibility for my actions. But I have recruited you for my purpose, and so I am also responsible for any consequences of your involvement. It was, and still is, my hope that when this is finished with you will be able to return to your life, minimally affected. And so I feel strongly that I must continue to provide you with only that information which I feel is absolutely necessary for you to help in this endeavor.'

'And I'll never know what happens at the *twelfth* hour?'

He turned to the window. 'I hope not.'

At that moment, Judaea's head lowered and Mary approached him. 'He won't speak with you anymore,' she said.

Judaea raised his head and fixed his stare upon her. The hair on her arms stood on end. Suddenly, she felt like a small animal that had just realized it had been spotted by a predator. Kadesh quickly drew her away from the table.

'Mary, you must not antagonize him,' Kadesh said.

'I know about the link between him and my son.'

Kadesh stared incredulously at her. 'Eh—'

'Tonight I made my son promise that he wouldn't communicate with Judaea anymore.'

'Have you really done this?' he breathed.

'Yes. No more secrets, Mr. Kadesh. No more games.'

'Believe me, Mary—this is *not* a game.'

'Whatever it is, my son's role in it is over.'

'Mary, I am sorry, but you do not understand. It is of paramount importance that Judaea continue to communicate with your son.'

'Then you knew.'

'Yes, I knew.'

'*Why didn't you tell me?*'

Kadesh was silent.

'Why is the link so important? Why have you kept this from me?'

'You already know why. There are many things that I would like to disclose to you, but as I have said, I strongly feel that I must not.'

Kadesh glanced toward the window.

'Why do you keep looking up there?'

'We have only until morning,' he said, rubbing his hand across his face. His hands pressed hard into his forehead and eyelids.

Anger churned within her. *Does he think I'm a small child that needs protecting?* she wondered. *It was you who came to me for help. You needed me.*

She turned her back to Kadesh and moved quickly to the table.

'You will never speak with my son again,' she said to Judaea.

Judaea bore down on her with the fullness of his glare, sending a chill spilling down her neck and back like ice water. She felt compelled to look away, but stood defiant and met his stare.

'I told him not to speak with you anymore,' she said.

Kadesh paced the room, casting alternating glances between Mary and Judaea, periodically touching his hand to his forehead as though trying to extract some guidance from deep within.

'The boy is no more,' Judaea said. 'You cannot do such a thing.'

'He's alive,' Mary said. 'I don't know why you believe what you do, but your information is wrong. Maybe it's your source,' she said, passing Kadesh a meaningful look.

'It is truth,' Judaea said. 'The boy is no more.'

'Your mind isn't right, Judaea. You can't trust your thoughts. You don't know my son, and you don't know me.'

'I know your face. I have seen it many times, alone and together with the boy.'

'When did you see us?'

Judaea looked to Kadesh.

'I don't know much about you, but I know enough,' Mary said sitting across from him.

'When you were alive, you preached about God, who you called *father*. You claimed to be mankind's key to salvation and eternal life. Many people believed in you. You had students who followed you and learned from your teachings. One night, you were betrayed by one of them and you were arrested. Do you remember?'

Only the sound of water gently trickling above passed through the interrogation room.

'When they came for you in your darkest hour, even your friend Simon Peter denied that he knew you. You knew that he would. Do you remember?'

Her voice seemed flat, void of any echo, as though a heavy blanket covered the building and muffled their sounds. Kadesh also seemed to notice the strange dampening of their sounds.

'Mary—,' Kadesh began.

'You were tortured throughout the night. Do you remember?'

Judaea's lips parted and the familiar hiss passed through the room, but his breath did not leave him.

'You were condemned. In the morning, you were brought to Golgotha. Roman soldiers made you carry a heavy beam on your back, across your shoulders—here.' She stood and touched the nape of his neck, where the skin was colored deep shades of purple and yellow.

'Even as you hung by your hands and feet, you wouldn't look into the faces of those who had gathered. You didn't want them to see your suffering. But there was no salvation offered to you from those who you helped, who you befriended.'

Through dispassionate, glass-like eyes, Judaea focused on her. He listened attentively, as if mesmerized.

'Where were your students or those who you helped? They *abandoned* you.'

'No,' he exhaled. 'I am not that man.'

As Mary recounted the brutal scene at Golgotha, the slightest shiver passed over Judaea. Knowing what would happen next, she called to him, but it was too late. His body tensed and seized, as though shocked with electricity. An instant later, he had again escaped into that enigmatic state beyond her reach.

She no longer held any doubt that the man across from her was the man from Nazareth who had walked the earth so many years ago. Yet something had happened to him: something terrible that was never recorded, or perhaps known. And now he sat before her in a catatonic state as though under a spell—the unliving shell of his former self. Ages stood between the man he once had been, and who or what he was now, centuries during which he appeared to have walked the earth, oblivious of his identity. Overwhelmed by the weight of the monumental task that lay before her, she bowed her head and cradled her face in her hands.

'I am sorry, Mary,' Kadesh said, placing a reassuring hand on her shoulder. 'This was to be my burden, not yours.'

She looked up at the strange man beside her, to whose plight she had become more and more sympathetic, and whose face now hung tired and drawn, as though he had aged years over the past hours.

'It is Him, isn't it?' she whispered.

'At this point, Mary, you know nearly as much as I do. Please allow me to retain as my own the little extra knowledge that I have. A gift to an old man?'

'It's almost morning,' she said, glancing at the window. 'Isn't it time to lay everything on the table?'

'Everything that can help us is already at the table,' he smiled sadly.

Judaea lowered his head.

Even through his silence, Mary could sense his discontent. She shifted in her seat and cleared her throat.

'Why are you communicating with my son?' she said.

'He is silent.'

'He won't speak with you anymore. I told him not to.'

The long silence that followed grew thick and heavy, surrounding them like a cage.

'You could not do such a thing,' Judaea said.

'Why couldn't I?'

'He is no more.'

She boiled with anger that choked her as it searched for escape. Desperately, she tried to maintain her composure, groping at the words that tried to follow, seizing them before they could escape and again confound her endeavor. But some of them were beyond her control and they slipped through her lips.

'He's not dead!' she said. 'You don't know him. You *never* knew him.'

'He was my son. He was lost to me.'

'He's not your son. He's *my* son. That's why he does what *I* ask of him, and that's why he won't speak with you.'

Suddenly, the lantern's flame shrank and the sole source of light dimmed. Turning quickly on his heels, Kadesh rushed to the lantern and removed it from the shelf just as the light was extinguished. They were left in nearly complete darkness.

'The oil is finished,' Kadesh announced. 'But do not worry, there is more!'

With the sounds of Kadesh fumbling behind her, Mary peered into the palpable blackness between her and Judaea and watched as his features emerged from within it, faded and ghostly. A cold chill embraced her, but Kadesh worked quickly in the darkness and soon the soft popping of the oilcan offered comfort.

'It is true,' Judaea said. 'You bore the child. But he is no more.'

'Don't say that. It's not true. He's alive, but he's very sick. I need you to help him.'

'I cannot.'

'You can. You had the power to heal. I believe you still have that power.'

'Your words are his,' he said, looking to Kadesh.

'No, they're my own. I need your help.'

A knot formed in her throat: a terrible, strangling sensation that momentarily took her breath away. She swallowed hard to clear it and to moisten her desiccated mouth, but she could not escape the awkward discomfort.

The darkness was suddenly filled with the fizzing sound of a burning match. Kadesh breathed a satisfied sigh as light from the lantern once again embraced them with a comforting yellow glow.

'I remember the boy and you, his mother,' Judaea said. 'But he is no longer among the living. This thing is true.'

'The only truth is that you will never communicate with him again, unless I permit it.'

'You do not have such power.'

'You know that I do. Twice already he's refused you.'

'No.'

'Yes. I told him not to communicate with you anymore. He's doing what I asked of him.'

A strange rippling wave seemed to pass through him: a barely perceptible shudder that displaced him unnaturally.

'You cannot,' he hissed.

'I can and I have,' she said, watching for the ripple to reappear. But only silence returned to fill the moments between their words.

'My son will not communicate with the dead.'

Kadesh shifted uncomfortably in his seat.

'I am alive,' Judaea said.

'You're not alive. Your life ended a long time ago. I don't know how or why, but only your body died. Somehow, your spirit still lives within it.'

Kadesh's warm hand touched her arm.

'Please,' he said, smiling down on her and gesturing for her to rise.

Again he led her to the far corner of the room, almost beyond the lantern's light.

'Mary, do you see what is happening?'

'Yes, I do.'

'I am very concerned with your approach. Anger is not the way.'

'Then show me the right way. I don't have much time left.'

'Then we must work together.'

'Together? We haven't been working together since I first came here. With your deceptions and half-truths, you've kept me in the dark. Even in here, you deprived me of light so I couldn't see the truth. But I can see the anger growing behind his eyes, and if all I can do here is anger him, then that's what I'll do.'

'Mary, you must not do that. You must be gentle with him.'

'Why? What are you so worried about?'

'He is not who you think he is.'

'Then who is he?'

Kadesh bowed his head. 'I cannot say.'

From across the room came the familiar hiss.

'You will tell him to speak with me,' Judaea spoke.

'No!' Mary cried.

Even in the dim light she could see his rage surface, churning and rolling like the growing waves of an angry sea. As he stared at her from across the room, again the strange ripple moved through him and he began to recede into the refuge of his altered state. She rushed to him and took hold of his arm before he seized.

'The people from the town gathered at the base of the hill to watch you pass,' she said. '*To Golgotha!* they chanted. There were children. They mocked you and threw stones at you. You recognized some of them, didn't you?'

His head moved from side to side, but the strange shudder that increased in frequency, and the tension that had grown behind his eyes, spoke for him.

'You were humiliated like a criminal, but you'd done nothing wrong. When they laid you on the cross, you looked to the heavens for mercy, but there was none. Even the One you called Father had abandoned you.'

'No,' he moaned.

Judaea's shoulders tightened and narrowed. Suddenly, his

head kicked back, his eyes rolled back and he again retreated from her voice.

'Mary, you must go now,' Kadesh whispered. He looked anxiously toward the window.

'I can't go now. I need his help.'

'Mary, this is not the way. I have been going like this for some time. We will not make progress tonight. He is like a fish that you can see just below the surface of the water, but when you reach your hand into the water, it disappears. I am sorry, Mary. It is too late. You must go now.'

'You worked hard to get me here, Kadesh, and now you want me to leave? Why can't you tell me what's going to happen in the morning? With all that I already know, what harm can it do?'

Kadesh shook his head and bit down on his lower lip. 'I cannot say.'

'You *can* say.'

'Please, Mary,' he said, leading her to the door. 'Please go. There is no more time.'

'I can't,' she said pulling away from him. 'If I go back with nothing, I'll lose everything.'

Kadesh's gaze danced between her and the small window.

'You must leave now,' he said and pulled the door open.

'What's going to happen?' she insisted, looking to Judaea, who remained in his stupefied state, his gaze frozen toward the ceiling.

Kadesh looked wide-eyed to the window and fixed his stare upon it, as though at any moment something terrible would come crashing through.

'I'm not leaving,' Mary said. 'I'm staying here for as long as it takes.'

A tear stood in the corner of Kadesh's eye. 'It was a mistake to bring you here,' he whispered, slowly shaking his head. He appeared old and frail. His lips were dry and cracked. As his tired eyes met hers, the skin on her arms and scalp tingled.

'This isn't *your* urgency, is it?' she breathed.

He closed his eyes.

'What's going to happen?' she said, moving closer to him.

He bit down on his lip and grimaced as if in pain. 'I should not have brought you here,' he said.

'What is it, Kadesh? What has he told you?'

Again Kadesh looked to the window, which now let through the faintest rays of morning light. He gazed at it for a moment, bowed his head and whispered in a barely audible voice.

'Soon after the sun rises, your son will perish.'

His words only slowly took shape in her mind. They coiled around her thoughts and squeezed them like a snake, invoking in her a terrible despondency.

'What?' she breathed.

'I'm sorry, Mary. You must fly *now*.'

She watched his expression for a sign of retreat, but he offered none.

'He can't know that,' she muttered through trembling lips. 'Nobody can.'

His mouth opened slightly, but no sound emerged. He bowed his head.

'It's not true. You know it isn't,' she said, seizing him by the shoulders. 'Kadesh!'

The slight man placed his hands over his face and bowed his head.

Tears crested the lips of her lower eyelids and streamed down her cheeks, falling through the coolness and bursting silently onto the cold, hard floor.

'He doesn't know those things,' Mary said. 'He can't. He doesn't know my son.'

Kadesh was silent.

As she gazed upon the strange man, the terrible sadness slowly transformed into rage. Vomit churned in her stomach as her anger welled, but she would not permit the indignity again. She glowered at Judaea, who remained in his unresponsive state.

'He can save him,' she hissed. 'I know he can. But instead

he wallows in self-pity. No wonder they killed him.'

'Mary, do not say such things!'

'Maybe you're right, Kadesh. Maybe he isn't who I thought he was. He's a rotting corpse possessed by evil.'

'Say no more, Maryam!'

Judaea lowered his head and glared at her.

He's mocking me, Mary thought. *He's denying my son of his future, just as he was denied his.*

She could no longer contain her anger. Anger not just for Judaea, but for everything and everyone. Anger for those who had failed them: for her husband who had died, and for their friends who had abandoned them. Surrendering to her rage, she ran to Judaea and slammed both hands down upon the table.

'CRUCIFY HIM!' she cried.

In the tiny fragment of time that followed, Judaea's mouth snapped opened, there was the sound of rushing air crackling electrically, and then a thunderous clap.

'*NO!!*' he cried.

A powerful force struck Mary. All the muscles in her body contracted simultaneously as she was thrown across the room to the concrete floor. Seething with pain, she rolled onto her back. All sound had disappeared except for a soft ringing in her ears. A thin stream of blood trickled out of her right ear and along the line of her lower jaw. She could hear nothing.

'Mary!' Kadesh cried.

Her lips turned pale blue. As she fought to regain her breath, she pushed herself along the floor with her feet, retreating crab-like from Judaea.

'Mary!' Kadesh cried again, grasping her by her shoulders.

Dazed and disoriented, she gaped at Kadesh, whose blurred face seemed to take on a thousand different forms before sharpening back into familiarity. With a great gasp, air rushed back into her aching lungs and her color was restored. Her breathing accelerated to a feverish pace.

'Deep and slow,' Kadesh said. 'You're hyperventilating.'

But his voice was a thousand miles away. She was fixed on

Judaea, who had risen from his chair and stood towering from behind the table.

Kadesh pulled her close. Placing his face only inches away from hers, he blew a strong puff of air into her face. For a moment she lost her breath, and she stared bewildered at Kadesh through soft and watery eyes.

'Mary,' Kadesh said pulling her to her feet. 'There is no more time. You *must* fly!'

He rushed her out of the room, but just as they reached the hallway, she stopped and turned to Judaea. For a moment, they faced one another in silence. She gazed across the room to the narrow window, through which came an ominous pinkish glow of morning. The air hissed as Judaea's lungs filled again, but Mary was gone before it stopped.

Kadesh and Judaea stood staring at one another as the sound of Mary's hurried footsteps faded down the hallway. All traces of her vanished as the outer door crashed.

Judaea gazed around the room. 'What is this place?' he said.

Kadesh bowed his head and trembled under the weak light of first dawn. A strange, uncomfortable smile spread slowly across his face.

'Purgatory, my Lord.'

❧ CHAPTER NINETEEN ❧

White Ashes

The sky was on fire.

Under the still quiescence of early dawn, large, heavy flakes like white ashes descended from the heavens, concealing all things they touched under a thin blanket of pure white. Mary stood just outside the door awestruck, gazing at her forsaken world that had been silently transformed into a wondrous scene of high contrast and smooth, even texture.

The dark alley appeared cleansed with the fresh coating of whiteness. Little could be distinguished beyond the narrow lane, but in the distance, rows of tall street lanterns were still visible, suspended high above the walkways, surrounded by halos of light cast out like silent spells upon the flakes as they fell. Across the lane, the long limbs of tall deciduous trees still heavily laden with thick, broad leaves hung over an old wooden fence, stooping precariously from the unfamiliar load upon them.

Mary turned her gaze to the disintegrating sky. Soft, light flakes fell upon her face. She wiped her hand across her cheek and watched as the icy particles turned into small water droplets on her fingertips. Her breath turned white as it met the crisp, cold air, rolling over her hands like puffs of steam from the nostrils of some mythical creature.

The aberrant cold seeped through her thin clothing and she shivered against it, awakening the dull aches in her bones. She pulled her thin travelling cloak around her and drew its large hood over her head. Casting a final glance over her shoulder at the grey edifice that held within it her lost hope, she stepped into the unfamiliar softness.

With the muffled sound of fresh snow crunching beneath her feet, she raced up the lane, kicking up icy flakes into the air and under her dress, where they melted against the bare skin of her inner thighs. Stride after stride, the wet snow offered tenuous traction to her numbing feet, which were unaccustomed to the icy surface. But as she rounded the corner from the lane onto the buried road that led to the hospital, her feet slipped out from underneath her.

Excruciating pain radiated up her right leg and buttock as she landed on the snow-covered road. She slid several feet on her side before stopping near the middle of the road. Slowly, she rolled over onto her back and faced the falling snow as dark and terrible thoughts permeated her mind.

Quick, Mary thought. *You need to get up.*

She tried to move her right leg, but it responded with intense pain that radiated like lightning from calf to buttock.

Valuable time drizzled away like rainwater on a windowpane. As she lay in the silent road, staring up at the sky, snow quickly covered her under a thin blanket of icy white and filled in her footprints, as though concealing her within the strange whiteness. Fighting the pain, she propped herself up onto her elbows and peered down the empty street, where the warm amber light from the baker's shop spilled out onto the walkway: a solitary sign of activity that radiated over the whiteness like an oasis. But it was hopeless. No one could hear her from that distance. She lay her head down into the snow and a silent cry escaped her.

Warm tears streamed down her temples, through her hair and into the snow. Her thoughts drifted away as the white flakes kept falling softly against her face.

She was a young girl again, sprawled at the bottom of the wooden staircase that had cast her down to the landing below. The terrible pains from her shoulder and the ribs of her upper back were too intense for tears. She lay against the cold floor, staring up at the speckled white ceiling.

'Mamma,' she mouthed at the falling flakes.

From somewhere near came the sound of her mother's footsteps, but even as deliverance drew near, Mary would not cry out. She would not share her suffering with anyone. Soon, she would be held against her mother's soft, warm bosom and she would be safe again. At the outermost edge of her vision she could see her approaching: a blurred figure slowly coming into focus…

From behind a thick curtain of falling snow, the mastiff emerged, the dark fur of its back and wrinkled forehead sprinkled with flakes of snow. It paused only a few feet away from Mary and lowered its massive head. She lay absolutely still, holding her breath as it moved slowly around her. Only her eyes moved, tracking the beast as it circled.

As if in a terrible dream, the mastiff walked along her incapacitated body, straddling her, trapping her within a cage formed by its powerful legs and long, broad torso. The glossy, dark fur of its chest stretched rhythmically as it drew the chilled air into its lungs and expelled it through its snout. Like the beast from her dream, its mouth opened; the white canine teeth of its upper jaws gleamed menacingly against long, black, drooping jowls.

But unlike in her dream of the tiger-like beast, in the twilight of the vanishing town there was no hero. No stoic image shimmering in the distant heat; no thunder of gunfire to rid her of the monster. Here her pains would end upon a bed of pure white, alone under the dim glow of early morning. She closed her eyes as the animal's breath spilled over her and condensed into a damp mist upon her face. Thoughts of her son took her away from that place as she waited for the pain to come, for the piercing of its long canine teeth through her skin, and the crush of its jaws closing around her neck.

But moments passed and the anticipated trauma did not come. Nothing followed but the self-induced darkness behind her eyelids, and the soft whisper of her own breath. No longer feeling the cold touch of snow on her face, she wondered if it was already finished: her life taken from her mercifully without announcement, ending like the passing of a season. Slowly, she opened her eyes and beheld the mastiff still looming above her, its massive body covering hers, blanketing her from the endlessly falling snow.

Clouds of mist burst forth from the animal's broad black snout, only inches from her face. But its breath was not rank like that of the beast in her dream. It was sweet like warm summer air after a light rain. She drew it in and her mind was filled with pleasant memories of the tender, serene moments cradling her newborn son.

Except for the broad expansion and contraction of its chest, the mastiff was still. As she gazed into its placid face, she understood. It would remain there, exactly as it was … waiting for her. She reached up and placed her hands around the mastiff's thick neck, locking her fingers together. As he raised his head, her hands sank into the loose folds of wet fur on the back of his neck, and her upper body was lifted away from the snow. With a powerful thrust of his hind legs, she was moving again, sliding on her cloak across the frozen ground.

The rush of wind made a pleasing sound in her ears that grew louder as the mastiff accelerated through the snow. His legs became a blur of movement draped on either side of her like a grey, translucent curtain. Cold air that flowed over her face brought tears to her eyes, obscuring her view of the mastiff as he lurched rhythmically forward.

The pain was gone. As the mastiff ran, she was no longer connected to the failed body that dragged along the snow-covered street beneath it. No longer was she a daughter, a wife, a mother. She was without identity—unaware of herself, like a newborn babe cradled in its mother's arms, satiated and content, its belly full of warm, sweet milk drawn from its mother's giving body. She was free again, released of all angst, relieved of the physical and emotional trauma that had plagued her almost every waking moment of the past few years. Like the great she-wolf of Romulus and Remus, the mastiff was her guardian and she a child beneath it. The bliss that now enveloped her so completely would be preserved forever in those moments.

But the falling flakes of ice soon began to pass by more slowly and the mastiff's legs became discernable once more against the whiteness. As he slowed to a trot, her cloak dragged awkwardly beneath her, tugging at her shoulders as it stuck to the frozen ground.

The mastiff raised his head as he approached the hospital, lifting Mary's shoulders clear of the hard edges of the stone steps. He seemed unaffected by the extra weight that hung from him. The muscles of his powerful legs and shoulders worked effortlessly as he ascended the steps. In only a few seconds, Mary was sliding across the grey slate tiles of the hospital's main entrance. The mastiff stopped just in front of the heavy wooden doors and bowed his head, resting Mary's shoulders onto the tiles. As if unlocked by some external force, her hands unclasped and she gently lowered to the floor. The mastiff raised his head toward the third floor and gazed briefly at Kaleb's window. Then with a powerful lunge, he bounded down the steps and disappeared into the stillness.

'Mary!' a voice called out.

Arianne emerged from between the large wooden doors, trailed by a soothing bright light that spread over Mary like warm water. She knelt by Mary's side and shivered.

'Mary, what's happened?' Arianne said, scanning the area.

'Arianne,' Mary winced, trying to get up. 'I've got to get to my son.'

Arianne embraced Mary and struggled to lift her to her feet, but even with Mary's slender build, she could not maintain a hold of Mary's icy cloak. Her face red with frustration, she looked into Mary's eyes. 'You're too heavy for me, Mary!'

At that moment, Muriel emerged from the doorway and swept upon them like a sudden breeze.

'I have her,' Muriel said in a calm voice.

With surprising strength and agility, Muriel wrapped her arm firmly around Mary and rose. Her soft face was unflinching as she bore Mary's full weight upon her slight frame. An instant later, the two women were passing through the hospital entrance hall.

The first light of morning had only just made its appearance in the grand foyer. A few of the elderly patients had already gathered to secure their places for the day on the wooden benches that bordered the open space. There they would pass the time reading under the ample natural light, talking to one another and watching strangers pass into their domain. Many strange things happened in that space, but nothing compared to the spectacle of the two young women racing through it. A pale, fragile man rose to his feet, mumbling and pointing a crooked finger at them as they passed.

Like dried leaves carried on a strong autumn wind, the two women swept through the foyer and ascended the marble steps. One flight after the other passed under their feet as Muriel flew upward with light steps.

The quiet corridor adjacent to the third-floor landing was hardly touched by the weak morning light that passed through the clusters of recessed windows set deep into the stone brick walls. As they passed under the amber light of the hallway lanterns, for an instant Mary recalled a small town she had visited as a child. There, lanterns mounted outside of the old shops threw a similar yellow-orange light against the walls of brick and stone, creating serene and welcoming warmth.

They soon arrived at her son's door, and Muriel lowered Mary onto her good leg.

'Muriel—,' Mary breathed.

'There's no more time, Mary.'

Mary peered through the somber light of her son's sanctum. Like a young bird abandoned by its mother, perched at the edge of its nest high above the forest floor, she felt unprepared for what lay ahead. Across the room, her son's small shape was still and silent under the thin woolen blanket.

Through the room's solitary window that had for so long brought the comfort of daylight and continued hope into their temporary haven, she could see colors of the sunrise spreading over the farmers' fields. In the distance, the sun peered from behind the horizon like a huge burning eye, searching for her son.

The room glowed as the morning light passed through the window. It found her son and awakened him with its touch. She forgot her pain momentarily as she rushed toward him, but her movement summoned the full wrath of her injured leg. She stumbled and fell to the knee of her good leg, landing at the edge of Kaleb's bed, her afflicted leg splayed out beside her. Terrible pain shot up her leg like strikes of lightning.

'Mumma,' Kaleb said in a tiny voice, 'I did what you said. I didn't let him in.'

'I know, angel,' she said, cradling his face in her hands.

No color remained in Kaleb's face, except for dark brown-blue semicircles that bracketed the bridge of his nose. His eyes were dull and lifeless. The tiny sparkle of hope that his effervescent spirit earlier that night had given her had disappeared into the blackness of assent. She took his hand and rested it in hers. He gathered his energy and drew a small puff of air into his lungs.

'Can we go home now?' he exhaled.

Mary's heart broke. She wept unrestrained, releasing her infinite grief over him. Viscous streams of despair seeped into her and coursed through her body like hot poison, dissolving away all residual happiness, all traces of hope.

'Mumma,' he breathed, 'I'm going to Puppa now.'

'No, angel,' she pleaded and squeezed his hand. 'Don't go—please don't leave me.'

Drawing on all his strength, the young boy inhaled slowly and deeply, but only the faintest whisper escaped.

'I can't help it.'

Mary convulsed with tears as she held his limp body against hers. He would fight. He would not leave her. He was a child and had many more years to live. He would one day carry her to her grave and stand over it, a strong and handsome man surrounded by a loving wife and beautiful children of his own. That was the proper order of life. It was his destiny. But as she looked upon his ghostly form, she knew his body had already surrendered. All that remained of her beautiful child was a tiny remnant of a bold and untethered spirit, barely clinging to the wilted body that had hosted it for just a brief time. Only her selfishness now stood in the way of its freedom.

'Okay, angel,' she nodded and wiped her tears away.

She reached into her pocket and grasped the scalpel blade she had removed from the surgical tray earlier that day. She felt no pain as she closed her hand tightly around it, drawing a thin trickle of blood from her palm. Holding her son firmly against her chest, she rocked back and forth and imagined he was drawn back into her womb. There, he was once again under her protection, her care, and she accepted all of his suffering into her.

'Go to him, angel,' she whispered. 'Go to him. Mumma's coming with you.'

❧ CHAPTER TWENTY ❧

Release

A palpable melancholy hung over the old stone hospital. Those in the foyer who witnessed the spectacle spoke in nervous whispers, as though afraid that somehow their voices might attract the same malice that had afflicted Mary. Frozen with uncertainty and fear, no one had moved to help her. Even Arianne, who was forbidden from leaving her floor, could only peer toward the empty stairway and listen for their movements above.

But not all was still. Just beyond the walls of the hospital, an unfamiliar presence approached: an unnatural thing that passed under the icy glower of the stone gargoyle. Silently, it crossed over the threshold from the frozen outer world and slipped into the détente of the warm sanctuary.

Large, down-like flakes continued to descend outside, but upon Judaea there was no ice or water. He left no trace behind. Like a light breeze, he moved through the foyer, passing unnoticed by all those who stirred within it. Only Arianne raised her head slightly as he approached, as though listening to a faint and distant sound, but at the slightest movement of his hand, her interest evaporated. With silent steps he ascended the marble stairs.

All along the third-floor corridor, the children's drawings flapped softly against the plaster walls. At the nurse station, Amira and McLeary spoke in hushed voices, respectful of the somber silence that embraced the ward. Only certain sounds that escaped their whispers traversed the length of the corridor, like a strange, subordinate language understandable only by the gentle breeze that flowed through the wing.

Judaea raised his head, as though perceiving something within the dry air of the third-floor landing. He paused only a moment and then continued along the hallway, his presence unacknowledged by the nurses at the far end of the wing.

Standing quietly on one side of the hallway, Muriel stared ahead, still as a stone sentry. When Judaea approached, she glanced at him and turned away, possessed with a slight smile. He stopped in front of her and gazed blankly. Her eyes darted over him, but she would not look upon his face. Slowly, her smile widened. She bowed her head, reached back and opened the door. With a slight nod, Judaea acknowledged her and passed into the room.

Bathed in the weak golden rays of early morning light, Mary sat upon the hospital bed, embracing her son's still body. Slowly, she raised her head and peered through red and swollen eyes toward Judaea as he passed through the doorway. He stopped a few feet away from her and looked upon the child. Mary held her son out to him, the boy's emaciated limbs dangling limply over her arms.

'Please,' Mary said. 'Help him.'

The air hissed.

'It is true,' Judaea exhaled, and placed his hands upon the child's head. He ran his fingers over the boy's small face, neck and shoulders.

The shadowy lids that covered the child's eyes parted and he looked up at Judaea.

'Puppa,' he mouthed.

Judaea touched Kaleb's dry lips. 'My son.'

'Have you come to take me to heaven?' Kaleb breathed.

'No,' Judaea said, a sullen look moving across his face. His chest broadened as he drew in the sterile air, and the strange, raspy sound again filled the room. 'Forgive me; I have forsaken you.'

Kaleb looked to Mary and then to Judaea. His shallow breathing accelerated. It was one of the few times Mary had seen him afraid.

'Puppa,' he said. 'You can't stay here. I'll be alone in heaven.'

Judaea rose to his full height, eyes wide and bright against his pale skin.

'No,' he said, anger growing behind his eyes.

Mary drew Kaleb closer.

'He shall speak with me,' Judaea said.

'Yes,' Mary said. 'He'll speak with you. Please help him.'

The same sallow look that had possessed Kaleb for the past weeks now passed to Judaea. In the morning light, he appeared worn and ghostly, as though the many years left behind had now found him. Again he caressed Kaleb's face.

'That I may touch him,' he whispered, 'this is worth *ten* thousand years of darkness.' He looked at Mary. 'You have shared my pain. Only you understand.'

'Please,' Mary said shaking her head. 'I don't understand.'

Darkness seemed to envelop them as Judaea backed slowly away, his gaze fixed on Mary.

'Then you *shall* understand…'

He inhaled deeply and seemed to draw in all that was around him—every scent, every sound, as if tasting them, savoring each sensation with his spirit—and for the first time, she saw him close his eyes. In that brief moment, a younger face seemed to emerge from behind his shroud of neglect: a striking face of simple elegance and profound beauty. Suddenly, she knew the reason for his haunting familiarity. She reached toward him, her lips parting to speak, when suddenly the fine hair of her arms stood on end. An instant later, a blinding pulse of bright, sparkling light erupted from him like an exploding sun.

Mary gasped as the energy passed into and was drawn

through her, like water into dry earth, tingling and soothing as it coursed throughout her body. Intoxicated with the foreign energy, she surrendered without resistance and instinctively released her suffering into it. And it accepted all. For that brief moment, or for an eternity—it was impossible to tell—she was empty. Nothing remained but the energy.

But as quickly as the energy came, so it retreated, leaving behind a void of infinite vastness, which drew into it strange warmth. More and more of it rushed into her, until she was filled with terrible pain as the warmth intensified into heat, and then rose from heat to fire.

The fire raged within her, consuming each element of her body. Far away in the infinite distance she could hear herself screaming, but only a faint voice returned. There was no escape from the overwhelming power that now engulfed her. With her son in her arms, she collapsed to the floor and succumbed.

When the pain subsided, Mary was no longer of any familiar form or substance. She was ether: lighter than air, unbound to matter. And now there was something else with her—or her with it, she could not tell, for the two were as one. The entity surged through her unabated, harboring within it most of what she once had been, and as it did so she was left with a profound emptiness. A *loneliness*.

At first there was only darkness. Then slowly, the world unfolded around her as an older, unfamiliar land. Everything appeared in a perfect and vibrant clarity, unlike anything she had ever experienced. But a new cruelty was also manifested. All things were now isolated from her, like distant specimens under a great glass dome. Of all the countless forms of life that teemed within her limitless vision, none held any significance for her. Even mankind, who now inhabited only small regions of the earth, was as intangible to her as she was to it.

But one of their kind was different.

In a large field of tall, golden grass, a small boy played. Like a lone point of bright light that shone through an endless array of colorless forms and shadows, he stood out. He ran through the field in a large, circular pattern, flattening the grass in his path. When he was finished with his design, he looked up to her from the center of a giant eye and laughed, 'I see you, I see you!'

She smiled with him.

And she knew the boy—in this form and as her other self, which had been formed of flesh and bone and was lost to her now. That other self loved the boy in a human way and knew him as her son, Kaleb, and although the boys were two, and separated by many centuries, they were the same in every way.

Since the moment of his birth, the entity that now possessed her had shared with the boy a unique bond: a common thread of spirit that formed an indelible link between them. Together, they spoke, employing words of an ancient, silent language.

He was the companion, the child gift who was most like one of her own kind, of which there were no more. Over the few years that marked the boy's life, they had become two halves of the same whole—the entity the spirit, and he the form. Through him, the entity lived another, vicarious existence: a life affected by physical forces it could not experience. He was its conduit to mortality, a delicate extension that linked it to his kind. Through that singular nexus, it learned of his kind and taught him of its ways. And in time, it came to love him.

But the boy was not of its kind. As the seasons of the earth folded one over the other, he changed with them. In what was the tiniest displacement of time to the entity, the boy became a man: one whose form was known to that which the entity now possessed, as *Judaea*.

The entity's strength was channeled through his voice, and his words became a unique power. With that power he drew the people to him and delivered the entity's messages to them. Many people came to love him and to know of the entity and its ways, and he did many great things in its name. He became a teacher of the people and they followed him as their rabbi, as a prophet.

Twelve men came to be his closest followers: disciples who would receive his special attention and spread the entity's words and its will far beyond the reach of one man alone.

But the Pharisees, the spiritual leaders of his time, cherished their power and control over the people, and became angered by his growing following. A dark shadow of jealousy came to possess them, and to it they fed their hatred.

The entity warned him of their malice and promised to bring upon them the most severe retribution, but he pleaded for their mercy. Out of its infinite love for him, the entity respected his wish.

Under the cover of secrecy, the Pharisees hatched a plot of betrayal. The entity apprised him regularly of their plans, but could not extinguish his conviction. It could only watch as the plot against him took shape and unfolded. And then, one night, they took him and tortured him, indifferent to their own laws and culture. Yet even with the heavy hand of their brutality upon him, he would not deliver them to the entity.

As he suffered, so the entity suffered, and a malignant contempt for all mankind was seeded; as the hours of his torture passed, from it a terrible anger grew.

Its presence was with him the morning they brought him to Golgotha and he was laid upon the wooden cross. As they drove the nails through his flesh, he could sense the entity's pain, and again he pleaded with it to withhold vengeance. But mercy was not the way of its kind, and as they impaled him upon the beams, its tethered fury raged.

It was a terrible thing to see him on that barren hill, suffering the indignity, to watch life drain from him, and to allow this to happen within reach of its omnipotence. But it understood his will. His mortal life was finite, but as a martyr his voice could live forever. And so by this end he could become like the entity.

From high above the tallest mountains to the east, it gazed down upon him. Amongst everything there was only he, nothing else. He was the beginning and the end, the atom and the universe. No longer could it witness his suffering, no longer could it contain its rage. With its slightest will, the sand around the hill rose into the air like a terrible cloud, but before it unleashed its fury, he looked up to it.

'Forgive them,' he breathed.

And he was gone.

Engorged with pain, the entity's rage welled and churned, spilling over the earth as an unnatural darkness. The air became charged, and prickled with the entity's fury. Lightning and thunder filled the sky. Hot rain fell upon the people as they scattered like insects to their shelters.

But no cover could hide them from the entity's vengeance. Upon them it would bring the fullness of its wrath. Rivers of molten rock would be summoned from the earth's depths and consume them. Brimstone would scorch their lungs as they gasped for breath and pleaded for its mercy, but they would be shown the same ruthlessness they had visited upon him. The sound of their suffering would fill the infinite void that had replaced his soothing voice. It would destroy them all—every man, woman and child—and the earth would again be cleansed of the pestilence that was mankind.

When the last person had descended the hill of crucifixion, the entity gazed down upon his lifeless body. Even as its anger roared, its love for him would not permit it to break its promise. It could not deny his final request, and with its retribution erase his echo from the earth forever. With no escape, the fury worked on the entity like a slow poison, corroding it, consuming it. And the entity did not resist.

When the entity later looked for him upon the hill, his body had been taken down from the wooden cross. It found him nearby in a garden tomb hewn from rock and sealed with a giant stone that it moved aside without effort. His body had been anointed with aromatic resins, frankincense and myrrh, and wrapped in white linen cloth from head to foot.

Without his comforting voice, the entity struggled in the coolness of the stone tomb, saturated with the toxin of its inescapable rage. Like a snake that senses the vulnerability of its prey and is drawn to it, despair coiled around and seized the entity within its dispassionate grip, its long fangs releasing its venom. Alone in the darkness, the entity remained with him, longing for his spirit to return from that place into which it could not pass, allowing the pain to engulf it. The poisons worked unabated, reducing the entity's spirit into its elemental form until all that endured was the emptiness of despair, and an insatiable longing for the one who had been taken. It yearned for its own end.

In the early morning of the third day of its suffering, when the weight of loneliness was greatest, the entity removed the burial wrappings from his flesh. It could almost feel his body, the core still warm against its spirit. Closer and closer it moved, passing over and through him, focusing on and binding to his remaining energy, which still glowed dimly from deep within. As the warmth faded like a vanishing beacon, it drew the entity further into him until his flesh surrounded it. At that moment, it let go of its suffering and abandoned all that it was.

And then there was nothing.

It took a few moments for Mary to become re-oriented with her surroundings and to accept again the burden of mortal flesh and modest spirit. Her body seemed awkward and slow, and she rejected it at first.

A few feet away, Judaea lay lifeless, just as she he had seen his body in the tomb.

A small warm hand touched her shoulder.

'Mumma?' came a soft and quivering voice. Kaleb stood next to her, shivering, his eyes glistening with tears.

'Kaleb!' Mary cried and grasped him by the shoulders. 'Look at you!'

As they embraced in the fullness of morning, she could feel the renewed strength in him and began to cry. A tingling sensation passed over her as she turned to Judaea's body, which had become translucent in the morning light. Like a dulcet breeze, the light passed over him, lifting his body and transforming it into glistening dust that rose high into the air around them. Locked in a tight embrace with their hearts pounding against one another, mother and son watched as the tiny particles that were Judaea folded into the air and vanished.

ও CHAPTER TWENTY-ONE ক

Revelations

'I've been manipulated.'

Mary stood in the doorway of the mock interrogation room, looking down on Kadesh, who was stooped over a sea of assorted clutter. She immediately recognized some of the items from the tiny storage room farther down the hall. The small wall lamp had been replaced with two larger floor lamps that burned at opposite corners of the room. The wooden table that Judaea had occupied was nowhere to be seen. If not for the distinctive window tucked just below the ceiling, the room would have been unrecognizable. Kadesh looked up, holding several tattered books in one hand. In the other he held a small desk lamp, its stained and yellowed fabric shade bent and torn in several places.

'Mary,' Kadesh said. 'What a pleasant surprise! I didn't expect to see you so soon. Eh, how did you manage to get in?'

'The door was open.'

'Oh,' he sighed. 'Of course.'

Carefully stepping over a stack of old wooden frames, he approached a decrepit three-legged desk that stood at one side of the room.

'Please,' Kadesh said, gesturing with the books toward the

desk. Noticing the books still in his hand, he placed them on the floor and balanced the lamp precariously on top of them.

Mary weaved her way through the clutter, taking little notice of the dusty items that bordered the narrow path. As she did, Kadesh plucked two chairs of questionable structural integrity from within the disarray and placed them on either side of the desk.

'Please,' Kadesh repeated, gesturing toward the chair nearest to her and pushing aside with his foot a small clock, a large candleholder and an inverted wooden crate from underneath the desk.

She unbuttoned her cloak and settled into the chair, which rocked and creaked beneath her.

'So, what can I do for you?' Kadesh asked, sitting down and smiling at her from across the desk.

'I have a few questions.'

'Oh, I see. Well, I hope I have the answers.'

'I believe you do. You see, there are a few unacceptable coincidences.'

'Eh, coincidences?' He blushed.

'—And they all center on you.'

'How do you mean?'

'Well, for one thing, it's quite a coincidence that you would be the one to find Judaea.'

'Really?' he said, appearing mildly insulted. He shifted in his seat. 'Why should this be difficult to accept?'

'On its own, it's not, but there are other coincidences that, when taken together, make it difficult to accept.'

She clasped her hands together and placed them on the table. 'It's also odd that we would have met before all of this.'

'Why is this so strange? Even Judaea had seen you before.'

'That's the third coincidence.'

Kadesh frowned, clearly regretting what he had just said.

'How is it that I would be one of only a few people who could help you—the mother of a child who had a unique link with Judaea?'

Kadesh blinked repeatedly, like a machine working through

a myriad of possible responses, pausing briefly over each one as they passed through his mind.

'Eh, this does not seem strange to me,' he said at last. 'After all, this is a small town.'

'Yes, it is—small and isolated. A place where secrets could be easily kept.'

'Eh—'

'These *aren't* coincidences, Mr. Kadesh. You knew about the connection between Judaea and my son *before* you first came to the hospital. You knew that Judaea would recognize me. That's why you brought me to him.'

Kadesh blushed and shook his head. She knew he felt cornered and was searching for some escape. He glanced at her, avoiding eye contact, then returned his gaze to the desktop.

She leaned in closer. 'It's also far too unlikely that the mother of the one person who could communicate with Judaea in that way would also be a psychiat—'

Mary froze in mid-sentence and stared, perplexed, at Kadesh. He closed his eyes and lowered his head, again shaking it from side to side. His shoulders narrowed like a guilty child's.

'But there aren't so many coincidences, are there?' he whispered and smiled. 'After all, you're not a psychiatrist.'

The words hung in the air like a lie, releasing a barrage of contradictory memories that spilled through her mind like leaves carried on an autumn wind. She gathered the recollections as they settled in disarray amongst her thoughts, like the clutter spread out around her. Slowly, they aligned and reconciled into the truth, and what she had come to believe these past hours melted away. Ashamed and embarrassed, she gazed into Kadesh's tired eyes as the clarity, elusive since she had met him, returned to her thoughts and memories.

'No,' she said. 'I'm a teacher.'

A wide smile stretched across Kadesh's face. 'It seems that despite my best efforts, there is very little you do not know about what has happened.' He traced his index finger along the wood grain of the desktop. 'Perhaps, about some things, you know even more than I.'

'I know what Judaea was,' she whispered.

'I can see that you do,' Kadesh nodded. 'He seems to have imparted to you some *special* knowledge.' The wooden chair creaked as he leaned back. 'You know he loved that boy as if he were one of his own kind ... as a *son*. But you were always *my* favorite—so sharp, so bright.' His lips quivered. 'It has been such a pleasure for me to see you again, Maryam.'

A pleasant sensation passed over her at the sound of that name.

'At that time, so many years ago, the people were like children,' Kadesh said. 'They did not know what they were doing. They acted only on instinct and allowed themselves to become like a pack of wild dogs, acting with one mind and one purpose: to destroy him. The leaders did not accept that He was working through him. They knew only that they had lost some of their control over the people.' He breathed deeply. 'Under the oppression of the Romans, the people had become thirsty for blood—even that of a lamb such as he—and so they were easily corrupted by the influence of a few. Even some of his closest friends came to believe that he should be destroyed. So they took him to Golgotha and there they crucified him.'

Mary vividly recalled the mob of her vision: its size, its immense power, and the danger she sensed as she stood within it. No longer a collection of individuals, it had become a single entity: a menace that acted with one collective thought and purpose, void of any conscience, capable of anything.

'But soon after his death, something very inexplicable happened: *He* disappeared.'

'He?' Mary said.

Kadesh's eyes brightened. 'Well, for lack of a better word.' He paused emphatically and shrugged his shoulders. 'In an instant, He simply no longer existed.'

There were no other sounds but the soothing trickle of Kadesh's voice, and Mary absorbed each word as she recalled her experience with the entity.

'I did not believe such a thing was possible,' he said. 'I am embarrassed to say that it was a very long time before it occurred to me what had happened, but by that time, He was lost to me.'

'Who are you?'

'But I have already told you—when we first met,' he smiled. 'I am *Gabriel.*'

The name rang in the air for a moment and then scattered like laughter into the clutter around her. Kadesh beamed proudly.

'You're an angel?'

A deep crimson blush washed across his face. 'Well, for lack of a better word, you may think of me like that. Yes,' he chuckled, 'I like that very much.'

Mary placed her hands upon her lap. The dampness of her cool palms seeped through her dress and cooled her thighs.

'Shall I continue?' Kadesh said.

'Please.'

'As the boy suffered, so too He suffered. And when the boy died, His pain was cast all around. His anger shook the earth and brought the elements down upon the people. They were very frightened and cried out for His mercy. But His pain was profound. A fury rose in Him unlike anything I had ever seen before, and I became very afraid for them.'

The terrible anger the entity shared with her still lingered. She shuddered at the thought of the malice that had swelled so dangerously under its power. She wanted to share the experience with Kadesh, to tell him what had happened, but knew it was a unique gift and would remain her secret always.

'And then He was silent,' Kadesh said. 'I believed He had found peace, but I was mistaken. I now suspect that He went to the tomb where they placed the boy. There, He rejected this world and somehow He merged with the body. He possessed it. I do not know whether it happened intentionally, but I now believe that when His spirit entered the body and mingled with the flesh, it became *entangled* within it.' He interlocked his fingers emphatically. 'When this happened, His identity was lost. The two had become one, and the man we knew as Judaea was born.

'All that He had as references for this world were those few fragmented memories that had not yet been lost in the wasting mind of the one He had loved so much. It seems that the possession preserved the flesh, just as it was in the tomb. By the time it occurred to me what had happened, He had already left the city. I know that He traveled east to the Dead Sea, but beyond this I know very little, for now that He was within flesh, He belonged to your world, and as such He was cloaked from me for the first time.'

'I searched for Him for many years, but I was looking for a grain of sand in the desert. It seemed an impossible endeavor. Many years of frustration passed before I had my idea.' He shook his index finger into the air and leaned toward Mary. 'I would bring forth the child again: the one of your kind who could communicate with Him, the one He loved. Perhaps, I thought, like a lure, the child would draw Him out from the shadows. So that is what I did.'

He sat back in his chair and folded his arms. 'Through you, I delivered unto Him the child—who is your son, Kaleb.'

'You?' she breathed. 'How can you do such things?'

Kadesh smiled. 'Not all secrets will be revealed today, Maryam. But I will say that such a thing is not easy to do. And it was not the first time—it was the third. *You* were the second.'

'Me? What do you mean?'

'Just as your son is the same child born unto the village of Bethlehem many years ago, so too are you the same mother of that child.'

'*Mary?*' she breathed.

'Yes.'

'It can't be true.'

'You are here, so it is true.'

In that moment, all thoughts dissolved away except for her visions of the ancient village and the crucifixion: detailed scenes so vivid with colors, textures and scents, they seemed like recent memories. Memories that were almost too complete. But how could they be hers? The memories of her life and her struggles, although painful to recall, were clear. From the events of her early childhood to the diagnosis of her illness, they were all hers. Yet she knew what he said was also true. Deeply immersed in her confusion was an immense joy in knowing that within her life and that of her son there had been hidden such a profound purpose.

'Why me?' she said.

'Eh, a boy needs his mother,' Kadesh blushed.

'I'm—a *clone*?'

'No, not at all,' he said, waving away the thought. 'A clone is a mere copy of the flesh. You are the same in both body *and* spirit.'

'And my name? How did I get her name?'

'I, eh—may have had some influence over that decision,' he said, blushing more intensely. 'I did like the name so much, and I had become rather accustomed to it. It didn't seem right for you to have any other.'

'You knew my mother?'

'Yes.'

Suddenly, she resented him. *He must have known of our struggles, yet he never intervened*, she thought. *If he can create life, what other powers did he possess but not use during my family's sufferings? Was he there to witness the death of Aaron? Could he have prevented it?* She quickly smothered the thoughts and accepted that there must have been some wisdom in the way things had come to be: wisdom beyond her comprehension.

'When you delivered your son into this world, I had only to wait near to you and see if my plan would work. And as you know, it did. He could sense the boy's presence, even from a great distance, and He was drawn to him. More recently, they began to communicate with one another through their thoughts only. It took Him years to travel here, but eventually he arrived. And on that day, I found Him—the Master of all things—amongst the shadows of this town, like a common vagabond. Even as I looked upon Him, knowing what I had done to bring Him here, it was difficult to accept what I saw.

'I brought Him here to help Him remember, but it proved a much more difficult task than I had imagined.' He ran his fingers through his silvery hair. 'The singular nexus between Him and your son was crucial to my endeavor, and it became the only tool that had effect on him. But your son's very unfortunate illness created an unexpected urgency, so I had to act quickly. I feared what would happen if the boy's voice became silent again.'

A heavy sadness passed over her as she thought of how close she had come to losing her son. A strangling sensation gripped her, and tears welled to the brims of her lower eyelids. She wiped them away before they fell.

'It was not my original intent to involve you,' he said, shaking his head. 'But it became imperative that I accelerate the process. I believed that if He saw you—if He spoke to you—it would help Him to remember, and that might free Him from the bondage of flesh. I hope you will believe that I tried to minimize your involvement in this and any effect it might have on you. This is why I prevented Him from seeing your son.'

The stream of revelations was difficult for her to bear, invoking a surge of contradictory emotions.

'Aren't you supposed to have wings?' she said, blushing at the ludicrous sound of her question.

Kadesh smiled. 'People see us as they wish to. Perhaps some would see us with wings.'

'Us?'

'Of course. Tell me, Mary,' he said, leaning toward her, 'what do *you* see?'

Embarrassed, she looked into his tired eyes. 'I see a kind gentleman.'

His smile faded ever so slightly.

'Look *deeper*,' he said and leaned closer.

She blushed and cleared her throat. It was like watching a stranger undress. She wanted to look away—to break his stare—but she held her gaze upon him, searching his face.

There was something about him. There had always been something about him. Even when they had first met years ago at the party, she had felt an unwarranted comfort in his presence—a certain ease. She gazed at him for what seemed like ages, smiling graciously into his wrinkles, until suddenly the years that masked Kadesh's face seemed to peel away like thin sheets of rippled ice.

And then she knew.

She was three years old, lying at the bottom of the wooden staircase. Intense pain radiated from her shoulder and upper back. Her mouth opened, but the pain was too great for a cry to escape. The sound of approaching footsteps was getting louder, booming down the wooden staircase like a rolling thunder. She could feel the vibrations through the landing. Her salvation had come, as she knew it would, as it always had. She held up her arms and mouthed *Mumma*, but a different face emerged...

'Puppa?' she whispered.

Kadesh smiled.

The familiar sting touched her eyes again as a salty stream of tears drew out from her the many pains she had suffered in her father's absence. Cradling her face in her hands, she purged herself of the guilt that had gripped her for nearly a lifetime, and as she did so a great weight lifted from her shoulders: the burden of believing she had been responsible for his sudden departure.

'He's dead?'

Kadesh nodded.

'He died when you were very young, Maryam. Not all young mothers possess the courage that is required to tell a small child that her father has perished. Perhaps this new knowledge will lead to forgiveness.'

In the warm darkness behind her hands, the memories of her mother, of her mother's pain, were recalibrated. She now understood the self-imposed isolation, her endless silence.

Mary rose from her chair, composed herself and moved

toward the door.

'Will I ever see you again?' she said.

A smile spread across Kadesh's face. 'Under the circumstances, I believe it is inevitable.'

She nodded and smiled. 'Thank you for what you've done.'

'No, Maryam—I thank you.'

❧ CHAPTER TWENTY-TWO ❦

The Beginning

'Well, look how handsome you are!' Mary said, stepping into Kaleb's hospital room, her arms folded across her chest.

Kaleb stood at the foot of his bed, neatly dressed in the modest clothes he had arrived in at the hospital months ago. His hair was freshly washed and parted to one side. In his hand he held a thin, beige coat adorned with large wooden buttons. A wide grin stretched across his face.

'I hardly recognized you in your own clothes,' Mary said, kissing his forehead. She brushed his hair back with the palm of her hand. 'Are you ready to go home?'

'Are you sure we can go home, Mumma?' he said as they moved into the hallway. He peered toward the stairway.

'I'm sure,' Mary said, putting his coat over him.

'Not so fast,' Amira said, suddenly appearing from his room.

'I'm sorry, Amira. I didn't know you were in there. I hardly recognize you out of uniform.'

'I'm not on shift, but I came over anyway. I wouldn't miss this for the world. This is something I'll tell my grandchildren about … if I ever get married!'

Laughing tearfully, Amira embraced Kaleb and pressed her lips to his ears. 'Were you just pretending to be sick all this time, little potato?' she whispered.

'No,' he whispered back.

'Hmm. Make sure you visit us. —Promise?' she said, wiping her tears away.

'I will,' he nodded.

McLeary left the nurse station and joined the group. Towering over Kaleb, she looked toward the far window and pressed her hand to her cheek.

'I hope Muriel said a proper goodbye to you two,' she said in a bold voice. 'The girl has terrible timing!'

'Yes, she did,' Mary replied, smiling down at Kaleb. 'And her timing was just fine.'

'Well, I guess this is goodbye, then,' McLeary said, extending her hand to Kaleb.

Unfamiliar with the formality, Kaleb hesitated briefly and then reached out for her hand. McLeary laughed out loud, knelt down and took his small face in her hands.

'Forty-two years, young man,' she said in a quivering voice. 'I've been a nurse since I was a very young woman—before your mother was born, and I've never…' McLeary's lips trembled as her eyes quickly filled with tears. She kissed him on the forehead and rose up with her chin held high. 'You're a very special boy.'

Kaleb took hold of his mother's hand and she squeezed gently. He started down the hallway, which was unusually quiet for early afternoon, then suddenly turned to Mary.

'I almost forgot!' he blurted and raced back into his room.

The women looked at one another. Amira shrugged and peered into his room. A few moments later, Kaleb emerged with the Mancala board, carefully leveling it so that the small black stones remained within their pits. He took a few measured steps but stopped to pass Amira a questioning look. She smiled and nodded. He continued slowly down the hallway, concentrating intensely on the board, and disappeared into the room two doors away.

'Hi, Kaleb,' Daniel said, swinging his legs over the side of his bed. He slid off and stepped toward the door, a smile spreading across his pale face. Kaleb held out the Mancala board.

'What's that?' Daniel asked, squinting. 'I don't have my glasses.'

'It's a game.'

'Thanks,' Daniel said, grasping the wooden board. But as he drew it towards him, Kaleb's grip remained firm. Bewildered, Daniel looked to Kaleb for a hint of play, but his face was solemn and deliberate. The boy tugged again at the board, but Kaleb held on. Just as Daniel was about to let go, Kaleb reached out and touched his wrist.

Daniel shuddered violently and collapsed to his hands and knees. The Mancala board tumbled to the floor, releasing the stones from their pits and onto the hard surface, where they danced in all directions. Trembling, Daniel stared wild-eyed at the floor, endeavoring to catch his breath.

'Goodbye, Daniel,' Kaleb whispered, and left.

Slowly, the young boy rose to his feet. He gazed at his wrist, turning it over, examining it as long-lost color returned to the skin of his hands and moved along his arms and neck to his face. Still shaking, he stepped toward the door and peered around the corner just as Kaleb took Mary's hand.

As mother and son walked together along the narrow hallway and descended the marble stairs, Daniel followed them with his eyes and smiled.

* * *

Many centuries ago, in a large field just inside the stone wall of an ancient city, a woman watches her child trample the shape of a large eye into the tall golden grass.

'I see you, I see you!' the young boy laughs at the sky in an ancient tongue.

He runs within the eye, stumbling with laughter, completing three circles before returning to his mother's hand. Around them, countless cicadas chirp incessantly into the rising heat of the day. A light wind carrying fine dust passes over the field and delivers to them the sweet scent of summer. As the young mother draws a veil across her face, her gaze turns upward to the clear sky and she wonders:

What will become of this?

THE END

ACKNOWLEDGMENTS

I would like to thanks the family members and friends who provided constructive feedback on this novel, and to Dania Sheldon, my editor, whose light touch made all the difference. But most of all I'd like to thank my wife, Vicki, for her unyielding support of this endeavor.

ABOUT THE AUTHOR

Mario A Kasapi was born and raised in Victoria, BC. He studied at the University of Victoria, and The University of British Columbia where he received B.Sc. and Ph.D. degrees in Science. He now lives in White Rock, BC with his wife and three children. For more information about this novel, please visit www.thesunrisesnovel.com.